HARD TO KILL

JAMES P. SUMNER

BOTH
barrels
PUBLISHING

Now, for something new...

PROLOGUE

The world burned before his eyes. Flames sprouted around him, forming walls that stretched up to the sky, igniting the clouds that darkened it.

He rested on all fours. His hands melted into the ground. His gaze darted frantically in all directions, searching for help or an escape. Embedded in the flames that confined him were the tortured faces of a million dead souls. They stared at him with empty eyes and shrieked with pain he instinctively knew he was responsible for.

He opened his mouth, anxious to unleash his own screams. To release the fear inside. To cry for help. But there was only silence. Yet, something caught in his throat, choking him. Not words. Not guilt. Something else. Something primal.

He looked down at the liquifying concrete beneath him. He wretched and gagged and watched in horror as cockroaches spewed forth from deep inside. His eyes bulged, threatening to burst from his head. He looked on helplessly as the creatures surrounded him, further encasing him in this inexplicable prison.

He looked ahead, searching the everlasting expanse for a sign of hope.

A child approached him. A young boy. His clothes were torn and stained, and his eyes glistened with tears. Slowly, he reached out. He saw the boy's mouth moving, yet he made no sound. He strained against the roar of the flames, against the restraints of the earth, silently imploring the child to talk louder.

No words came.

Instead, the child unleashed a howl that melted the skin from his bones. He looked on, helpless, as the small body crumbled to dust before him, trapped inside the echo of the ungodly cry.

In that moment, he realized the dead still scream long after they're gone.

HARD TO KILL

ROACH: BOOK 1

1

_____

October 27, 2019

The man's body lay motionless. A barely perceptible rise and fall of his chest was the only sign that life still resided within. Slow, rhythmic breaths settled in time with the ticking of the broken air conditioning.

A steady trickle of saline traveled along an IV line, dripping into his bloodstream via the cannula inserted into the back of his hand. Fresh bandages covered almost every inch of skin. Only his eyes and mouth were exposed.

It wasn't much of a life, but it was a life nevertheless.

A nurse entered, looking weary and uncomfortable as she began another long shift at the end of another long week. Her uniform hung shapelessly on her body. It was spotted with dark patches of unavoidable sweat—a consequence of the oppressive heat.

She wasn't young but had aged well. The few lines on her face betrayed her years and told a story of dedication, rather than strife. However, today, she was tired and disinclined to hide it.

She moved to the bedside, expertly checking the machines that hummed and clicked, exactly as she had done three times a day for the past month.

Nothing had changed.

She couldn't help asking herself if this seemingly futile exercise was worth it. No one knew who the man was. It was unlikely anyone knew he was there. It appeared he was clinging to life for no other reason besides habit.

As she switched out a fresh bag of solution for the IV, she looked down at the body and let out a tired sigh. She followed it up a moment later with an apologetic smile, as if he could hear her thoughts.

"Good morning, you stubborn bastard," she said.

Her voice was friendly. She spoke quietly, despite the mystery man being the only patient in the small room.

She adjusted the pillow beneath his head, fluffing it to remove the dent in the middle where he had been resting.

"There you go. Nice and comfortable. You're healing well, y'know? Those bandages should be coming off in the next day or two. Then we can finally look at that handsome face of yours."

"Has he talked back yet?"

The nurse turned, catching her breath. Then she rolled her eyes and smiled through mild embarrassment.

"Doctor Monroe, I didn't hear you come in," she said.

He smiled, friendly and warm. "Clearly."

Monroe idled into the room, walking with effortless and patient steps. A man who understood there was no reason to rush anywhere. He wore a yellow shirt, paled with age, beneath an open white coat. Also, black pants and shoes. There was no tie around his neck. His collar was unfastened, revealing more of the coarse bristle that coated his face and throat. His eyes were soft and kind, almost out of place on his otherwise hardened face.

"Any change?" he asked, retrieving the medical chart that hung over the bottom railing of the bed.

The nurse shook her head. "No. Same as always."

Monroe sighed. "Well, no news is good news in his case."

"Doctor, do we..." She hesitated. "Is there a way to find out—"

"Who he is?" Monroe nodded. His smile was one of understanding. "Probably. But it's not our place to find answers to those questions. We're here to keep him alive and help him heal. That's it."

She turned to face him. "I know. I'm sorry. But what if he doesn't wake up?"

Monroe placed a friendly hand on her shoulder. "Then we will never know who he was or where he came from, and we will carry on regardless. We provide discreet healthcare to a... *niche* clientele. The people who pay us for this service do so because they trust us. We never ask questions, and nothing good will come from starting now."

"I just feel bad for him. No one's come looking for him."

Monroe shrugged. "Maybe that's for the best. While we have a good idea *what* happened to him, we don't know how or why. Perhaps it should remain that way, hmm?"

The nurse nodded.

"Come on," he said. "We have work to do, and your friend still has healing to do."

The pair of them left the room, disappearing along the corridor outside.

The man in the bed remained still as always, save for his stubborn, shallow breathing. His arms lay exposed on top of the bedsheet. Natural muscle strained against the bandages.

On his right hand, as fresh saline dripped into him, his index finger twitched. A tenacious tremor, barely visible—the sign of a fight not yet lost.

The nurse returned later to repeat her routine of checking the machines and topping up the IV. The air inside the room was stifling, which meant she needed to change the bedsheets every day.

She negotiated the fresh bedding around the man's solid frame on autopilot, having faced that challenge countless times before. As she pulled the clean blanket over the body's feet, she saw one of them twitch. A movement so small it wouldn't have registered in her periphery.

Her brow furrowed with confusion when it twitched again a moment later.

Perhaps a subconscious tick of a restless nerve, she thought. *It happens.*

She glanced up and saw a pair of unblinking brown eyes staring back at her.

The nurse shrieked, clasping her hands to her mouth.

A monotonous moan escaped his dry lips in response.

"You're awake!" she exclaimed.

Her words barely registered over the perpetual echo of a dying scream inside his head. Consciousness washed over him, tugging him awake like a lazy tide trying to drag him out to sea.

A gradual awareness of discomfort and aching caused his heartbeat to quicken, amplified by a pulse of dull pain flooding his body. He instinctively tried to control his breathing, feeling overwhelmed by the rush of sensations he wasn't prepared for.

He swallowed. His throat was coarse and dry.

The world around him settled into focus. Equipment buzzed and blipped to his right. He heard the faint rattle of a tired air conditioning unit.

He closed his eyes and let his mind wander, hoping it would stumble upon the events that had brought him to wherever he was. But the more he tried to remember, the more he came up empty. There was a gaping hole where his memories should be, as if someone had deleted a file from a hard drive but left the folder in place.

His eyes opened again. He took a deep breath to subdue the rising panic inside him.

"Where am I?" he asked.

His question seemed to fall on deaf ears. The nurse gazed at him with wide eyes, frozen to the spot. The only movement was from her mouth.

"You're... you're awake?" she repeated.

The man shifted in his bed, shuffling to sit upright and find a modicum of relief for his aching body. "Yeah. Apparently."

He tried to smile but found he couldn't. It was as if the muscles required hadn't been used in so long, they had forgotten what a smile was. Instead, he felt he simply looked bewildered.

"Please, where am I?" he asked. "What... what is this place?"

His own voice felt foreign to him. The unfamiliar sound, tone, and accent further added to his disorientation.

"I can't believe you're awake," muttered the nurse, mostly to herself.

She shifted her gaze between the man and the door, caught between the urge to run and the urge to stay where she was. The result was a visible hesitation. She simply rocked her weight from one foot to the other.

Finally, her instincts took over.

"I should get Doctor Monroe," she said, her voice still little more than a vacant whisper.

She paced quickly out of the room. The man reached out in a futile gesture to stop her.

"Wait! Don't..." He paused to let out a sigh of defeat and frustration. "...go."

He slouched against the soft pillows behind him, searching for the right position to alleviate the soreness he felt in every inch of his body. He eventually settled for everywhere simply hurting a little bit.

He closed his eyes again and let out a heavy breath.

"Great."

2

He awoke with no sense of how much time had elapsed since the nurse ran out on him. Consequently, it wasn't clear to him how long the man had been standing in his doorway.

He sat up again, wincing first with frustration at having fallen asleep, then as an acknowledgement of the fresh bolt of pain that plunged through his chest. His body tensed with instinctive caution. The new arrival approached the bed with idle steps. He had his hands clasped behind his back and a practiced smile on his face.

"I'm Doctor Monroe," he said after a moment. His voice sounded whiskey-rough, like the bark of an old dog. "How are you feeling?"

"I'm fine," he replied with a poor attempt at stoicism.

"That's encouraging to hear."

The man shifted in his bed, searching for comfort as he sat upright.

"Where am I? How did I get here? And why am I..." He looked down at his arms and body. "Mummified?"

Monroe's smile softened and grew wider. "One thing at a

time. Let's start with something simple. Can you tell me your name?"

The man frowned as he searched the clouded recesses of his mind for the answer.

After a moment, he gave up.

"No, I... I don't know," he said regrettably.

Monroe nodded. "That's okay. I expected as much. What's the last thing you *do* remember?"

The man leaned back against the pillow, allowing his head to loll to the side. His gaze drifted to a random point on the ceiling, away to his left. His vision blurred as he fought against his own mind to recall something—*anything* —of any substance.

He looked back at Monroe. "Nothing. I can't remember anything."

The doctor nodded once more. "That's fine. Don't worry, okay? Post-traumatic amnesia is a relatively common side effect. Now you're awake, most of your blanks should fill themselves in over the next few days. Just try to relax and let it happen."

The man furrowed his brow. "A common side effect of what?"

Monroe took a deep breath. "You've been in a coma for the last month."

"Seriously?"

"You arrived here in one of the worst states I've seen in a long time. First- and second-degree burns covered most of your body. There was a bullet in your left thigh. Another in your chest. You had cuts and bruises all over. You also suffered a head injury, resulting in a severe concussion. You looked as if you'd been hit by a train."

The man let out a heavy sigh. "I sure as hell feel like it right now, let me tell you."

He took a moment to let the doctor's words sink in.

"Burns and bullet wounds?" he said eventually. "What the hell happened to me?"

"I honestly don't know," replied Monroe. "But the surgery to remove the bullets was successful. You were fortunate. They didn't cause any permanent damage to the muscle or bone. Most of the lacerations healed on their own. A couple needed stitching, but that was it. The burns were mostly treated with ointments and antibiotics. You had one that was a little more severe, on your left shoulder. That required a simple skin graft to prevent too much scarring. We kept you bandaged longer because you were comatose, but by all accounts, you were quite lucky."

The man rolled his eyes. "Yeah, real lucky. So, what is this place?"

"This," he explained, gesturing to the room, "is a privately funded medical facility roughly twenty-five miles off the coast of Pattani."

The man stared blankly.

"Thailand," Monroe continued. "This hospital isn't open to the public. Our patients are... not typically fans of law enforcement, shall we say."

The man did not understand, and the struggle to do so gave him a headache.

"How did I get here?" he asked. "And why would I be brought somewhere like this? What the hell did I do?"

Monroe took a heavy breath. "Private security is big business in this part of the world. A couple of contractors happened across your body just outside a forest in Cambodia. They dropped you off on our doorstep. My guess was they assumed you were one of their own. Maybe they felt honor-bound to help a fallen brother. I don't know. They didn't say, and I didn't ask. But that was a little over four weeks ago, and you've been here ever since."

"Huh."

"As for what you did, or how you came to be lying unconscious and on fire in Southeast Asia, I honestly couldn't tell you."

The man nodded slowly. "I see."

"I appreciate this is a lot to take in," offered Monroe.

"You think?"

Monroe took his sharp tone as a sign their conversation had lasted as long as it needed to for now.

"Try to relax and rest up," he said, getting to his feet. "Tomorrow, we'll get those bandages off you, maybe look at starting some basic physical therapy."

"Therapy?" His eyes bulged in their sockets with instant panic. "What, am I paralyzed or something?"

Monroe flashed a comforting smile. "Not at all. But your muscles haven't been used in a month. You need to warm up a little before you go running any triathlons."

The man nodded, relaxing. "Ah, yeah. Makes sense."

"The nurse will be in soon with some food for you. Try to take it easy, okay?"

As Monroe turned to leave, the man called after him.

"Hey, Doc, you said this place was privately funded. Who by, exactly?"

Monroe smiled. Polite and professional with no humor. "Honestly? I don't know and I don't ask. Probably best you don't either."

He rolled his eyes again. "Yeah. Right."

He sank back into the pillows with a heavy sigh and stared up at the ceiling. He focused on a small stain on one of the tiles until his vision blurred. He slowly clenched both fists, fighting against a rising anxiety in his chest.

Monroe looked on, observing the struggle his unknown patient was trying to control. He found himself feeling sympathy for the man who, by all accounts, should be dead. But he would likely make a full recovery, save for some mild scarring. He was impressed by his patient's instinctive resolve. He had seen cases like this before, though not often. The adjustment period after waking from a coma was always tricky. Some people reacted with fear and uncertainty. Others with anger and frustration.

This patient was among the latter.

He couldn't imagine what must be running through his mind right now.

"Just try to relax, all right?" said Monroe finally. "Let your body and your mind rest. There's no hurry."

"Thank you," he replied with a heavy sigh. "I don't mean to sound... I don't know... ungrateful. I just—"

Monroe held up a hand, cutting him off. He smiled again, warmer this time. "Don't apologize. I'm a doctor. I'm used to patients who don't like the fact they need treatment. Trust me."

The man regarded him for a moment, then broke into a deep chuckle.

"Fair enough."

Monroe nodded and left. The man shifted until he found a position that relieved enough pain for him to relax, then closed his eyes.

Monroe sat behind his desk in the small, airless room he called his office. With the stub of a cigar clamped between his fingers, he leaned back in his chair and stared absently at the photograph beside his computer.

The wood frame had faded and chipped over the years.

The photo's color had yellowed from too much time in direct sunlight. He looked at the image of his younger self. He'd had more hair, less waist, and the enthusiasm of a man who believed he had it all figured out.

By his side in the picture was a tall woman with long, curly blonde hair that rested just below her shoulders. She wore a lab coat and a pencil skirt. They were holding hands, like the loving husband and wife they used to be.

He took a long drag of his cigar and blew the thick, blue-gray smoke up to the ceiling with a long breath. He remembered her smile. She was always a good-looking woman, but that smile could light up a room the moment she entered it.

Behind them stood the medical facility he was sitting in. The opportunity to set up their own practice overseas had been too good for either of them to pass up. They were young, idealistic, newly qualified doctors out to make a difference in the world. They were both devoted to their work.

Him more so than her.

He worked every hour he could, focused on turning their private medical practice into a profitable business. But he did so at her expense. Months of neglect turned into years. Eventually, he caught her sleeping with one of the male nurses. She cited a loveless marriage as an obvious justification for her infidelity and said their venture wasn't worth what it cost them.

She left, taking her father's money with her. With the bulk of their investment capital gone, Monroe struggled to keep the facility afloat. When the opportunity to tend the wounds of injured mercenaries off the books presented itself, he had no choice but to take it. The money was good, and as his reputation grew, he became more protected from the dangerous world in which his patients lived.

That was over fifteen years ago.

He stubbed out the remains of the cigar in the glass ashtray beside him. He caught himself thinking back to his earlier conversation with his nurse. About not intervening in their mystery patient's life. About not asking questions. Despite his experience and professionalism, he had grown fond of the mystery man. He and his nursing staff shared a hushed support for him. Seeing him now, awake and lost... he felt compelled to do something.

Being a doctor was all he had. If he were going to continue letting it consume his life, maybe it was time he found a way to help people outside of the practice too. After all, he didn't treat a global network of mercenaries without getting to know a few people.

Monroe reached for his phone and dialed a number from memory.

"Hello?" said a female voice. The tone was cautious and restrained.

Monroe smiled. "Hey, Val. It's me."

There was a low, audible sigh of relief. "Clyde, is that you? How you been, sweetie?"

"Oh, you know, I keep on keeping on. Business good?"

"You know it, sugar."

"Listen, I was hoping you could do me a favor. I need to keep this quiet, and I'd owe you."

"Clyde, honey, I'll just deduct from all the favors I owe *you*."

The pair shared a laugh.

"Fair enough," continued Monroe. "I got a patient who just woke up from a coma. Been out around a month. He's experiencing some memory loss..."

"And you want me to see if I can ID him?"

"Could you try?"

"Put everything you have into a draft e-mail on the usual account, no matter how small or insignificant. I'll pick it up and take a look. Give me twenty-four hours, okay?"

Monroe grinned. "You're the best, Val."

"I know," she replied, then hung up.

He sat back in his chair and spun around to face the window. He stared out at the dry trees and grass, baking beneath the scorching afternoon sun.

It couldn't hurt to ask. He just hoped his mystery patient could handle potentially finding out something about himself he might not like.

3

The man looked at himself in the bathroom mirror. His hospital gown clung to his bulky frame, resting just above the knee. The short sleeves revealed his large arms—muscular but not defined. In the reflection, he saw the nurse and Doctor Monroe standing in the doorway, looking on patiently, holding the bandages that had been carefully removed only moments earlier.

He was initially anxious about them being taken off. He had imagined the worst in terms of potential scarring. The reality wasn't nearly as bad as that. Aside from a thin layer of hardened tissue on his forehead and right cheek, he looked the same as he had before.

And therein lay the biggest shock of all.

He stared into the brown eyes of a stranger, which stared right back. He was unfamiliar to himself. Not bad-looking, he thought. A strong jaw, chiseled features, some stubble... nothing to complain about.

He just wished he knew more about the man looking back at him.

"Are you okay?" asked Monroe with genuine curiosity.

The man poked and prodded his face, as if searching for a button that would activate his memories.

"I think so," he replied vaguely. "I mean, I don't look like I've been injured, which is something... right?"

Monroe smiled. "It is. As I said yesterday, most of your wounds were superficial. You were always going to heal as good as new. At least physically."

"I think you look handsome," added the nurse.

Monroe glanced sideways at her. She caught the look and shrugged.

The man felt his freshly unwrapped cheeks flush with color. He looked away from himself, fixing the nurse's reflection with a grateful gaze.

"Uh, thanks, Nurse... um... Nurse..."

"Conrad," she replied. "But you can call me Clarissa."

Monroe took a deep, audible breath.

"Will you stop?" he hissed playfully. He stepped inside the bathroom and dumped the pile of bandages in the trashcan. Then he looked at the man's reflection. "This is a big step, I know. Seeing yourself for the first time since waking up can be overwhelming. But this point is usually when patients start to see some of their memories returning. Seeing themselves can act as a catalyst. Just remember what I said, okay? Give it time. This is a marathon, not a sprint. You'll get there."

The man inhaled a weary breath. "Yeah, I know, Doc. I'm just—"

"Frustrated?"

He chuckled. "Yeah, something like that."

"Now come on. I believe you have a physical therapy session."

"I do." He spun on the balls of his feet to face the doorway and Nurse Conrad. "Go easy on me, okay?"

She smiled, feeling her own cheeks heat up. "I thought you were supposed to be tough?"

He smiled back. "Working on it."

He shuffled back into his room and over to the bed. He sat down heavily, tired from the exertion.

Monroe followed, heading for the door and stepping out into the corridor. Nurse Conrad idled by the bathroom door.

"Your chariot awaits," said Monroe.

A moment later, a tall, lean man wearing clean scrubs that were maybe three sizes too big for him appeared in the doorway. He was pushing a wheelchair.

"This is Somchai," announced the doctor. "He'll be your physical therapist."

The new arrival smiled without a word, leaning slightly on the handles of the chair.

The man looked at him and nodded a brief greeting. Then his gaze drifted to the wheelchair. His shoulders slumped forward in pre-emptive defeat.

"Is that necessary?" he asked.

Nurse Conrad moved to the side of it and smiled at him. "You can always walk..."

He stared over at the bathroom for a moment, then back at her. He rolled his eyes. "All right. Fair point."

Monroe looked on as Somchai and Nurse Conrad helped the patient ease himself into the chair. The three of them then headed out into the corridor. The faint smell of disinfectant tugged at the man's nostrils.

Same smell, any hospital in the world, he thought.

Monroe stepped back to let them all pass.

"I'll call back later to see how you got on," he said as they made their way down the corridor, toward the therapy room.

The man waved a hand casually for Monroe to see before they disappeared around a corner.

Flanked by Somchai and Nurse Conrad, the man shuffled tentatively toward his room. He leaned wearily on his walker after a grueling, intensive few hours. As he made his way along the featureless, bland corridor, he glanced to his sides, offering a grateful and determined smile to each of them.

"Thank you," he said to Nurse Conrad when they stopped outside his room.

She grinned a silent *you're welcome* and blushed.

He let out a pained sigh as he turned in the doorway to face Somchai.

"You... you're evil. I don't like you."

Somchai was tall and wiry, yet deceptively stronger than his frame suggested. Despite a heavy accent, he had a competent grasp of the English language. He had been working with him on his exercises.

He laughed from the belly. "No pain, no gain! You will be tap dancing again in no time, my friend!"

His words were slow and measured, as if to ensure they were pronounced correctly in his broken accent.

The man smiled. "I'll settle for walking unaided some-time soon."

Somchai shrugged and laughed.

Nurse Conrad chuckled. "The way you're going, it won't be long at all. Just try not to push yourself too hard, okay?"

The man nodded courteously. "Yes, ma'am."

He turned and walked tentatively into his room, leaving the nurses to their duties. He collapsed onto his bed and rolled awkwardly onto his back. His heavy eyes closed almost instantly.

———

The low rattling of the HVAC unit was barely audible over the dull murmur that rippled around the room. Three levels below the bustling streets of New York City, beneath one of the tallest buildings to stand against the iconic skyline, seven analysts hunched over their workstations. Each station consisted of three large monitors, a keyboard and mouse, and a webcam positioned on the rim of the middle screen.

Streams of data flowed over the displays on each desk, scrutinized by the expert that occupied it.

The small team was comprised of a mixed bunch of people. Men and women. Young and old. No obvious imbalance of race or gender. Just seven people who were there because they were among the best at what they did.

The desks formed a tight horseshoe, with three along each side and one at the end, by the door. Covering the far wall was a large bank of screens. Some were blank. Some showed satellite imagery and news channels from around the world.

The young man sitting at the end desk tapped feverishly away on the keys as he worked to filter the influx of information before him. A short ping on his left monitor distracted him. He looked over, irritated by the interruption.

There was a pop-up box in the center of the screen, dominated by a red triangle with an exclamation point on the left-hand side.

The young man frowned. "What the hell..."

He clicked the alert, which brought another screen to the forefront of his middle monitor. He quickly scanned the data. His eyes grew wide. He swallowed hard. A thin film of sweat appeared instantly on the back of his neck.

"Oh, man."

He opened a number pad and tapped in a short code. His webcam illuminated as a video call rang out on his screen. He swallowed hard again as it was answered.

The man who appeared on the screen looked frustrated by the call. His pursed lips formed a thin line on his clean, chiseled face. His dark eyes narrowed.

"What is it?" he asked.

The young analyst took a deep, calming breath. "Mr. Crow, we've had a hit on one of our algorithmic searches."

His expression remained the same. Unimpressed. "And?"

"It came from Thailand, sir. A phone call to someone on our watchlist."

"Who?"

"Valerie Edwards."

A minute twitch of his eyebrow was the only sign his interest was piqued. She was a former CIA analyst who had been on their radar for over a year as a potential recruit.

"I'll be right down."

The call cut off. The analyst got to work, bringing up screens and programs and maps summarizing all the information from the alert, ready for...

Brandon Crow.

The door burst open. Crow strode in with the confidence of someone who knew he was unquestioningly in charge. The atmosphere in the room tightened.

Crow was tall, a shade over six-four. A flawless

complexion masked his years. His tailored suit clung to his sculpted frame.

"What do we have?" he asked.

The analyst waved him over. He pointed to his screens as Crow appeared next to him. "The call came from a medical facility near Pattani, Thailand."

Crow paced back and forth behind the analyst's chair, like an impatient tiger waiting for lunch.

"What type of facility?" he asked.

A few key presses later, satellite imagery filled the large screens along the back wall.

"Privately funded. Believed to be used by mercenaries as a place of refuge."

"And who placed the call?"

More tapping. A picture and a profile appeared beside the map.

"Doctor Clyde Monroe, born November ninth, 1956. Divorced. No children."

"How does he know Valerie Edwards?"

"Still working on the connection, sir, but it was definitely her. Voice recognition software matched at ninety-seven percent."

Crow stopped, staring thoughtfully at the satellite imagery of the area.

"Zoom out," he said.

The screen panned out, revealing the Gulf of Thailand. His eyes zeroed in on the land across the water.

Cambodia.

Phnom Penh.

He let out a taut breath. His eyes narrowed with concern. "What did the call say?"

The analyst stumbled as he sifted through the data on his own screens.

"Come on!" urged Crow, impatience clear in his voice. "What did they say?"

With a nervous cough, the analyst said, "Monroe asked Valerie to find any information she could about one of his patients."

"Which one?"

"We don't know, sir. And neither does he. The patient woke from a coma yesterday and is apparently suffering from memory loss."

"How long was he in a coma?"

"Monroe said about a month."

Crow connected dots in his mind that only he knew existed. It took seconds for the picture to become clear.

"Okay, listen up," he said to the room. "This is now a live operation. I want a team on the ground at that facility in twelve hours. I want eyes and ears inside the building ASAP. I'll be coordinating everything personally from this room. No one leaves. No one sleeps. Hell, you piss under your desk if you have to. There is a high priority target inside that hospital, and he needs eliminating. Questions?"

The young analyst looked over. "Sir, can we... can we do that? What if one of the agencies finds out? Or... or GlobaTech? I mean, we're not sanctioned to run independent operations like this, are we?"

Without hesitation, Crow reached beneath his suit jacket and retrieved a gun. He placed the barrel to the analyst's head and pulled the trigger. The shot was deafening inside the small, underground room. The young man's body lurched to the side, collapsing in a lifeless heap on the floor beside his chair.

Crow holstered his gun and addressed the room again.

"Any more questions?" He was met with silence. "Good. Now get to work."

4

October 29, 2019

The world still burned. The sky still glowed red behind low clouds made of dark smoke. Walls of flame continued to border the horizon in all directions, enclosing him in his own personal purgatory.

He was still on his hands and knees, still staring at the ground through tears of regret as he melted into it, like resting on concrete quicksand.

The noise of the roaring fire was deafening. Faces continued to gaze at him, locked in horrifying screams that could no longer be heard. He looked around at them. The demons that guarded his prison remained, but they were silent.

They were losing their power.

Ahead of him, a young child ambled toward him. His skin was still bruised and blackened by smoke. His expression was calm. The eyes offered a dark, emotionless gaze aimed in his direction but without the focus they once had.

The boy held out a hand to him but not with the intention of taking his. Instead, he pointed, mouthing inaudible words. He followed the boy's finger, looking down at his own chest—the object of the child's attention. Immediately, he felt pain. Tension began to consume his entire body. He opened his mouth to shout for help, but his words were trapped, blocked by something in his throat.

He coughed and wretched, straining and tearing his stomach muscles until he expelled the sickness within. A thick, black stream of cockroaches spewed forth, covering the earth around him. The final bug flew from his lips, propelled by the scream that followed it.

The sound of his own voice startled him. He shouted again, testing to make sure it wasn't a fluke. Once more, his scream was heard.

He laughed and looked up at the boy, who stared back impassively. The boy lowered his arm to his side, turned, and began to walk away.

"Hey, wait!" called the man.

The boy didn't hear him. Or perhaps he simply chose not to listen.

He looked down and reached for a cockroach, grabbing it gently between his finger and thumb and lifting it to his face. He examined it curiously. Its legs moved, desperately searching for traction.

Smiling, the man tossed it aside. It landed without acknowledging the fall and scuttled away. Then his attention turned to the earth beneath him. His fingertips were now pressed on solid ground, as if the earth was healing itself.

His landscape was changing, evolving around him. He brought a knee up to his chest and planted his foot firmly. He tested his weight and his strength to support it. He pushed himself upright, standing tall and turning a slow circle. The walls of fire began to shrink.

It filled him with hope.

He ran after the boy, reaching out to place a hand on his shoulder.

The boy turned and looked up at him with the same sad eyes as before.

"Wait," said the man. "Where are you going?"

"Home," whispered the boy. "Come with me."

The man shook his head, confused.

"I... I can't. I need to find my own home."

"Roach."

"What?"

The boy pointed at him.

"Roach," he said again.

The man looked down to see a lone cockroach clinging to his chest.

The boy stepped forward and took the man's hand in his. "Time to wake up."

The man frowned. "What do you mean?"

"Wake up," said the boy patiently. "Wake up. Wake up..."

The man's eyes snapped wide with confusion as he was violently pulled from his deep slumber. Doctor Monroe was standing over him, pushing his shoulder to rock him awake.

"Wake up!" he hissed.

He saw the panic in his eyes and the sweat on his brow.

"What? What is it?" he asked.

"You have to move. You must hide. Now!"

He shifted himself up in the bed, rubbing his eyes to help them adjust to the unwelcome influx of fluorescent light.

"What are you talking about? What's going on?"

"They're here. They're here for you. You have to hide!"

"I... I don't understand. Who's here?"

He heard a distant sound, which he immediately identified as gunfire. The short, loud triple-crack of bullets triggered a sense of familiarity. A previously clouded instinct he could now embrace. But with it came a flood of knowledge that momentarily stunned him. A respect for the danger he now understood he was facing.

He rested back against the pillow as a wave of dizziness washed over him.

Monroe threw the covers back and moved his legs over the side. Then he reached over, grabbed his wrists, and dragged him upright.

"There's no time," he urged. "You need to move now, or they will kill you."

His mind snapped back into focus. He stared at the doctor. He felt his jaw clench with desperate yet measured intention.

"Okay, let's go."

Three men swept through the wide, minimalistic reception area in a tight triangle formation. Dressed head to toe in black, unmarked outfits, they moved like deadly shadows seeking to extinguish the light around them.

The two security guards who occupied the front desk had been riddled with bullets the second they got to their feet. No hesitation. No remorse. Just necessary casualties of a mission that must succeed.

A corridor branched off on either side of the desk, leading further into the building. The man at the tip of the spear looked at each one in turn as the sound of faint screaming echoed along them.

News of their arrival had traveled quickly around the facility.

Beneath his mask, the man known as One felt a discreet smile creep onto his face. He knew he had already outsmarted and defeated any potential adversary. Prior to entering the building, the team had secured the perimeter and sealed all other exits from the outside with chains and padlocks. The only way out was through them.

He relaxed his broad and commanding frame, allowing the suppressed SMG he carried to hang from its shoulder strap. The two men with him did the same.

He glanced to his left.

"Two, wait here," he ordered with an authoritative tone. "Anyone who isn't with us comes through here, you drop them. Understood?"

His teammate moved back and positioned himself centrally in front of the main doors, tightening his grip on his own weapon.

One turned to the other man.

"Three, you're with me." He gestured to the corridor on the right with an upward flick of his head. "Sweep and clear every room. No survivors. We'll reconvene on the upstairs landing at the opposite end. The target is above us, in a room against the eastern wall."

They exchanged a simple nod of understanding, then moved for their respective corridors. They held their weapons once more in a firm grip, leveled and pointing forward, moving in sync with their eyeline.

One moved at a steady pace, aware of every sound and movement around him. The thick soles of his combat boots muted his steps on the stained floor tiles along the narrow corridor. He paused at every door he came to, nudged it open with the barrel of his gun, and peered inside to make sure it was empty.

The second room he came to wasn't.

He pushed the door open, expertly checking his angles before stepping inside. It was a small office, consisting of little more than a plain desk with a laptop stood open on it. The window behind it had the blinds closed. The room opened out to his left. He saw the nurse standing with her back to the corner, her hands pressed to the wall. Silent tears streamed down her face from eyes held wide with fear.

Knowing how intimidating it would look while wearing a full mask, he tilted his head slightly. It was an unspoken acknowledgement that he was about to kill her and felt completely indifferent about it.

Nurse Conrad clasped a hand to her mouth, muting the whimper that escaped her lips. She closed her eyes, forcing more tears to flow down her face.

Quietly, she prayed.

One paused for a moment, looking at the nurse with curious apathy as she silently confronted her own mortality. He had seen the same reaction a thousand times before. It never helped.

Wrong place, wrong time, he thought. *Sorry, sister.*

He tapped the trigger three times. The single-round bursts punched into the nurse sequentially and without compromise. The first two hit either side of her chest, forcing each shoulder to lurch back into the wall, leaving splashes of dark blood behind her. As she opened her mouth to scream, the final round smashed into the center of her forehead. Her eyes managed to roll halfway back into her skull before she slid to the floor, resting in a lifeless heap.

He moved back into the corridor as the sound of similar gunfire came from the other side of the building.

Everything was proceeding as planned.

The man stumbled and shuffled as fast as he could. He leaned on Monroe's shoulder as they made their way toward the doctor's office, situated at the end of the corridor.

The sound of gunfire somewhere below made them stop for a moment. Three bullets. Precise. Deadly. They exchanged a worried glance.

He pushed his body to support as much of his own weight as he could as they neared the door.

"I don't want to hide in your goddamn office," he protested. "I can help."

Monroe pressed on. The thin film of sweat on his brow glistened in the fluorescent lights overhead.

"How... exactly... could you help?" he managed between deep, desperate breaths. "You can... barely walk. Besides, they won't find you... in here. Trust me."

Monroe unhooked the man's arm and guided him to rest against the wall outside his office. He fumbled for the key to the door.

"Who are they?" the man asked. "Do you know?"

"I have no idea, but that's the least of our concerns." He turned the key and thrust the door open. A blast of chilled air conditioning hit them from within. "Come on."

He moved to offer his support again but was pushed away. The man stood upright, using the wall for balance and support.

"I can do it," he said.

His jaw muscles clenched with determination. His body ached and resisted the effort, but he walked regardless. He understood he had no choice but to find the strength he needed.

He reached for the back of the chair facing the desk, desperate to lean on something for a moment's respite. He looked around the office. The desk and chairs. The window and the air conditioning unit. The two large bookcases to his left.

Something was off, but he couldn't place what it was.

"What's going on here?" he asked.

Monroe locked the door behind them and moved around his desk. He shifted his weight restlessly between each leg, as if resisting the urge to pace. "What do you mean?"

He was avoiding making eye contact.

"There's something not right here," said the man.

"Yes... there are men with guns attacking my hospital!" Monroe snapped.

"No, something else. Something in here. What are you hiding, Doc? What did you do?"

Monroe hesitated a moment before letting out sigh of resignation. "This is... this is my fault."

The man forced himself upright again. He pushed the chair away to remove any further temptation to rest on it. "What makes you say that?"

Monroe looked away. "I... I reached out to an old friend yesterday. Someone I've gotten to know well over the years. Someone I trust. I asked them to dig around and see if they could find any information about you. See if we could find out what happened. I... felt sorry for you and wanted to help."

"And you think whoever's firing guns downstairs is here because of that? You think they're here for me?"

"Of course, they are, dammit!"

The man ignored Monroe's short tone. "But why would someone want to kill me? Did you find something out about me?"

"No, I never heard back from my contact. But think about it... I place a call and mention you, then less than twenty-four hours later, we're under attack?"

"So, this is my fault?"

"What? No, of course not. You don't remember anything. But... look, this is how it works, okay? Whoever is here is likely here on behalf of someone else. Someone who tapped into my phone call yesterday. It's unlikely my phone line has a pre-existing bug on it, which means whoever heard my call was made aware of it because it was flagged up to them. That means some computer, some algorithm somewhere heard something on my call it didn't like."

The man stared at the floor.

"You know an awful lot about this spy stuff, considering you're a doctor..." he mused.

Monroe shrugged. "You don't work in a place like this for as long as I have without getting to know a few things."

"So, you think I'm on some government watchlist? Who the hell am I, Doc?"

"I don't know, but whoever's here isn't playing around. They're clearly here to kill someone, and the odds are it's you. You need to leave."

The man looked around again. "And what do you suggest, exactly? Aside from the fact I can barely move, I'm in a hospital gown and locked in your office with armed hostiles between me and the main entrance."

Monroe opened a desk drawer and took out an envelope. He held it in his hands for a moment, feeling the weight, running every possible outcome through his mind. Finally, he held it out to his patient.

"Take this," he said.

The man did. "What is it?"

"It's two thousand U.S. dollars. It should be enough to get you out of the country. Go anywhere. Start a new life. Just... get away from here and don't draw any attention to yourself. Ever."

He shook his head, struggling to keep a handle on what was happening.

"I can't take this," he said. "Why do you even *have* this kind of money lying around anyway?"

Monroe smiled humorlessly. "Sometimes remaining favorable to a naturally untrusting clientele isn't cheap."

The two men held each other's gaze for a long moment. An entire unspoken conversation transpired between them. Gratitude. Appreciation. Understanding. Acceptance.

The man nodded a silent *thank you.*

Outside, another short burst of gunfire rang out, much closer this time. A man's voice yelled out before being cut short by another bullet. Both men recognized it as Somchai's.

Monroe hustled over to the bookcase from behind his desk. "There's no time to lose. Come on."

He pulled a book at his eye level toward him. A latch clicked. The bookcase popped open from the wall. Monroe pulled at the edge, creating a gap big enough to fit through.

The man looked around the room again.

That's why it looked strange, he thought. *The outside wall seemed bigger than the interior. Now I know why.*

"What's this? A panic room?" he asked.

Monroe shook his head. "Not quite. It's an escape tunnel. Leads you down to the basement and under the grounds of the hospital. It brings you out about a quarter mile east, just before the local village."

"But... how? Why?"

"The basement level was completely blocked off when we bought the building, many years ago. No access except for this one door. Originally, it was an indulgence of mine. A boyhood fantasy, if you will. But when the nature of my business changed, it seemed like a sound investment. I had the bookcase installed as a false door. The whims of an aging fan of spy fiction, I guess."

He smiled weakly.

"Come with me," urged the man. "You don't need to stay here."

"Yes, I do, son. If we both go, they'll know we're on the run. If I stay, I can say you left weeks ago and buy you some time."

"But—"

"No buts. Now go, while you still can."

Without giving him a chance to argue, Monroe ushered him through the gap, careful not to topple him in his weakened state.

The man placed his hand against the cold, damp brick for balance. There was a passage ahead of him that led to a staircase, which disappeared to the right. Clutching the envelope of cash, he stared back through the gap at the face of the only friend he had.

"I'm sorry this is happening because of me," he said.

Monroe let out a taut breath. "It's not. It's happening because of me. Now go. Good luck... and Godspeed."

He pushed the door closed, engulfing the man in darkness.

After hearing the latch click back into place, he sat behind his desk and reached for the phone. The line was dead. He figured as much.

There was a noise outside his office. He looked up and

saw two dark outlines in the frosted glass. He held his breath, his gaze transfixed on the door.

A second later, the door burst open, tearing from its hinges. Two men entered, holding SMGs loose but ready in front of them.

Three stood guard in the doorway, his back to the frame, so he could see both the room and corridor outside.

One stepped up to the desk and removed his mask. He grinned at Monroe.

"What's up, Doc?"

5

Monroe gripped the arms of his chair. The new arrival loomed over him, smiling with menace from across the desk.

"Who are you?" he asked, using every ounce of physical and mental strength to remain calm. "What do you want with me?"

The man in front of him narrowed his eyes, still smiling. Except now he appeared smug, like he knew something no one else did.

"My name is of little consequence," he replied. "But you can call me One. My friend over by the door? That's Three. And you... are Doctor Monroe."

Monroe took a short breath. "You seem well informed."

"Oh, I am. Now..." He took a seat opposite. "Me and you are gonna have a little chat."

At the top of the steps, behind the hidden door, surrounded by darkness, the man leaned against the cold brick wall. Mostly for support. Partly to think.

Everything had happened so fast. The doctor had woken him, panicked. There was gunfire throughout the hospital. He had been bungled through a secret doorway to hide because his life was apparently in danger.

He closed his eyes.

What the hell is going on? he wondered. *If this is really my life, I don't want to know who I am.*

His hand squeezed almost involuntarily at the envelope of cash.

Maybe I don't have to...

He took a slow, deep breath, conscious of making any noise. He stood upright, placing a hand on the wall for steadiness. As his eyes adjusted to the gloom, he noticed a sliver of light, like a pale yellow string held up against the night sky. He followed it to its origin—a spy hole in the door.

He frowned, hesitating for a moment. Then he moved toward it, taking each step carefully so as to remain silent. Slowly, he placed his eye to the light. The lens wasn't concave, like normal. It was like looking through a magnified keyhole. He could see the room. The armed man clad in black standing by the door. Monroe behind his desk, talking. The man with no mask.

One.

His eyes popped wide. His jaw hung loose. He clasped a hand to his mouth before the gasp could escape. He forgot himself and fell to the cold, hard floor. He remembered he didn't have full use of his legs only when he landed.

He scurried away from the door until his back found the wall. He dropped the envelope and clutched at his head as an intense pain devoured his skull. He gritted his teeth, desperately fighting to stifle a scream of agony. It was as if his mind had awoken, and an unfiltered, uncontrolled stream of data was gushing into it.

And just like that, he remembered everything.

"Tell me, Doc, where's the patient?" asked One.

"You'll have to be more specific," replied Monroe. "Assuming you haven't killed any of them, there were six currently receiving treatment here."

"That's funny." He leaned forward. "Don't try to be funny. You know exactly which patient I mean."

Monroe regarded him as he weighed his options. He fought every urge he had to glance at the escape door.

"I have a hunch, yes," he said after a few moments. "If you mean the patient who was suffering with amnesia, he's gone."

One flicked an eyebrow. "Gone?"

"Yes, gone. He was brought in here... oh, just over a month or so ago, now. Poor sonofabitch was in a coma. Shot up and burned, found somewhere in Cambodia. Two mercenaries brought him in. Guess they figured he was one of their own. I don't know and I didn't ask."

"You didn't ask? What kind of doctor doesn't ask about their patient's history?"

"Excuse me—I'm a great doctor, thank you very much. However, this isn't your typical hospital, and my patients aren't your typical patients. Sometimes conventional rules don't apply here. But I'm guessing you already know that."

One nodded. "I do."

"So, why are you here? If you know what this place is and who funds it, why risk attacking it? Retribution for this will be... I imagine... unpleasant."

One shrugged. "I don't know who funds your hospital, but then, neither do you. Not really. You don't ask questions to preserve your reputation. I get that. I respect it. Truth be told, I've known fellas who found themselves here on occasion. You're doing an honorable job, Doc. But now isn't the time for misplaced confidence and concerns about your reputation. See, you don't need to worry about getting any future business right now. If you don't start being honest with me, you won't have a future. Am I being clear?"

"Crystal," replied Monroe. "But I don't know what you want me to say. The man you're talking about woke from his coma a little over a week ago. He was... distressed. He couldn't remember anything of importance—his name, what happened to him, how he got here... nothing. We tried to calm him down. He panicked and ran. Haven't seen him since. Hell, he could be a thousand miles from here by now."

"Yes, he could. Except he isn't, is he?"

"W-what do you mean?"

"I mean, as liars go, you're not the worst I've seen. But you *are* lying, Doctor Monroe. Now stop insulting my intelligence and tell me where he is."

Monroe let out a short, stubborn breath. "Why?"

"Because I want to talk to him."

"Talk?"

"Okay, fine. *Kill*. Are you happy now?"

"Ecstatic."

One leaned forward again with a sudden movement. He slammed his hands down on the desk and slowly pushed himself to his feet. "Tell me where he is!"

Monroe held his gaze defiantly. "I... don't... know."

One reached behind him and drew the pistol holstered to his back. He aimed it with infinite steadiness at

Monroe's face. "I know you're lying. You know you're lying. You probably know *how* I know you're lying. Stop doing what you're doing right now and tell me where the patient is, or I will shoot you. And look at my face, Doc—I'm *not* lying."

Monroe's stoicism finally gave way to an understandable and human fear. "T-tell me who you are. What do you want with him?"

One smiled humorlessly. "Who I am and who I represent are not your concern. I was tasked with finding him and killing him—which, honestly, I thought I'd already done."

Monroe's fear gave way to surprise. It was an almost throwaway comment, but to him, it changed everything.

"What do you mean?" he asked.

"See, your boy used to work for me. He was part of my team. He messed up on a job, and I had to put him down. Turns out, he's a stubborn bastard, which is why I'm here. Been looking for him ever since Cambodia. Now I know he was here yesterday. Tell me where he is now, and maybe... *maybe* you won't suffer."

Monroe ran a hand over the coarse hair on his face, stalling as he thought of the best way out of the situation. If there even was one.

He soon resigned himself to the fact that there likely wasn't.

"He left in the early hours this morning," he said with a sigh. "I told him I'd inquired about who he was—which is how you found him, I'm guessing? He was worried about drawing any unwanted attention to this place, so he left. I urged him not to go. He's still healing and far from a hundred percent, but he was insistent. Guess he had a point..."

One looked at him. He figured the doctor was lying, but

he couldn't be sure. If he was, it was a much better lie than the first one he told.

He lowered his gun slightly, distracted by his own thoughts.

If the doctor was telling the truth, they were wasting valuable time. If the patient was still injured... still unsure who he was... he wouldn't have gotten far in less than a day.

He looked back at Monroe, re-establishing his unwavering aim. "Where did he go?"

Monroe shrugged. "Out the main entrance and right. After that, I don't know."

"You didn't try to stop him? Or follow him?"

Monroe shook his head. "I have obligations to more patients than just him. If he wanted to refuse further medical treatment, that's his choice."

"Damn, Doc. That's pretty cold. What about that hypocritical oath you took?"

"You mean Hippocratic?"

One shrugged. "Whatever. Either way, you're no longer any use to me."

He fired twice, putting two rounds in Monroe's chest. The force of the impact sent him flying back against his chair, toppling it over. He landed out of sight behind the desk.

One turned away and headed for the door.

"Come on," he said to Three as he passed him. "We've got some legwork to do, apparently."

He waited fifteen minutes before opening the door and walking gingerly back into Monroe's office. He headed straight for the desk and collapsed to his knees beside the doctor's body. He felt the thick wetness of blood stain through his thin hospital gown but paid it little heed.

Monroe's eyes were wide, as if transfixed on an unseen horror above him. His breathing came in short, desperate rasps.

The man placed a hand firmly on the chest wounds. "Jesus, Doc, what were you thinking?"

Monroe let his head roll to the side. He stared up at his patient. "They... they... were going to kill me... anyway. Had to... to... hide... you."

"It'll be okay, Doc. Just take it easy."

The man lifted his hand. The blood loss was significant, and the wounds were critical.

Damn it.

Monroe tried to reach for him, but his hand fell short, instead landing on his bent knee. He gripped it as hard as he could. "They... they... knew... you. Must... run."

The man took the doctor's hand and squeezed it gently. He smiled to offer comfort. "I know he did. I heard everything. But it'll be okay. It'll all be okay. I'm going to fix this, I promise."

Monroe's eyes fought to roll back inside his head. "H-how?"

The man smiled. "Because I remember, Doc. I remember everything. Seeing him must've been a trigger. It hit me all at once. I know what happened to me. I know why. I know who the men were and who sent them. I owe you my life, Doc. I swear to you, I won't let what happened here be for nothing."

Again, Monroe tried to lift his hand. "W-who... are... you?"

The man held Monroe's hand once more before resting on his chest, pressing it down on the wounds. It would only be a matter of minutes now. He would wait with him. He didn't deserve to die alone, not after everything he had done to help him.

The man held Monroe's gaze and took a deep breath.

"My name's William Roachford," he said as he shifted to sit down beside him. "But my friends call me Roach."

SIX MONTHS LATER

6

The glass exploded under the impact of the man's body, scattering thousands of shards across the sidewalk. The sounds of the city's nightlife drifted into the bar—the hustle of people shuffling toward their next drink, the distant wailing of sirens, the lazy crashing of a calm tide on the nearby shore...

...and the grunt of a semi-conscious man landing awkwardly on the sidewalk.

He rolled over on his front, pressing his hands to the ground to push himself up on all fours. Glass tore at his palms, but he ignored it. A combination of alcohol, anger, and fear numbed his senses.

The crowd of people who had been walking by when he made his surprising exit stopped, forming a wide circle that spilled into the narrow road. A mixture of concern and excitement filled their hushed murmurs as they collectively reached for their cell phones.

The man brought one knee to his chest. He planted his foot firmly and glanced behind him at the door he never got the chance to use. Gritting his teeth and scowling through the pain, he forced himself upright. He turned as another man stepped out to the street.

Roach stopped just in front of the doorway to the bar, feeling the first crunch of shattered glass beneath his boot. He rolled his right shoulder, relieving built-up tension in the muscle caused by the exertion of throwing a grown man through a window. His T-shirt looked small on his bulky frame. Months of having little else to do besides work out had paid off, toning and defining his already impressive physique.

"Are you out of your goddamn mind?" yelled the man. Blood from his palms dripped to the ground.

Roach shrugged. "You were asked to leave. You didn't. I made you. Get over it and go home, Eddie."

Eddie stepped forward, fists clenched. "Who do you think you are, huh? My friends are in there, and when they come out, they're gonna—"

"Escort you home," interrupted Roach.

Eddie smiled. "I don't think so, asshole."

Roach held his gaze, keeping any trace of emotion off his face with practiced ease. "Wanna bet?"

He heard movement behind him and stepped to the side as two more men bustled through the doorway. One moved to Eddie's side. The other stopped in front of Roach, posturing as he tried to stare him down.

Roach leaned slightly to look past him. He gestured at Eddie with a nod, then straightened and fixed the man before him with a stare so cold, it could sink the Titanic.

"Your friend's done for the night," he said. "He's clearly

had a few too many. Make sure he gets home safe, would you?"

The man remained unfazed. He was marginally taller than Roach and about as broad. His skin was a dark olive. While Eddie was a tourist, probably American, Roach suspected this guy was a local, meaning he may not have understood everything he just said to him.

Not that it mattered. Roach was fluent in another language that was universally understood and arguably better suited to situations like this. Learning it had been easy. There were fewer words.

He held the man's gaze, studying his body language in his periphery. He saw the muscles in his arms tense and flex. His weight was shifting between legs. His breathing had quickened.

He was preparing to fight.

Roach raised a questioning eyebrow. "You sure you want to do this?"

The man looked around. Seeing the crowd seemed to spur him on. Pride replaced logic. There was no backing out now.

Roach took a deep, patient breath as he waited for the inevitable attack.

No more words.

The man moved his right arm. There was little wind-up. His feet stayed rooted to the spot.

Amateur, thought Roach.

He almost felt bad for the guy.

Almost.

He stepped forward, left leg first, and turned his torso clockwise. He brought his left arm up and stepped into the man's body. As the blow connected with his shoulder and upper arm, Roach snaked his hand around the man's neck and clasped the base of his skull. With effortless strength, he forced his head down. He brought the knee of his back leg up to meet it. The man's nose and cheekbone smashed into the thick, unforgiving bone of Roach's patella.

They caved as if made of sponge.

Roach discarded the man's now unconscious body to the side. It crashed unceremoniously to the ground.

He directed his attention to Eddie and his remaining friend. "I said... go home."

The other man stepped forward. He was shorter and slimmer than the first but just as angry.

"All right, don't..." muttered Roach with a frustrated sigh.

The man stormed toward him. Roach stepped to meet him, jabbing the outer groove of his palm and thumb into his throat. The man's eyes bulged as he began choking from the blow. He immediately staggered back, clasping at his throat.

Roach followed it up with a sharp elbow, smashing the area where it met the forearm into the man's temple. The bone there was thick and calcified. It was like swinging a brick at a bunch of grapes.

Minimum movement. Maximum effect.

Two men now littered the street. The crowd collectively took a step back, giving the scene an even wider berth.

Eddie didn't move. He stared at his friends. His expression had changed, resembling a deer caught in headlights.

Roach stared at him. "Like I said. Go... home."

His words were measured. His tone was even and his breathing calm. There was no sign he had expended any energy at all.

Eddie spun on his heels, crunching the glass beneath his shoes, and ran.

Roach watched him disappear around a corner, then turned back to the bar. He delicately stepped over the two bodies and walked back inside.

"You could've at least thrown the guy through the open frickin' doorway!" yelled Sam, the bar owner.

Roach sat calmly on a stool at the end of the bar. He rested an arm on the damp surface, surveying the crowd. He listened without looking.

"Sorry," he replied. "It was a heat of the moment thing."

"I mean, Jesus Christ, Roach—that's the third time this month!"

He finally turned his attention to his boss, a man he had come to regard as a friend. Sam was in his early fifties. He had moved to Greece a few years ago and taken over Squares, a bar on the island of Corfu. It was prime real estate, situated on the East coast, on the main strip between Old Town and Faliraki.

Roach had arrived there a week or so after leaving the hospital in Pattani, by way of a haulage ship from Tunisia. Corfu was a resort town but without the attraction of night-clubs from the East and the crowds from the West. Busy but manageable. It was easy to lie low in a place like Corfu.

Squares was the first place he saw. He sat down at the bar, ordered a beer, and struck up a conversation with Sam. He was hired that day.

Roach shrugged. "I told you, get some saloon doors fitted. Makes evicting assholes easier. Plus, it'll give the place some character."

Sam threw his head back and sighed at the ceiling before moving back behind the bar. He picked up a towel and began cleaning a glass. "This place has all the character it needs. The only thing missing is a doorman who doesn't enjoy watching me hire a glazier every goddamn week."

Roach turned to face him and smiled. "I wouldn't say I enjoy it. Although, it's nice to talk to someone other than you every once in a while."

"Whatever, wise-ass. It's coming out of your pay."

Roach flicked an eyebrow at him. "No, it isn't."

Sam held his gaze for as long as he dared. Then he looked away, slung the towel over his shoulder, and produced a bottle of beer from beneath the counter. He popped the lid and slid it over to Roach, who caught it graciously.

"Whatever," he said with a resigned sigh. "You're still a wise-ass."

Roach tipped the neck of the bottle toward him. He took a generous swig, then turned to look back at the crowd of patrons, all happily going about their evening.

Amazing what throwing an asshole through a window will do to keep people in check, he thought.

———

Eddie stumbled along the narrow alley, searching for the darkest spot, so he could piss. The adrenaline had worn off, and he hadn't drunk enough beer to numb the pain that wracked his body following his trip through the window.

He absently traced a hand over the wall beside him, occasionally using it to steady himself. His feet shuffled along the cobbled ground as he muttered angrily to himself.

"I'll show him. Who does he think he is, treating me like that? I'm gonna sue his ass for assault. Yeah, that's what I'll do. First thing tomorrow, I'll go to the police and report his ass. That'll teach him."

He heard a noise behind him. Footsteps, it sounded like. He glanced over his shoulder but saw nothing. Streetlamps were few and far between in the network of alleyways behind the buildings leading out of the town center. While most served as shortcuts, some were simply an alternative to the main streets.

And like anywhere else in the world, a few were best avoided.

He heard footsteps again. They were more distinctive this time. He stopped and turned, fumbling with his zipper as nature's call became too urgent to resist. The path behind him was shrouded in shadow.

"Whatever," he mumbled. "Assholes."

Eddie turned to face the wall, resting a palm flat against it. He looked down, focusing on the task at hand. The warm evening breeze brushed his hair. He looked absently around, sighing with satisfaction at the overdue relief.

He looked left, at the path ahead, and—

"Christ!"

He jumped, startled by the appearance of a man standing merely a few feet from him, watching him silently. Eddie looked down, catching his breath.

"Ah, jeez... I've pissed on my goddamn shoes!" He zipped up and turned to the new arrival. "What the hell are you doing, just standing there like some pervert? Where the hell did you come from, anyway?"

The man took a step back, his face covered by the darkness. His clothes were indistinct but not typically suited to the climate.

"My apologies," he said.

He was American. His accent was familiar. *Brooklyn, maybe*, thought Eddie.

"Whatever, man." Eddie pushed past him and continued on.

The man followed, quick-stepping to draw level with him. "I saw what that doorman did to you back there. That shouldn't be allowed."

Eddie looked over at him, relaxing. "I know, right? It's assault. That's what that was. Outright assault."

"You drink in there a lot?"

"A couple of times a week, yeah. I'll tell you one thing—I won't be drinking in there again!"

"I don't blame you. So, that doorman... he worked there long?"

Eddie shrugged. "I've been in town a couple of months. Extended vacation. He's been here at least as long as I have. Why?"

The man shook his head. "No reason. But... I'm going to have to ask you not to report him to the authorities."

Eddie stopped and turned to face his new companion. "What? Why? You know him?"

"Not personally. But friends of mine do, and they would prefer it if he remained unknown to the local police for now."

"Why?"

"Let's just say now isn't the time for him to draw any attention to himself."

Eddie waved a hand dismissively and began walking away. "Screw you. That bastard threw me through a window! His ass belongs in jail."

The man watched Eddie go, allowing him to get a few paces ahead before setting off after him. He reached behind him and unsheathed a knife from his belt. The blade was like a mirror. It glistened in the moonlight.

He kept pace, staying five or six steps behind Eddie, until they approached a large clump of bushes on the left.

Only then did he speed up to close the gap.

7

April 17, 2020

Roach was sitting outside, watching as two men finished fitting a new window to the front of the bar. Through the glass, he stared at the large TV mounted on the wall inside the bar. Usually, it showed sports, which attracted the tourists. Otherwise, it displayed a local station and provided background noise during the quieter times.

Today, it showed the news.

The early afternoon sun scorched his shoulders. He sipped his cold beer, watching the screen intently as it showed live coverage of various 4/17 remembrance services from across Europe.

He couldn't believe three years had passed since it happened. The world was still rebuilding itself, physically and emotionally. Everything changed that day.

Roach leaned back in his chair, allowing his head to rest on the edge of the wicker chair, just beyond the protective cover of the canopy. He closed his eyes and let the sun burn down on his face. The noises of the world around him faded until nothing but the crashing waves of the nearby ocean filled his ears.

After everything he had been through in recent months, even after a full recovery and a fresh start, there were times when it felt alien to him to remember details from before his accident.

There were times when he wished he couldn't.

His mind wandered, recalling his own whereabouts when 4/17 had happened.

Paris, France.

He had been running a surveillance op for Tristar Security. Despite having been with the private security firm for a few years by that point, it was his first solo contract. An arms dealer was in the city, selling three crates of automatic weapons to a group of Albanians. An anonymous third party had hired Tristar to capture photographic evidence of the deal.

The mission had been going well, but then all hell had broken loose. The sky burned as the world was reset. He was lucky. Most of Western Europe survived unscathed. There was a suspected terrorist attack in Prague about a week after, but that was it.

The Middle East and Asia, however, had been devastated. India, Pakistan, Afghanistan, Russia, China, parts of Japan, North and South Korea... all suffered immeasurable loss.

And America. Texas was completed flattened. New Texas has barely begun to rise from the ashes. Roach was born and raised in Dodge City, Kansas—a country boy who grew up working the farm. That one had literally hit too close to home.

He opened his eyes and took a sip of beer. The memorial service continued on the TV.

He shuffled his chair around, putting his back to the bar, and stared out at the town around him. Early afternoon on a Greek island was typically quiet outside. The unforgiving sun blasted the earth with its dangerous temperatures. Locals and tourists alike sought refuge in shade or indoors until later. The town came alive in the late afternoon and flourished until long past dusk.

Roach took a deep breath and wiped a film of sweat from his brow. He glanced over his shoulder at the digital clock on the wall behind the bar.

1:19 p.m.

Ninety-two degrees.

He went back to watching the thin crowds amble past. Families, young couples, friends, retirees... all enjoying this little slice of paradise without a care in the world.

He envied them.

The chair next to him scraped across the ground. Sam placed two fresh beers on the table, then lowered himself heavily into the seat. He sank into it with a weary sigh. "Tell me, Roach. Why do you spend your downtime where you work? You not got anywhere else you'd rather be?"

Roach smiled. He finished his beer and gratefully picked up the new one. He tipped the neck of the bottle toward his friend, who clinked it with his own.

"Not particularly," he replied.

"Well, if you don't mind my saying so... that's kinda sad."

"What can I say? You have a nice bar."

Sam scoffed. "No, I don't. I have a cheap bar."

"Is there a difference?"

"Around here? Not really. Kinda why I bought the place."

They held each other's gaze for a moment before breaking out in laughter. Comfortable silence fell across the table. The two men had enough mutual respect for each other to not question when they needed to contemplate things to themselves.

A woman walked by wearing corked, open toed heels and a short summer dress that waved lazily in the gentle sea breeze. She wore a large straw hat and oversized sunglasses. As she drew level with the table, her head turned toward them. She lowered her glasses with a subtle movement of her hand, looking directly at Roach. She smiled. He smiled back. The woman walked on.

"Holy hell. How do you do that?" asked Sam exasperatedly.

"Do what?" replied Roach with a genuine frown.

"That woman could've set the goddamn sun on fire, she was that hot. How'd you get her to look at you?"

Roach shrugged. "I didn't do anything..."

"Bullshit."

"What? I'm just sitting here, same as you."

"Uh-huh. So, why did she look at you and not me, huh?"

Roach raised an eyebrow. He looked down at himself. His black tank top was stretched over his bulky, toned frame. His camo shorts rested just below his knees, displaying his strong, defined calves.

He looked across at his friend and boss. Sam's thinning hair was matted to his scalp with sweat. He wore a bright Hawaiian shirt, half-fastened over a mesh tank top, which strained to cover an impressive beer gut. His khaki shorts finished halfway up his thighs and were at least three sizes too big. He wore white sports socks and Croc sandals.

Roach shrugged and returned to his beer. "It's a mystery..."

Sam cleared his throat, feigning offence. "You cheeky sonofabitch!"

Roach smiled to himself.

"What time's your shift tonight?" asked Sam.

"I start at eight, unless you want me in sooner."

Sam got to his feet. "Hell, you're here anyway. May as well start earlier. You want some food?"

"Sure. Thanks."

Sam headed inside the bar, then returned fifteen minutes later with a burger and fries. He lay the plate unceremoniously in front of him without a word.

"How much is it?" asked Roach.

Sam placed a hand on his shoulder and smiled. "Shut up and eat, kid."

Roach nodded his thanks and tucked into the food. He took a deep breath as he chewed, admiring the view in front of him. A dusty strip, palm trees, a beach, the ocean... he was a world away from who he used to be. He never allowed himself to fully relax, fearing complacency. But he made sure he took the time to enjoy the freedom he had.

Sam's voice interrupted his musings. "Forgot to say, somebody dropped this off for you this morning."

He produced a small brown envelope and placed it beside him.

Roach stared at it, confused. "What do you mean? The mailman left it?"

"No, some guy came in just as I was opening for breakfast. Asked if this was where Mr. Roachford worked. I assumed he meant you, so I said yes. He put that on the bar, said to make sure you got it, and left without so much as a *take it easy.*"

Roach put the half-eaten burger down on the plate and

pushed it away from him, staring intently at the envelope. He was reluctant to even touch it.

Who knew he was there?

No one that he was aware of.

He had been careful. He had covered his tracks ever since he left Thailand, leaving dummy trails in case One and his team from Tristar were still looking for him. He had been vigilant to the point of paranoia ever since he had arrived on the island. He had seen nothing that worried him or triggered any alarm bells.

He picked up the envelope, turning it in his hands.

It wasn't heavy. Nothing was written on it.

"What did the guy look like?" he asked.

Sam shrugged. "I dunno... normal height, normal build, sunglasses... just a guy. Why? What's wrong?"

"Nothing. I just... wasn't expecting any mail."

He went back to his burger but glanced at the envelope out of the corner of his eyes, as if expecting it to move toward him.

"Well, aren't you gonna open it?"

"Yeah, when I've finished lunch."

Sam shook his head and walked away.

Roach checked over his shoulder to make sure he was alone, then picked up the envelope. He tore open the end and peered inside.

"What the..." he muttered.

He tipped a USB flash drive into his hand. He double-checked there was nothing else inside before examining the drive more closely. It was black. No markings or branding of any kind. Maybe four inches long.

It looked like any other flash drive he had ever seen.

Instinctively, he looked around the bar, then along the strip outside in both directions.

There was nothing suspicious. Nothing stood out. He was confident he would see someone who didn't belong. It's what he was trained to do.

He shoved the drive into his pocket and stared absently at the table as he finished his meal. His mind raced, asking every question he had without answering any.

Questions soon turned to frustration, which then evolved into anger.

He had been careful. He had kept to himself. Only dealt in cash. No cell phone. Limited interaction with people. Nothing personal or familiar. Yet, someone had found him and left a flash drive for him.

Why?

Brandon Crow awoke to the sound of a phone ringing. He lifted his head slightly to see past the woman that lay beside him and check the time.

7:47 a.m.

He reached over her to grab the receiver. He answered the call as he shuffled upright in his bed. "What?"

"That's not polite, is it?" said the voice on the other end, calm and confident.

"It's too early for pleasantries. And it's definitely too early for games. Who is this? How did you get this number?"

"Brandon, relax. You'll wake your friends."

Crow bolted upright, glancing first at the woman to his left, then to the one on his right. Both were naked and sound asleep.

He looked around his apartment. Whomever he was speaking to could see him. He had his own internal security, and his residence was regularly swept for bugs and surveillance equipment, so he knew that wasn't it. The window wall in the bedroom of his penthouse apartment overlooked Battery Park and the bay beyond, but he was seven floors up. It was possible they were looking through a scope from somewhere but unlikely.

"Okay," said Crow finally. "You have my attention. What do you want?"

"I want to help you."

"Why?"

The voice laughed. "Not really the question I was expecting."

"What?" Crow shuffled down the bed, so as not to disturb his companions, and got to his feet.

"When people offer help, the usual response is to ask *how* they can help, not why they're helping. You're clearly a businessman."

"Seeing as you called my private number, I figured you know exactly who I am."

"Oh, I do. Brandon Crow, Head of Logistics for Tristar Security. A private security firm whose dubious reputation is cemented by the fact they give ambiguous and deceptive job titles like *Head of Logistics* to people who essentially have free reign to do whatever the hell they want... legal or otherwise. Sound about right?"

Crow padded through the living room and into the kitchen, where he prepared a pot of coffee. "If you're trying to impress me, you're not. Now get to the point. I'm a busy man."

"I'm sure you are. Okay, to business. I've found something you've been looking for. More specifically, some*one*."

Crow stopped. "Who?"

"William Roachford."

Rage and resentment washed over his face. He clenched

his fist and moved to slam it on the nearby counter, only to stop himself inches from the surface. Instead, he rested it there as he fought to remain calm.

"And what makes you think that name means anything to me?" he asked.

"Brandon, please. We both know it does, so let's skip the flirting and go straight to third base, shall we?"

"Okay…"

"I have information that you want."

Crow straightened, smiling humorlessly. "You do. And what, may I ask, do you want in return for sharing this information?"

"Now *that*, Mr. Crow, is the question you should be asking."

8

The sun was setting as the evening crowds gathered. The deep orange disc sat on the horizon, casting a picturesque glow on the restless ocean.

The temperature remained claustrophobically warm, despite the increasingly late hour. The strip outside Squares was busy, filled with a constant stream of people ambling in both directions.

The bar was slightly busier than usual. Roach could always tell when a flight carrying new tourists had arrived earlier that day. The young men and women Sam employed to tend bar were hard at work, serving one customer after another without reprieve.

Roach rested against the doorframe, just inside the entrance, arms folded across his chest. He kept one eye on the patrons inside and another on the crowds passing outside. He typically worked with just one other guy, Hector. He was a local, born on the mainland, but moved to

Corfu in his early twenties. He was somewhat of a dreamer, Roach thought, but a nice enough person and handy in a scuffle.

He hadn't seen Sam for a few hours. Probably in his apartment upstairs, he figured.

The evening had been uneventful so far. Roach paid extra attention for any sign of Eddie. After the previous evening, he half-expected some kind of attempt at retribution. It wouldn't do the guy any good, but it's a hassle he could do without.

The quiet time had allowed him chance to think. He had been preoccupied ever since opening that envelope and seeing the flash drive, which still rested in his pocket. He had so many questions but couldn't focus on any one of them long enough to figure out an answer.

Roach considered himself a logical thinker. He believed that common sense and intelligence were different, and someone rarely had both. His naturally analytical mind looked at the facts and made decisions based on what he saw. By his own admission, he struggled to sometimes think outside the box. Still, despite any shortcomings, he felt confident he had consistently done everything right. He did everything he had been trained to do in order to remain invisible.

How the hell did anyone find me? he pondered. *And what could be on that flash drive that's so important, someone tracked me down just to give it to me?*

However, that was a problem for another time.

Roach's attention was drawn to two men standing by the bar, shouting at each other. One shoved the other, who shoved back. Their faces were contorted with anger, no doubt fueled by alcohol. Their raised voices were beginning to attract attention.

He sighed and placed his index fingers between his lips, whistling loudly.

"Hey!" The bar went deathly silent. The two men turned in unison. He pointed at each of them in turn. "Don't."

The men looked at each other, exchanging a long, tense stare. Then they turned away without another word. A few people looked over at Roach, but most simply went back to their drinks and conversations. The indecipherable, collective rabble resumed its previous volume, and the evening carried on without incident.

Hector made his way across the bar toward Roach, smiling.

"Damn, man. That was... impressed? Impressing? Impressive?" he said. English wasn't his first language, and his Greek accent meant he stumbled on certain words.

Roach nodded, returning the smile. "The last one. And thank you. Nothing, really. Reputation counts for a lot in this line of work."

"Not sure the boss man needs two of us with you here, hey?" he laughed.

"You kidding? I couldn't do it without you, Hector," replied Roach.

He turned and stepped into the threshold, gazing absently out at the strip as it approached its peak level of activity. He scanned the crowd, partly from habit and partly from boredom.

Something caught his eye. It stood out enough to register in his mind as out of the ordinary. Plus, since receiving the flash drive, anything out of the ordinary was suddenly much more interesting to him.

He searched the crowds again, looking to find whatever it was that just registered in his periphery.

In a sea of movement, it's the stillness that cannot hide.

He saw something that wasn't moving against a backdrop of things that were. No, not something...

Some*one*.

He stepped outside and turned left. His attention dragged a millisecond behind his gaze.

After a moment, he saw it again.

Male. Tall. Shaved head. A piercing stare that lost none of its intensity as it traveled across the strip to rest on him.

"You okay?" asked Hector, disturbing him.

"What? Yeah, I just..." When Roach looked back across the strip, the man was gone. He sighed. "Never mind. It's nothing. Must be tired."

"Whatever, man."

Roach stepped back inside, leaned against the doorframe, and looked casually out across the busy town.

He was certain he had just seen a ghost.

A half-hour crawled by. Roach patrolled the inside of the bar. It was spacious enough for maybe sixty people to sit comfortably, leaving enough room for a makeshift dancefloor in the middle.

He wandered back and forth like a tiger waiting for lunchtime, one hand buried in the pocket of his shorts, twiddling the flash drive between his fingers. He grew anxious to see what was on it, but at the same time, he was reluctant to give in to his curiosity. He knew nothing good would come from knowing what information he had been anonymously given. He just wanted to be left alone. He just wanted to—

He stopped by the bar, facing the entrance. Three men had appeared. The first remained outside. Another had stepped inside but lingered by the door. The third was walking casually toward him. The recognition was instant. He knew the man who approached. It was the same man who had come looking for him in Thailand. The same man who killed Dr. Monroe to get to him. The same man who had put him in that hospital in the first place.

It was the man known to him only as One.

He wore black combat pants and boots with a thin, gray long-sleeved tee. A gold chain hung around his neck. He was smiling, clean-shaven, and cocky as he neared.

Roach remained rooted to the spot, analyzing the situation. He had no idea how they had found him, but that was a question for later. His immediate concern was the people in the bar. There was no doubt One and his team were here to kill him. Not bring him back. Not interrogate him. Kill him. If they tried that in a crowded bar, there would be chaos and casualties.

One stopped short and sidestepped over to the bar. He rested on his elbow as he leaned over the counter to address the young girl working on the other side.

"I'll have a mojito, please. Extra mint, extra lime." He looked at Roach. "What'll it be, partner?"

"I'm good," replied Roach, never taking his eyes off him.

"Just me, then," he said, redirecting his attention to the barmaid.

The girl walked away to prepare the drink. One stared ahead, looking at the rows of spirits mounted behind the bar without really seeing them.

"Wondering how we found you?" he asked.

"Not really," said Roach.

"You sure? It's a helluva story."

"I'm sure it is. But I don't care."

One turned to him, standing tall and squaring his shoulders. They were both roughly the same height and build. "You shouldn't have run, Billy."

"The name's Roach. Only my mother calls me Billy."

"Oh, yeah. Tell me, how is the old girl?"

Roach took a small step toward him, closing the already narrow gap between them. His fists tightened. "Choose your next words *very* carefully."

One held his gaze and stood his ground. "I'm not one of the locals in this piss hole you call a bar, Billy Boy. I taught you everything you know, remember?"

"Not everything."

One smiled. "We'll see."

"You here to take me back?"

"Nope."

"Right. Loose ends?"

"Yup."

"*Your* loose ends, specifically. Tell me, how much shit were you in after Cambodia?"

One slapped his palm down on the bar in a flash of anger. "Not as much as you would've been if I hadn't put you down!"

"Uh-huh. Except you didn't, did you? That can't look good."

"Boy, you have no idea how many people want you dead right now."

Roach shrugged. "Don't much care, either. Seriously, how could you go along with what happened back there? Those were GlobaTech personnel we took out!"

"I didn't care then, and I don't care now. Neither should you. We were there to do a job, which we still managed, no thanks to you."

"We weren't in the Army, for Christ's sake. The private sector doesn't have the authority to carry out operations like that. Hell, the military doesn't, for that matter. Didn't any of that seem a little off to you?"

"Listen, Billy, we can stand here debating all night long, but it would be a pointless exercise." He reached over to the bar, retrieved his freshly made mojito, and took a sip. "Ah, perfect. Now, you have until I finish this delicious cocktail to tell me what you've done with the flash drive. If you don't—"

"You'll what? Kill me? You should probably threaten me with something you're actually capable of."

One smiled again, but this time, there was no humor on his face. "No, Billy Boy. If you don't tell me, the team and I are going to execute everyone in this bar... just like I did with your doctor friend back in Thailand. I think I'll start with the pretty young thing who served me, which would be a real shame. That bitch can make the hell out of a mojito."

Roach believed him. He knew him well enough to not doubt a single sadistic statement he uttered. But he couldn't risk a fight. Not in the bar. He might get the advantage against One, but Two and Three were nearby and undoubtedly armed. They would open fire in a heartbeat.

"I don't know what you're talking about," he said after a moment.

One sighed. "Sure, you do."

"Okay. Why do you want it so bad?"

"Because I've been sent to retrieve it. And to kill you. So, that's what I'm gonna do."

"Well, aren't you the good little boy, playing at soldiers? How about I jam that mojito down your throat and stomp a hole in your chest?"

"Don't be stupid, Billy Boy. Pretty sure you know I've bolted the rear exit closed from the outside. You're outnumbered, outgunned, and surrounded by civilians. I imagine you care more about them than I do, you goddamn boy scout. There's nowhere to run. Come with me, give me the drive, and I'll end it quick. Two to the head down some alleyway. You won't feel a thing."

"Well, aren't you the gift that keeps on giving..."

Roach heard movement behind him. He glanced over his shoulder to see Sam appear in the doorway behind the bar.

The scene froze for a long moment before Sam broke the silence.

"Everything all right here, Roach?" he asked.

"Peachy," replied Roach.

"Who's your friend?"

"No one. Definitely not a friend. In fact, he was just leaving..." He turned back to One. "Weren't you?"

One feigned choking on a mouthful of mojito.

"Are you kidding me? Now the gang's all here? Not a chance." He looked at Sam. "Tell me, tubby, is this your bar?"

Sam ignored him. "Roach?"

"I know," said Roach. "I'm handling it."

"Oh, are you?" asked One. "Sorry, I didn't realize. Tell me, how *exactly* are you handling it?"

Roach didn't hesitate. He lurched forward and grabbed One's shirt and collar with both hands. The move took One by surprise, but he recovered quickly and gripped Roach by the throat.

They bullied and jostled for an advantage as Roach forced them toward the entrance. Patrons dove out of the way. Chairs were scattered across the floor. He pushed on, forging a path across the bar. Each of them exchanged short blows to the face and body. Jabs and uppercuts tested every angle, looking for a way through to cause damage. They began circling, reinforcing their grips on each other's clothing.

As they neared the door, Roach caught a glimpse of Three moving out onto the strip. He was no doubt regrouping with Two, waiting for the opportunity to smother him. To kill him.

He planted his lead foot on the floor and spun sharply, changing direction and pulling One off balance. He seized the opportunity and lurched forward, dragging One with him. They exploded through the window, showering the people sitting outside in glass as they crashed into them and through the table. They both landed shoulder-first on the unforgiving ground, still warm from the day's sun.

Inside the bar, screaming sounded, and the concerned chattering grew. Sam held his hands up to his head, his eyes wide with shock and disbelief. "My goddamn window! Jesus Christ!"

Roach and One struggled to their feet. The people around them had formed a wide perimeter.

Same shit, different night, thought Roach as he stepped toward One. He knew he had no option but to stay close, take the fight to him, and hope the others didn't risk a shot. He landed a couple of well-placed, powerful shots to the face.

One was staggered, but he stayed vertical. He countered with a shot to the gut that winded Roach. He reached behind him, drew a gun, and took aim. Roach saw it and grabbed his wrists, forcing his arm into the air as he squeezed the trigger.

The shot was loud, amplified by the night. It echoed around the strip. A roar of panic rose from the crowds. Almost immediately, sirens sounded in the distance.

Roach and One wrestled to a standing stalemate,

fighting for control of the weapon. Roach knew he had to lead the men away from the bar. Away from the strip. They were here for him. He wouldn't allow anyone to get injured because of a fight he unwittingly brought to their doorstep.

He delivered a stiff kick to One's groin, followed by a knee to the side of his face. As One stumbled back, he dropped the gun, which Roach quickly scooped up. Without looking, he emptied the magazine in the direction of Two and Three, forcing them to seek cover behind the low wall that separated the strip from the beach.

As the hammer thumped down on an empty chamber, Roach turned and ran, knowing the others would follow. He tossed the empty gun over a wall as he passed, sprinting as fast as his body allowed.

He needed to lead them out of the town, away from everyone.

Then he needed to kill them.

9

He didn't bother looking behind him. Roach knew One and his team wouldn't be far behind.

He slowed enough to take a sharp left, diving through a slim gap in the middle of a group of people out for the evening. Long, shallow steps led him down to a courtyard filled with haphazardly parked cars. The buildings were various shades of yellow, beige, and white. Graffiti decorated almost every wall, visible in the fluorescent glare of the lone streetlamp.

He paused, looking around at each of the three paths that led out of the area—left, right, and straight ahead. As he tried to plot the best route to take, a commotion sounded somewhere behind him. He glanced back to see One barging through the group at the top of the steps, sending some of them flying to the ground.

Roach darted to his right. He picked up pace again as he passed under a decaying stone arch and entered another courtyard. This one had a clear exit ahead of him. It led back out to the section of road running parallel to the boardwalk and seafront.

He didn't know where the others were, but One continued to gain ground. As he chanced a look over his shoulder, the whipcrack of a gunshot rang out. He ducked, and the bullet splintered the plaster and brick of the wall inches to his right.

Seems he's found another gun.

Ahead of him was a place that rented scooters. Two young men had just pulled in to return theirs. The road was busy with nighttime traffic, mostly cabs and bikes. The sidewalks were even busier with the evening crowds.

He made a call.

Another bullet whizzed past him, punching into a parked car just ahead. The dull thunk as it punctured the bodywork was loud, prompting the two men and the bike attendant to look over.

Roach made a beeline for the nearest of them. He shouldered him out of the way and stepped onto the scooter in one motion. The key was still in the engine. He started it up and accelerated away just as One emerged from beneath the arch, only a few yards behind him.

He threaded through a narrow gap and merged onto the main road, heading away from the town. The scooter wasn't fast, but it was agile, which counted for more in heavy traffic.

A third gunshot behind him made him glance over his shoulder. The other young man was lying on the ground. One had commandeered the second scooter, causing two cars to collide as he set off in pursuit.

Roach weaved through the traffic, attracting confused looks from pedestrians and blaring horns from drivers. But as long as One followed him, he didn't care.

He knew the freeway was half a mile ahead. He also knew he had to do something long before he got there. He could only assume Two and Three were following somewhere behind him in a car, which meant he wouldn't stand a chance on the open road.

More gunshots narrowly missed their mark. Roach leaned forward, his chest inches above the handlebars, trying to make himself as small a target as possible.

Up ahead on the right were steps leading down to the harbor. He was familiar with them. They were steep, opening out onto a boardwalk that had a selection of seafood restaurants overlooking the bay. It was wide enough for a scooter.

His speed had turned the warm evening breeze cool, and it gnawed at his exposed arms. In the distance ahead, he saw the unmistakable flashing lights of the police. Two cars, it looked like.

That made up his mind for him.

He leaned right, guiding the scooter toward the steps. He waved his hand in front of him, signaling to the people nearby to move.

"Get out of the way!" he yelled.

The scooter clipped the low curb, leaping slightly through the air. It landed awkwardly, forcing him to wrestle it back under control seconds before descending the steps. He sat forward, lifting off the seat a little as he entered the tricky decline.

Behind him, One followed.

Bullets pinged off the handrail that split the center of the steps, inches from Roach's arm, as gunshots continued to ring out behind him.

He saw a couple ahead who had yet to notice him approaching at speed.

"Move!" he shouted.

The man grabbed the woman and fell to the side

milliseconds before Roach whizzed past, followed closely by One.

As the steps ended and the ground leveled out, Roach squeezed the brakes. He leaned his weight to the right, planting his right foot as he slid the back end of the scooter out. He whipped around in almost a full three-sixty and turned back in the direction he had come from, along the boardwalk. It was wide, with a waist-high railing separating the short drop to the water on the left. However, tables and chairs from the scattering of restaurants made it narrower. It would be harder to avoid the people.

Roach scanned the layout in front of him. There was a turn up ahead on the right, between two restaurants. An opening underneath a bridge led to an internal courtyard bordered by bars on all side. He was almost certain there was a way out on the opposite side that would lead him back to the main strip.

Almost.

He was running out of boardwalk. He obviously couldn't turn around. He had to gamble on *almost*.

He took the right turn, bursting into the courtyard and sending the throng of people fleeing in all directions. He sounded his horn; the high-pitched honk helped motivate everyone to clear his path.

He was right. As he entered from the South, there was a ramp to the Northeast that led back to the main road.

Roach glanced behind him as he turned, forced to drive through the designated seating area of one of the bars. One was close, having just entered the courtyard. He continued, heading up the ramp. He left the ground again as he reached the top, flying across the lane of incoming traffic. He landed just in front of a cab on the opposite side of the road, which screeched to a halt as he accelerated back toward the main strip.

Roach needed a plan to end this. One wasn't about to give up, which meant—

A hail of automatic gunfire rang out. A staccato roar of bullets peppered the road around him, pulling him from his thoughts. He looked around to see an open-top Jeep directly behind him. Three was driving. Two was shooting.

So, that's where you two went...

He began weaving around the cars in front of him, across both lanes. He went as fast as he dared, eager to make himself as hard to hit as possible. Ahead of him, the road was about to run straight through the town center, parallel to the strip where Sam's bar was. Where he imagined the local police were.

As the road began to dogleg right, a gap appeared in the traffic beside him, bringing with it an opportunity.

Roach moved across and slammed on his brakes. Smoke erupted from the small, thick tires, leaving a dark stain of urgency on the blacktop. The Jeep came up on him fast, drawing level almost immediately. He accelerated again to keep pace alongside them, alternating his gaze between the vehicle and the road ahead.

In the passenger seat, Two was reloading his GlobaTech G1 machine pistol. He and Roach locked eyes for a long moment.

They were coming up on a stoplight that was preparing to change. The crossing had a large group of people on either side, eager to start walking.

He knew he had to make his move.

He stood up on the scooter, gripping the throttle until the last possible moment. Then he reached out, grabbed the frame of the Jeep, and stepped into the back seat. No hesitation. No doubt. Just a singular purpose and no option but to succeed.

With his back leg still hanging over the side, Roach reached around the seat and clamped his hand on Two's throat, squeezing with all of his strength. He pulled the man toward him, pinning him against the seat.

Two struggled against the ungodly hold, maneuvering in his seat to bring his right arm up and aim the gun behind him.

Roach had expected it. It was the obvious and only option. He swung his loose leg inside the Jeep and took hold of Two's wrist with his other hand, thrusting his arm skyward as he squeezed the trigger.

They blasted through the red light as an arc of gunfire peppered the dark blue sky. The crowds by the curb scattered. Three drove with one hand, reaching feebly to intervene on Two's behalf. But it did nothing.

Roach tightened his grip. The force he could apply with one hand was vice-like. He relieved Two of his weapon and tossed it behind him. Then he reached around with his other hand, battling past Two's flailing arm, and clasped his palm firmly over the nose and mouth. He pulled back with all his body weight. Even over the noise of the night, he heard the seat straining against the bolts affixing it to the floor.

Three looked panicked. He could see his teammate losing the struggle. He looked back and stared at Roach, who stared back with eyes as cold as ice. No emotion. No anger or pleasure in what he was doing. Just the unwavering certainty of a man doing what he knew must be done.

Three looked back at the road just in time to avoid the braking car in front. He veered across to the other lane, gunning the engine to overtake. Then he moved back and narrowly avoided an oncoming bus.

"Let him go!" he screamed.

He yanked the wheel left and right, rocking the car, trying to shake him off. It did nothing.

Roach leaned back, bringing both knees up to help push him farther away from the seat. He felt Two's windpipe caving beneath his hand. The flailing had almost completely ceased. Little oxygen was making it into the lungs.

"Damn it, Four! We were on your side! Let him go!" yelled Three.

Through gritted teeth and a clenched jaw, Roach turned his head and stared blankly with wide, wild eyes. "Only side I'm on is my own. And my name isn't Four. It's... Roach!"

A sickening crunch momentarily silenced the world around them. Roach fell back against the rear seat. Two's throat had been completely crushed, unable to withstand the pressure any longer.

He was dead.

Roach lurched forward. He dove between the gap in the seats, reaching for the wheel. Three clawed at his face while trying to maintain control of the vehicle. However, fighting one-handed didn't work for long.

The road straightened again, leading away from the nightlife, past the high street stores that had closed for the evening. The sidewalks weren't as crowded, and the road wasn't as busy with traffic.

Roach saw his opportunity.

Each man had one hand on the wheel and used the other to alternate between delivering short blows to each other's face and trying to protect his own.

Roach also had the additional struggle of trying to maintain balance. He was resting on one knee, with his front leg threaded between the seats, planted in the passenger footwell. Doing so meant he was naturally falling into Three, which required the use of his back and stomach muscles to remain upright. The added strain made the close quarters battle all the more difficult. He knew he needed to end this as quickly and safely as possible.

Up ahead on the left, he saw a low building made of dirty white brick. Its shutters were pulled down and fastened shut for the night. There was no one walking past it.

He delivered a short elbow to Three's temple, momentarily disorienting him. He quickly unfastened Three's seatbelt, then switched hands. He used his left hand to turn the wheel sharply as he clamped his right against the carbon fiber frame of the Jeep. They shot across both lanes at speed, mounted the curb, and plowed headfirst into the metal shutters.

The impact brought them to an immediate stop. The momentum crushed Roach against the frame, knocking the wind from him, despite his best efforts to brace himself.

Three was catapulted forward. He flew through the space where the windshield would normally be. He collided heavily with the metal shutters, smashing his head and neck into them before rolling down to the ground.

Roach didn't hesitate. He jumped out of the Jeep and dashed around the hood. Three was clawing his way up on all fours, seemingly with little energy and strength to manage.

Roach delivered a stiff kick to his ribs, forcing him to roll over and lie flat on his back. He then straddled his chest, crouching over him with one knee resting flat on the ground.

He unleashed two thunderous blows. His fist throbbed as it hammered down into Three's face. The first shattered his nose. The second split the skin across his cheekbone.

"How did you find me?" he asked.

Three spat blood out over his lips and smiled.

"You have a... lot of enemies, Four. Lot of people... want you... dead."

"What do you mean? Isn't Tristar just tying up loose ends? We all know what we did in Cambodia was wrong. I know why One tried to kill me back then. Isn't that why you're here? To finish the job? Tell me how you found me!"

Three shook his head. The slightest of movements.

"This is... bigger than you. The flash drive... they want it back. They won't stop. We will... keep coming."

Roach hesitated. He believed him. But it didn't make sense. He understood why he was a target, but this felt like something else. Something bigger. This was about more than him. He needed to find out why.

He placed a hand around Three's throat.

"Tristar are going to keep sending people after me, huh? Maybe I should leave them a warning to show that's not a good idea."

Three's eyes went wide. The color drained from his face, making way for a pure, primal fear.

Roach set his jaw. His right hand balled into a fist so tight, his knuckles turned purple. He took one deep breath. Only one. He wanted to be left alone. He wanted to hide. He didn't cause trouble for anyone. When he remembered who he was, he ran. But someone brought the fight to him, and he couldn't let that stand. His enemies needed to understand he was off limits.

He needed to send a decisive message.

He smashed his fist down hard, further opening the gash

on Three's cheek. Another blow blackened his eye. A third broke the cheekbone completely.

Three tried to fight back. To protect himself. But the crash had dazed him too much. A concussion wouldn't have chance to take hold, but the symptoms were there. He couldn't lift his arms enough to do anything more than a feeble slap.

Roach continued hammering down, feeling more and more bones cave beneath the severity of his punches. He didn't feel anger toward his former teammate. He didn't feel... anything. An arctic calm engulfed him as he beat the man until his knuckles bled.

After a few long moments, he stopped. His hand pulsed and ached. He looked down to see nothing but a corpse. Its face was distorted, misshapen, and unrecognizable beneath a mask of dark crimson.

Then he heard it. The sound his mind had locked onto.

One's scooter.

He drew Three's gun from the holster strapped to his thigh and stood, spinning around to level the gun at the road behind him. It was the first time he had paid any attention to the world around him since veering off the road. A few people stood watching. Others were running and screaming.

He ignored them.

One slowed as he approached the scene, his face visibly concerned. The world seemed to slow to a crawl. As he and Roach locked eyes, Roach opened fire. With a loose aim, he peppered the scooter with bullets. A round punched through One's shoulder but didn't knock him down. Instead, he revved the engine and accelerated away.

Roach traced him with his aim, firing until the gun clicked empty. He watched until the scooter disappeared out of sight before wiping the gun down on his shirt and tossing it beside Three's body.

As the world around him resumed its usual speed and faded back into existence, the sound of sirens registered. They were loud. Close.

He glanced back at Three. He felt nothing. He took no pleasure in beating a man to death with his bare hands, but he understood it needed to be done. Now whoever sent One and his team might think twice before sending anyone else. That dead body sent a clear message to anyone that wanted him dead:

Leave me alone.

10
_____

The sun had barely begun to rise on a new day, yet the temperature was already soaring into the early eighties. The pale light reflected off the ocean's surface. The beach was filling up with families and sun worshippers alike.

The laid-back atmosphere of the small town had gone. The air sizzled with a palpable tension. People walked on edge, whispering to each other as they navigated the streets with fresh paranoia. Parts of the strip remained cordoned off following the previous nights' events, including Sam's bar.

Frustrated and uncomfortable, Sam sat beneath a canopy outside a competitor's bar, waiting for his breakfast to be delivered to his table. He was mostly shaded, though that did little to reduce the heat.

His food arrived. Despite his hunger, he had little in the way of an appetite. A combination of heat and anxiety meant a hot breakfast wasn't as appealing as it usually was. But he forced himself to eat.

He sat beside the balcony rail, which overlooked the street. It was only a handful of steps higher than street level, but it gave him an improved view. He saw Roach walking toward him. He wore a baseball cap pulled low, a plain T-shirt, and thin white cargo pants.

That is about as incognito as he is ever going to get, thought Sam.

Roach climbed the steps and took a seat opposite without a word. The waitress came over and asked if he would like some coffee. She was Caucasian but had the permanent tan of someone who had lived and worked on the island for a number of years. She looked the tired side of forty. The friendly smile was more habitual than genuine.

He nodded a silent *thank you*, and she disappeared again.

Sam didn't look up from his plate.

"You okay?" he asked.

"Yeah," replied Roach. "Thanks for meeting me here."

"It sounded urgent when you called at Christ-knows-what-time this morning. What was I gonna do? Say no?"

"Well, I appreciate it. I know things got a little out of hand last night."

"A little out of..." He looked up and pointed at Roach with a forkful of bacon. "You tore up half of Corfu from what I heard!"

"It's... complicated."

"No, Roach. No, it isn't. That window company I seem to hire every other goddamn day, it's run by two brothers—local guys. Nice guys. Thanks to you, I'm on a first name basis with them both, and I'm putting their kids through college!"

"Calm down, Sam. You'll have an aneurism."

"Don't tell me to calm down, all right?" He paused to

take a sip of coffee. "What happened last night, Roach? Who was that guy?"

"He's... someone I used to work with. You might say we didn't part on the best of terms."

"Bullshit. I don't know all that much about you, but I suspect I know you better than most. You're a helluva door-man, and you're a nice guy. I respect your privacy by not asking too many questions."

Roach let slip a small smile.

He glanced away, feeling awkwardly humbled. "Thanks, Sam."

"You're welcome. But that's why I know all this 'we didn't part on the best of terms' bullshit is exactly that." He leaned forward, lowering his voice to little more than a whisper. "You attacked that guy, Roach. I saw you. You went for him first, and you both fought like you were trying to kill each other."

"It was me or him, Sam. I had to get him out of there before he started hurting innocent people. I couldn't wait around to be a gentleman about it."

"Well, ain't you all noble?" He gestured to Roach's bruised and swollen hand. "That looks painful. What did you do, beat somebody to death?"

It was meant as hyperbole, but Roach didn't correct him. He simply stared at him, no emotion in his eyes. It was an unspoken request not to ask questions he didn't really want the answers to.

"Holy hell..." muttered Sam. "Well, thanks to your antics, my bar, along with half the strip, is a goddamn crime scene right now. I'm losing money every second I'm sat here instead of serving beer, so what the hell is going on?"

As Roach was about to speak, the waitress returned with his coffee. He took it gratefully, then added some sugar before taking a sip. He then took a deep breath before telling Sam everything that happened six months ago.

Sam stared blankly at the cold plate of food in front of him. He watched as each drop of condensation from the glass of water in his hand splashed onto a half-eaten slice of toast.

He hadn't moved in almost five minutes.

Roach looked on patiently. There wasn't much to recount from his time in Thailand. He was asleep for most of it, and he left three days after waking up, leaving behind the dead bodies he felt responsible for, along with every memory of who he used to be.

He had arrived in Corfu about a week after that, and from that point on, Sam knew everything.

Although, it was still a lot to take in.

Finally, Sam looked up. His expression remained unchanged. "So, you're... what, exactly? Some kind of soldier gone AWOL?"

Roach shook his head. "No. I was trained by Tristar Security. They're a private security firm. You could say I'm closer to a mercenary than a soldier."

"And those guys from last night... they were sent to kill you because you're a loose end?"

Roach leaned back and let out a heavy sigh. "That's what I thought, yes. I still don't know how they found me, but I figured that was the only reason they were here."

Sam furrowed his brow. Focus replaced confusion. "You figured?"

"They were quite insistent about taking the flash drive from me. Seemed to me like tying up loose ends was nothing more than a nice bonus. The mission was that drive."

"How did they know you even had it? And if it's so important, why would it be sent to you? What's on it? And who sent it?"

Roach smiled empathetically. "Sam, take a breath. I've been asking myself those exact questions all night, and I'm still no closer to answering any of them. Which reminds me... did you bring it?"

"Bring what?" Sam rolled his eyes a moment later. "Oh, yeah. Sorry."

He reached beneath the table and picked up a shoulder bag. He rested it across his lap to open it, took out the laptop, and slid it across the table.

"Here," he said.

"Thanks," replied Roach. He lifted the lid and powered it up.

Sam cleared his throat. "Just, ah... just don't look in the folder named PRIVATE, okay?"

Roach looked at him over the screen, an eyebrow raised. A wry smile spread across his lips.

Sam coughed again. "Just financial stuff, that's all. For the bar."

"Uh-huh..."

Roach reached into his pocket and took out the flash drive. He held it between his finger and thumb, regarding it with a mixture of intrigue and skepticism.

"You sure they're not coming back for that thing?" asked Sam, gesturing toward it.

Roach shrugged. "I doubt it. I killed two of them last night. The guy I fought in the bar got away, but my guess is he's gone to report back to whoever sent him. He failed to complete either objective in spectacular fashion. Plus, this is now the third time he's had orders to kill me and the third time he hasn't. He'll have some explaining to do."

"So, you did... y'know... kill them?"

Roach looked over again. His expression remained neutral. "I did. Like I said, it was them or me. Not a difficult decision."

"Jesus."

Sam looked around absently, trying to process that someone he regarded as a friend not only killed two people but seemed worryingly at ease with it.

"Do you have a VPN on this thing?" asked Roach, pointing to the laptop.

Sam frowned. "A what?"

Roach sighed. "The program you most likely turn on to bypass your ISP's built-in security when you want to look at your... financial stuff. You know... for the bar."

Sam glanced away sheepishly, feeling his cheeks flush with color. "Um, yeah... it's the blue icon, bottom right."

Roach activated it, then pulled the protective cap from the flash drive and plugged it into a USB port.

"Why do you need the VPN anyway?" he asked.

Roach didn't look up from the screen. "I'm connected to a public Wi-Fi server. There's no protection on there, which means anyone with a smartphone could feasibly see what I was doing. I don't know what's on this drive, but I'd rather no one else saw it. Including Tristar."

"How would they know you were even looking?"

"I'm not sure they would. But if they sent my old team to retrieve it and kill whoever had it, chances are it's either information about them that they don't want public or information they're eager to have for themselves. Either way, adding some security to mask what I'm doing seems like a smart move."

He fell silent as he explored the contents of the drive.

"Shit," he said after a minute.

"What?" queried Sam.

"Everything's encrypted. This will take some time."

"Can you... I don't know... un-encrypt it?"

Roach peered over the screen at him. "I think you mean *decrypt* it. And yes, I can. Maybe."

"Can I help?"

Roach smiled. "Thanks, but no."

Sam thought for a moment, then looked inside the restaurant and caught the attention of the waitress. She made her way over.

"Can I get two more mugs of coffee please?" he asked.

She smiled and headed back inside.

He looked at Roach and smiled. "See? I can help."

It took almost an hour to decrypt the flash drive. Roach had some technical and analytical skills but not to the level needed here. However, he did still know how to remotely access software installed on Tristar's mainframe. He felt comfortable that he had masked his activity well enough to sneak in and begin decryption.

"I'm in," he announced.

Sam looked up from his newspaper and squinted. The sun had moved during the time they had been sitting there, so it was now mostly shining in his face.

"Good going," he replied. "You... ah... you mind if I have a look?"

Roach shuffled to the side, a silent invitation. As Sam moved around, Roach began navigating the various folders, looking for anything that stood out as important enough to kill him for.

"It looks like an info dump from one of Tristar's secure

servers," said Roach. "I guess that means my old team was here to retrieve, not acquire."

"So, someone hacked Tristar and copied a bunch of files?" said Sam. "Why send that to you?"

"I'm not sure," replied Roach. "Seems to be contract reports, mostly. Although, the bigger question is how did whoever hacked them know I was here?"

"Yeah. What type of contracts do the reports relate to?"

"Tristar took almost any kind of job, from personal security detail for a VIP to helping destabilize foreign governments—and everything in between."

"Is that even legal? I thought they're just a private security firm. They're not exactly GlobaTech, are they?"

"Not even in the same ballpark. I had a hunch there was more going on than they told the public... or their contractors, for that matter. But the money was good, and I was never asked to do anything I had a problem with, so I carried on regardless."

"Right up until you were shot and left for dead, you mean?"

Roach glanced across at Sam and rolled his eyes. "Yeah, right up until then."

"So, what exactly were you doing in order to get... y'know?"

"We were sent to retrieve some cutting-edge technology that had been stolen. The brief said it was being stored in a warehouse in Phnom Penh. Cambodia. One—the guy from last night—said our orders were to kill anyone who showed up. As we were getting ready to leave, a unit of GlobaTech personnel arrived and began conducting a sweep, reporting their findings in real time. We had our orders, but that didn't sit right with me. Turns out, questioning things isn't good for your health."

"Jesus," muttered Sam, staring blankly at the screen.

"Hmm, I wonder..." Roach trailed off as he redirected his focus to the laptop.

"What?"

"I'm looking to see if the official report of that mission is on here."

"Is it?" asked Sam after a few moments.

"I can't... wait—here it is."

Roach opened the file and scanned the report.

"That's bullshit!" he said finally.

"What've you found?"

"According to this, we were there to protect a farming operation from a rogue faction of the Royal Cambodian Armed Forces that were stealing supplies from local villages. No mention of a warehouse. No mention of the stolen tech. No mention of a GlobaTech presence. That doesn't make any sense."

"Why would they lie about your mission? Retrieving stolen technology sounds like a perfectly legitimate thing to me."

"Yeah, unless..."

"Unless what?"

"Unless we weren't there to retrieve it."

"You think you were there to steal it?"

"From GlobaTech... quite possibly, yes. It would explain why the report has been manufactured. But it doesn't explain what's so important about this drive. Only reason I know that report is false is because I was there. No way of knowing if any others are, so Tristar can't be worried about people reading them."

He flicked through the other folders on the drive. Much of what he saw was meaningless to him. Financial records, personnel data... he knew what the information was but saw no value in it.

"What's that folder there?" asked Sam, pointing to the screen. "What's Orion?"

"No idea," replied Roach, opening it.

They began looking through the files it contained, scanning them one after the other, working their way down the list. The document fifth from the top stopped them in their tracks.

Sam's eyes were wide. His mouth hung open. "Do they mean Orion, as in Orion International?"

Roach shrugged. "Apparently. According to this, they've had surveillance ops in place on Orion International... that's bold."

Sam nodded. "Yeah, no kidding."

He had just been reading about them in the paper. In fact, they *owned* the newspaper. Orion International was one of the biggest conglomerates in the world. Based in Singapore, they owned news outlets, TV stations, and holding companies all over the globe. Orion was owned by a reclusive group of billionaires and had always been the subject of speculation and conspiracy in the modern media.

"Hang on a second," said Roach.

He clicked back through the folders until he found the financial records. This time, he studied them more closely.

"Tristar aren't surveilling Orion," he announced a few moments later. "They're owned by them."

Sam leaned back in his chair, letting out a heavy sigh.

"This is insane," he said. "Are you sure?"

"It says it right here. Tristar Security is listed as an asset of a shell company that is ultimately owned by Orion International."

"What does all this even mean?"

"It means if Tristar really was in Cambodia to steal technology from GlobaTech, it's unlikely they were doing so for their own purposes. Not only do Orion own them, but they've taken measures to hide the fact they do. It's a justifiable assumption to think someone in Orion knew what Tristar sent me and my team to do. If that's the case, why would a company like Orion risk stealing from GlobaTech?"

Sam got to his feet and paced back and forth along the balcony. He stopped just before he ran out of shade to retrace his steps back to the table.

"This is getting pretty heavy," he said. "You should get rid of that goddamn drive right now."

"Not until I find out how and why it was sent to me," replied Roach.

"But this is some crazy, top-secret, industrial espionage-type shit, Roach! I want nothing to do with this."

"Sam, relax. You *don't* have anything to do with this. I'll make sure none of this finds its way to your doorstep again. You have my word."

"But they've already sent three men to get that thing, and they were prepared to kill for it. How can you be—"

He was interrupted by Roach's hand snapping up to request silence.

"What now?" he asked.

Roach was transfixed on the screen. He had opened his own personnel file. He was listed by Tristar as a high priority target. Excessive use of force had been authorized in order to terminate him. Authorized by a name he recognized.

Brandon Crow.

He had little interaction with him during his time with Tristar, but he knew the man by reputation. He knew if Crow was involved, he was in more trouble than he realized.

He found himself thinking back to the previous night, to the message he sent using Three's corpse. He began to question if the message was loud enough.

He then noticed an appendix on his file. It was a reference to a contingency operation called Rising Sun. Roach went back into the operations folder and searched for it. He knew what a contingency operation was. He had carried out a couple of them with his old team. If a contract Tristar assigned someone was deemed to be a particular level of risk, they would draw up one—sometimes more than one—CO. A back-up plan should the primary mission fail.

Operation Rising Sun was apparently the CO should One and his team fail to kill him, which they did.

He read the brief.

Tristar had an asset stationed in Tokyo. If One failed to kill him and retrieve the drive, the asset would carry out the CO. They would travel to the States and—

Roach leapt to his feet, yanking the drive from the laptop. "I have to go."

"What?" asked Sam, startled and confused. "What's going on? What was on that drive?"

"I might already be too late. They've had at least twelve hours."

"What are you talking about, man?" Roach went to move past him. His face was etched with focus and panic. Sam grabbed his arm as he drew level. "Roach, what is it?"

Roach turned and looked him dead in the eye. His heart rate increased with each beat. "There's a plan in place, should they fail to kill me. Which they did, last night."

"What's the plan?"

"To kidnap my sister and use her as leverage against me. Someone from Tokyo has been assigned to do it."

"Jesus Christ! I'm sorry, man. I didn't even know you *had* a sister."

"I haven't seen her in a long time. But I have to assume Tristar knows I'm still alive, which means they could already have her. I have to go. Thanks, Sam. For everything."

He walked down the steps to the street and turned right, heading back past the balcony where he and Sam were just sitting.

Sam leaned over the railing. "Where are you going?"

Roach spun on the spot, walking backward. He looked at the only friend he had and knew he would never see him again. "Home."

11

The elevator descended smoothly, silently. Brandon Crow checked his reflection in one of the mirrored walls. He straightened his tie. Checked his hair was neat. Tugged lightly on the cuffs of his shirt, pulling them stylishly into view from beneath his suit jacket sleeves, revealing his thousand-dollar cufflinks.

The Tristar offices in New York stood on the corner of East 23rd and 3rd, three blocks from Madison Square Garden. Standing nineteen stories high, it was a modest building compared to some in the city, but it towered over most in the nearby area.

Crow was heading to one of the sub-basements, three levels beneath the busy streets of Gramercy Park. The doors slid open. He stepped out into the hallway. The walls were painted off-white and devoid of any decoration. His footsteps echoed as the heels of his shiny black George Cleverley shoes clicked on the dull gray tile.

He followed the corridor around to the left and stopped outside a door flanked by two men in matching uniforms. They wore dark camo pants, combat boots, a bulletproof vest over a long-sleeved tee, and assault rifles. The man to Crow's left leaned over and opened the door for him.

He stepped inside. Another man, dressed the same, stood in the corner. Crow gestured with a circular motion of his hand. The man knew that was a sign to cut the security feed to the interrogation room. He quickly muttered into the radio pinned to his shoulder, and a moment later nodded confirmation.

Crow wandered idly over to the table in the middle of the otherwise empty room. There was no two-way mirror. Nothing on the painted breezeblock walls. Just the table and a chair on either side of it.

He glanced behind him as the door closed, then sat down, relaxing back and crossing his legs. He exuded patience and control and power. He clasped his hands on his lap as he looked over at the man sitting opposite him, tied to the other chair.

One had been beaten severely. Both eyes were blackened. The right one was swollen almost entirely shut. Blood trickled from his nose and mouth. Bruising was visible, ranging from deep yellow to purple and black. If it wasn't for the restraints behind him, he would undoubtedly have fallen out of the chair.

Crow scratched absently at his eyebrow, breathing slowly, measuring what he was about to say.

"You know why you're here, right?" he asked finally.

One didn't respond. Not through stubbornness or pride but because he didn't have the strength to shake his head.

"You failed to kill this prick six months ago," Crow continued. "And you failed to kill him..." He quickly checked his watch. "Seventeen hours ago. So, either this guy is the greatest asset we ever produced, or you're an incompetent asshole. Which is it?"

One opened his mouth to speak. A sliver of thick blood dribbled onto the table. He coughed and spat some more to the side. His head lolled around until he was able to focus using his one good eye. "S-sir, he—"

Crow held his hand up. "Oh my God, this is painful. Don't bother trying to speak. What I'm going to say is rhetorical and doesn't require your input. You're an incompetent asshole, and you let the two remaining members of your squad be killed by a goddamn doorman. Am I missing anything?"

One went to respond. A bubble of blood formed on his lips. He coughed again. "Mr. Crow, I—"

Crow leapt to his feet with a speed not befitting his demeanor. He glided toward One, placed a hand on the back of his head, and smashed his face into the table with frightening ferocity. The sound of One's nose shattering echoed around the near-empty room.

He lifted him up again. His face was a bloody mess. The stain on the table was significant.

He leaned close. "Do you understand what 'rhetorical' means? I said I don't need you to respond. I need you to—" He slammed his face down once more into the table. "—listen!"

Crow stood, composed himself, then sat back down opposite One.

"I've done my best to clean up the mess you caused in Greece," he continued. "As I'm sure you can appreciate, that's not the kind of publicity Tristar wants. We know Roachford still has the flash drive, although we still don't know how he got it. I now have to—"

His phone starting ringing.

He took it out and glared at the screen, frustrated by the

interruption. However, his expression softened when he saw who was calling.

Crow let out a taut breath and got to his feet. He looked over at the man in the corner and gestured to One. "Clean this shit up, would you?"

The man nodded. Crow turned and left the room. As the door closed behind him, he heard the muted burst of a suppressed gunshot. He answered the call as he strode away from the guards.

"I was wondering when I was going to hear from you," he said.

"Your boys made quite a mess in Corfu, didn't they?" said the voice.

Crow hadn't heard from the mystery man since the initial call a couple of days prior.

"I'm handling it," said Crow.

The voice scoffed. "This is you handling it, is it?"

Crow stopped. "Hey, remember who you're talking to, all right? A deal's a deal, but understand I have the information you had, which means you're relying on my goodwill to uphold my end of this. There's nothing stopping me—"

"Brandon? Shut up. I don't work for you, and you don't intimidate me. Yes, I told you where Roachford was, so you could go and kill him. But that wasn't all the information I had. That wasn't all you wanted to know."

Crow's jaw clenched. He hated playing games.

"Okay, enlighten me," he said begrudgingly.

"I've known where that piece of shit has been for months. Why do you think I waited until now to tell you? Hmm?"

"I don't know... boredom?"

"No, numbnuts. Opportunity. I'm a broker of information. His location wasn't valuable enough to share. So, I waited until it was."

"And what makes it more valuable now?"

"The fact he has recently come to be in possession of a certain USB device."

"How do you know about that?"

"Because I know who gave it to him *and* how they obtained it in the first place. You think it's a coincidence it was given to him specifically?"

"Apparently not."

"No, it's not. Tristar has never done things in half measures. It seems that also applies to making enemies."

"Okay. So, who—"

"Don't be silly, Brandon. Remember who *you're* talking to, hmm? I told you where that sonofabitch was. You agreed to kill him. Me sharing more information with you is reliant on you upholding your end of the existing deal. I need to know dealing with you is good business."

Crow turned a slow circle, staring blankly at the walls and ceiling, fighting to keep his rage and frustration in check. "Fine. But how do I know the rest of the information is good?"

"The first piece was, wasn't it?" countered the mystery man. "This is what I do for a living, Brandon, and I make a shit-ton of money from it. I wouldn't risk soiling my reputation by lying. You want to find out who hacked you and gave what they stole to *him*, you kill him first. Then you will need to find a significant amount of money..."

"Sounds to me like there might be some history between you and Roachford. You want him dead so bad, why not just do it yourself?"

"Why go to the trouble myself when I can get someone to do it for me? This way, he dies, I stay clean of any involvement, and I set up an opportunity to make an obscene amount of money. Sounds like a no-brainer to me, Brandon. I thought you were a businessman?"

"Fine. I'm working on it. I know where he is now. It's only a matter of time."

"Good. I'll be watching."

The line went dead.

Crow looked at the phone for a moment, then pocketed it and headed for the elevator. He hit the call button and stood restlessly. He despised incompetence, and he despised being played, especially by someone he didn't know. The sooner Roachford was taken care of, the sooner he could find out how the data was stolen from them.

The people he answered to were far less forgiving than he was.

The elevator arrived. The doors slid open, revealing a woman. She wore tight jeans tucked into black knee-high boots with a thick sole. A low-cut top was visible beneath the dark combat vest she wore. Her slim, toned body had obvious muscle. Her hair was bobbed, cut to just above her shoulders. It was the color of fall leaves. Dark eye makeup accentuated her cheekbones and drew attention away from the jagged, circular scar above her eyebrow.

A tattoo of a butterfly was partially visible beneath her hair, on the right side of her neck.

She was Jay, his personal security detail.

He stepped inside. Jay hit the button for the fourth floor without a word.

"What's happened?" he asked.

"Sir, one of our analysts says he has an update on the target," she replied.

"Wonderful."

Three minutes later, he strode into the room as Jay held

the door for him. The atmosphere changed in a second. All chatter stopped. A collective intake of breath could be heard.

Crow ignored it. The last time he was in this room, he had shot and killed a young analyst who had asked too many questions. Since then, the team had been working around the clock to track and monitor Roachford's movements.

"Somebody has something?" he asked.

A woman sitting to the right put her hand up. She was visibly shaking.

He moved over to her, standing behind her and looking at her bank of monitors. "What?"

She cleared her throat. "Well, sir, the target accessed the flash drive a little over fourteen hours ago."

He leaned forward, scanning the information on her screens. "Are you sure? How do you know?"

"As a s-safety measure, we install algorithms... viruses, basically... in certain folders that contain sensitive information. Should we ever have a data breach, we can access those files without detection on the foreign network. It allows us to see when certain information is accessed and by whom."

"I'm familiar with the Trojan Protocol, yes. So, what did he access?"

"First, he used a backdoor to access one of our decryption servers, which allowed him to open the files. We can only assume he looked at everything, but we know for definite he accessed... this."

She clicked through a few screens and brought up a folder, which immediately triggered a log-in screen and a restricted access warning. Crow knew which folder it was, and he knew what it contained.

He took a tight, frustrated breath. "Where is the sonofabitch now?"

"We piggy-backed an NSA satellite since ours are monitored. We tracked him to Corfu International Airport. He boarded a British Airways flight to London. A few hours later, we saw security footage of him purchasing a ticket to Kansas City. That's roughly an eleven-hour flight with a layover in Chicago. With no delays, he should land at KCI tomorrow morning. I can try to—"

"That's fine," he said, cutting her off. "I know exactly where he'll be going when he lands. Exceptional work."

Crow headed for the door, then stopped alongside Jay.

"I want you on the ground when he lands," he whispered. "Our asset in Tokyo has located the secondary target, so we know where he's likely to be heading. You're to follow him. We have a small field office in the area. I'll arrange to have a squad standing by for you."

Jay nodded.

"You're not to make a move unless I tell you to. I want updates every thirty minutes once you have him, okay?"

She nodded again. "Understood."

Crow gestured to the door with a small flick of his head. "Go."

He glanced back at the team of analysts working feverishly behind their desks. A smile crept onto his face.

Got you now, you bastard.

12

He was surrounded by walls of bones that stretched to the sky, beyond the reach of his vision. Near darkness consumed him. Only a sliver of light penetrated his cage. A thin line on the ground in front of him offered a glimmer of hope that somewhere outside, the world still existed.

That hope still existed.

When he closed his eyes, he saw figures surrounding him, dancing in the perpetual shadows. Faces of those he had hurt. Those he had killed. Their eyes burned with rage and pain. The demons beside them laughed as they juggled all the souls he had sent them.

Deep inside him, he felt a struggle, a tug-of-war between guilt and justice, each vying for his own soul. He had never taken pleasure in anything he had done. He had only ever done what he believed was necessary, but he knew necessity didn't justify evil.

The ground beneath him began to burn, melting the aged concrete to mud. The weight of his burdens was too considerable to bear. He slowly sank into the earth, feeling himself being pulled from beneath, dragged down by consequence.

He tried to scream. Tried to beg. To plead for understanding.

But the sound never came. Not here.

The only sound was the cries of anguish and torment that flooded through the walls, drowning him where he sat.

He looked down. His legs were submerged in the molten earth. He struggled to free himself, but it was no use.

It was never any use.

And that's when He appeared. He descended from the infinite sky to float above him. The hood was pulled low, obscuring His face. But the voice was familiar. It was always the same.

"You will never be free," He said. "Don't you understand? You will never be free of this place."

His eyes bulged as he tried to speak. Tried to force his words out through the blockage in his throat. Like pressure building in a narrow pipe, his chest swelled. His jaw tightened, and his fists clenched...

And he screamed. Like a banshee, his wail exploded. The walls of bones shook and crumbled. The sliver of light expanded. The faces of the figures and their dancing demons recoiled. The world around him shattered, taking his prison along with it.

The ground split, and he pulled himself up, standing tall before the hooded figure.

"I am free," he said.

The figure pointed a long, inhuman finger. "You will never be free! Your screams will always falter and fade. The walls will always rebuild. You beg for mercy, yet you never seek forgiveness. This will always be your aberration."

He shook his head. "I do not require forgiveness. I will not apologize for doing what I believed I needed to, despite the consequences. I no longer wish to suffer. I no longer believe I deserve to. But I won't deny what brought me here."

"Is that how you justify your actions to yourself? By saying they were necessary?"

"Yes. Because I'm the only person I need to justify my actions

to. *I know why I'm here, in this place. But now I'm ready to leave.*"

The figure moved closer to him. The hood brushed the cold skin of his cheek. The figure whispered, "You are not strong enough to leave..."

The man stared deep into the emptiness inside the hood and whispered back, "Watch me."

He turned to walk away, stepping over the piles of bone and rubble and into the light that shone beyond his bondage. The hooded figure reached out, grabbing his arm...

Roach snapped awake in his seat, his eyes wide with disorientation and surprise. The stewardess was leaning over him, smiling, her hand on his shoulder.

"I'm sorry, sir," she said in a soft voice. "You need to put your tray table up. We're preparing to land."

Roach nodded absently. "Ah, yeah... sorry."

He shuffled upright in his seat, looking around and re-familiarizing himself with his surroundings.

Having spent the last thirty-six hours on and off various airplanes, he had no idea of the time. But that didn't matter to him. He knew he didn't have a choice.

The plane landed without issue. Passport control went smoothly. He had traveled using the fake documentation he had acquired not long after arriving in Corfu. He knew he needed to prepare an exit, should the day ever come when he had to move on. His contact hadn't let him down.

He had no luggage with him, so he was able to forego the crowds and the stresses of baggage claim and head straight outside. The temperature in Kansas City was vastly different from the soaring Mediterranean heat of the Greek

Isles he had grown accustomed to. Despite still being relatively warm for the time of year, he found himself shivering.

Roach got into a waiting taxi, sat back, and looked ahead, making eye contact with the driver by way of the rearview mirror.

The driver, an overweight man in his early forties who was long overdue a shave, looked back at his fare with a smile. He noticed the vacant stare, the deep tan, the minor shaking...

Tourists, he thought.

"I need to head over the border," said Roach. "I'm heading to an address in Topeka."

"You got it, pal," said the driver. A few moments later, they were merging into the stream of traffic trying to leave the airport. He called over his shoulder. "So, where you flown in from?"

Roach glanced at him before staring back out the window. "Greece. By way of London."

The driver let out a low whistle. "That's some flyin' you done there, pal. I could tell you'd come from somewhere warm. Yes, sir, this breeze can be a shock to folks stepping off a plane."

Roach murmured a response, feeling in no mood for conversation.

"So, Topeka, huh?" pressed the driver as he effortlessly navigated the afternoon traffic. "Not much in the way of tourism there..."

"I remember," replied Roach. He realized he had maybe a thirty-minute ride, which would likely go smoother if he was courteous. "I was born near there."

"No kiddin'? I wouldn't have pegged you as a country boy."

"That's me. Well, I grew up in Dodge City, so I'm more of a farm boy, I guess."

"I don't get out that way much. What brings you back? Business or pleasure?"

Roach took a deep breath, pained with a cocktail of emotions—guilt, uncertainty, fear, anger. "Family."

"Hey, that's great, man. I hope you enjoy your stay. Who knows? Maybe you'll decide you prefer it over that Greek sun, eh?"

He laughed at his own joke. Roach smiled politely but said nothing.

The rest of the journey was accompanied by an easy silence. The unfamiliar cityscape faded away as they headed west along I-70, across the flat, unspoiled farmland, all the way into Topeka. He quietly hoped he had remembered the name of the place correctly. He had only visited once, many years previously.

The taxi pulled over, and the driver turned in his seat. He pointed across the street. "There you are, pal. Millbrook Care Home."

"Thanks for the ride," said Roach, distracted.

He paid him, including a tip, and opened the door.

"You need me to wait around?" asked the driver. "I don't mind."

Roach looked back and smiled. "Thanks, but no need. I might be a while."

He got out and stretched, glancing up and down the street. His cab drove away. He crossed over and headed up the short driveway of the care home. It was a low brick building on a large plot, with a well-maintained garden and flowerbed surrounding a sign welcoming visitors. When he reached the entrance, he looked over his shoulder, quickly casting an eye along the street again. Then he disappeared inside.

The black rental slowed to a stop, pulling up to the curb three car lengths from where the taxi had driven away. Behind the wheel, Jay dialed a number on her cell phone, watching intently through the windshield.

"It's me," she said when the call was answered.

"Have you found him?" asked Crow impatiently.

"He's just gone inside a care home."

"Good. Sit tight and let me know when he leaves."

"Of course, sir."

The line went dead. She tossed the phone onto the seat beside her, adjusted herself in her seat, and waited.

Roach looked around the reception area for a nurse. It had been years since he was there last. Nothing looked familiar. The carpet appeared new, perhaps recently cleaned. The walls had fresh paint and pictures hanging in nice frames. A pleasant scent lingered in the air, like potpourri. Or maybe just a strong air freshener designed to smell like a spring meadow.

"Can I help you?" asked a friendly voice.

Roach snapped out of his daze and focused on the nurse who had appeared beside him. She seemed friendly. Perhaps a little tired but welcoming nevertheless. Mousy blonde hair tied into a long ponytail complemented her dark blue eyes. The maroon tabard clung to her frame. He figured her for late twenties, maybe early thirties.

His mind wandered as an image of Nurse Conrad distracted him. She was friendly too.

"Sir? Is everything okay?" asked the nurse.

He shook his head to refocus. "Hmm? Sorry, yes. I'm here to see Annabelle Roachford, if possible?"

The nurse's expression softened. Her smile broadened. "Aww, Bella will be thrilled to have a visitor!"

Bella?

"Are you a relative?" she asked.

"Ah, yeah... I'm her son," he replied.

The nurse's smile faltered ever so slightly. She recovered quickly, but Roach saw it.

"How's she doing?" he asked.

"She's fine. She's comfortable and happy here. She... ah... she talks about you often."

"Yeah?"

"Mm-hmm. Quite a bit, actually. Perhaps we should talk in the office first... before we go to see her?"

The nurse set off along the corridor that branched away to the right. Roach followed without needing the invitation.

"Is everything okay?" he asked, unable to hide the sudden concern.

The nurse stopped outside a door halfway along on the left. She gestured inside. "Please."

She shut the door behind them. It was a small waiting area of sorts. Matching sofas faced each other, separated by a low coffee table with magazines spread across it. A small kitchenette was to the left. There was a single, wide window with vertical blinds.

Roach took a seat. The nurse sat opposite.

"Is there a problem with the money?" he asked. "The payments should come through every month automatically. It's been that way for years without any—"

The nurse held her hand up. "The payments are being received without any issues, Mr. Roachford."

"William, please."

He thought it appropriate to use his actual name, under the circumstances.

She smiled again. "Of course. I'm Nurse Lane, but feel free to call me Rosalyn."

Roach nodded. "So, what's wrong?"

"I know it's been a while since you... or anyone, for that matter... has been to visit her. Another nurse and I are assigned to look after your mother specifically. We don't have many residents here. I appreciate the living costs sometimes put people off." She smiled weakly. "So, the staff, we... we get to know our residents well. I understand her daughter calls once a month, but—"

"But what?"

"But her condition is worsening. What do you know about dementia, William?"

He shrugged. "Let's assume I know nothing of consequence."

"Okay. Well, dementia is measured in a number of ways. Here, we focus on the patient's cognition and functioning— their ability to go about their normal, everyday lives. The symptoms they portray are scaled using a CDR... a Clinical Dementia Rating. One is for the early stages. Things like mild confusion, lack of concentration, forgetfulness."

Roach nodded, following along.

"Two is the mid-stage. More severe disorientation, greater difficulty recalling memories or information, occasionally mood swings. And three is late stage, where there is little awareness and almost no ability to look after themselves."

"Okay..."

"Over the last few months, I'm afraid your mother has progressed to CDR-2. She copes well. She's a much-loved member of our home. But she does struggle, and I'm sorry to say that she's unlikely to improve."

He leaned back against the sofa cushion and stared at the coffee table. He felt overwhelmed by guilt. He should've been around more. He and his mother had barely spoken since his trial, all those years ago. He had been home just once after that, to help her move into the care home. Rebecca was away at college, so the responsibility had fallen to him. Even then, the two of them said almost nothing to each other. He had been too stubborn to try and resolve things between them. She was his mother, and he had turned his back on her the way he felt she had on him.

Had he contributed to her condition?

The nurse sat forward, reaching out with her hand to attract his attention. When he looked up, she was smiling. It was warm, comforting. "Your mother is well looked after here, I can assure you. I know I speak for my colleagues when I say we all care for her way beyond the boundaries of our profession."

Roach nodded. "Thank you, Rosalyn. That means a lot."

"Come on. I'll take you to her."

She stood. He followed her back along the corridor, through the reception area and some double doors, and into a common room.

Lots of large windows provided plenty of natural light in the room. It was a sizeable space, divided into four main sections, with each one occupying a corner. Top left, there was a large TV facing a wide, spaced semicircle of reclining chairs. Maybe half were taken. Bottom left was a group of tables, each with four chairs, along with two bookcases full of books, games, and crafts. Bottom right seemed to be some kind of therapy group. A young man wearing a similar tabard to Nurse Lane was demonstrating stretching exercises. A handful of residents mimicked him. And top right...

Sat with her back to the doors, staring out the window, was his mother.

He followed Nurse Lane across the room, lingering a couple of paces behind. His heart began to hammer inside his chest. He felt apprehensive. The guilt, perhaps. His palms were clammy.

The nurse approached her chair and placed a hand gently on her shoulder, so as not to startle her. Annabelle Roachford looked up, a semi-vacant expression on her face, as if she had been slowly pulled from a deep sleep.

"Hi, Bella," she said. "Do you remember me? It's Rosalyn."

After a moment, a smile crept across her face. "Why, of course, dear. Rosa."

She smiled patiently. "You have a visitor. Someone special's come by to see you."

"To see me? Oh, how lovely!"

Taking his cue, Roach stepped around Nurse Lane and stood by the window. Annabelle looked up at him with a blank expression. There was no sign of familiarity or recognition at all.

Seeing the look on her face pained him. He took a breath and smiled, waving tentatively at her.

"Hey, Mom."

13

"How've you been, Mom?" asked Roach, taking a seat beside her.

Annabelle looked at him blankly. It was as if she was staring through him. After a long moment of silence, she slowly reached out, patting the back of his hand with hers.

"Are you looking for your mother, dear?" she asked innocently. "You're a big, handsome boy, aren't you? You shouldn't lose your mother, you know."

She looked away, resuming her vacant gazing through the window, admiring the garden outside.

Roach sighed. He felt his heart sink in his chest. The guilt wouldn't go away. He glanced up at Nurse Lane, who stood a respectful distance away. A silent plea for help.

She crouched beside the woman's chair, placing her hand gently on her arm. "Bella, *this* is your son. William. You're his mother. He's here to see you."

Annabelle turned to her, confused. Then she looked around at Roach. He saw nothing in her eyes. No recognition. No familiarity. Just a flickering candle where the full light of life used to be.

It broke his heart.

Annabelle turned back to the nurse. "I used to have a son, you know. Yes, strapping young man, he was. All the potential in the world, that boy." She reached out and grabbed her wrist. "He was a murderer, you know? Went to jail. I think he might have died there. And good riddance. Damn murderer, he was."

The color drained from Nurse Lane's face. A mixture of embarrassment, shock, and concern. She cast her gaze to Roach, who couldn't think of anything else to do besides shrug and look away sheepishly.

"Bella, sweetie, your son is sitting right there next to you," said Nurse Lane. "He's come home to see you."

Annabelle ignored her, resuming her inspection of the garden outside.

Both Roach and Nurse Lane got to their feet and stepped away to the side.

"I'm really sorry," she said. "You've caught her on a bad day. This can happen every now and then. She just needs some time."

Roach nodded. "I understand that. Unfortunately, time is something I don't have. I need to talk to her."

"Is... is everything okay? I mean, sorry—I know it's none of my business. I just thought maybe I could help. I know your mother pretty well now."

"I have to find my sister. I've not seen her for a long time. I don't know where she lives, what she does for a living... nothing. I know Mom knows. I just have to... get the information out of her somehow."

"Your sister... it's Rebecca, isn't it?"

Roach nodded. "Becky, yeah."

"We have her details on file. She's down as the emergency contact. I can get them for you if you—"

"Billy?"

They both stopped and turned.

Annabelle was staring up at him, her eyes cloudy with tears. "Billy, is that you?"

He moved to her side and smiled. "Yeah, Mom, it's me. Hey."

She reached out and placed a cold, weak hand on his cheek They held each other's gaze for a long moment, then the silence was broken by the dull, hollow clap of her slapping him across his face.

"You should've rotted in prison for what you did!" she screeched.

Shaken and angry, she moved to get to her feet. Nurse Lane rushed to her side and helped ease her back into her seat.

"It's okay, Bella. Just relax, okay?" she said patiently. "No need for you to get up."

Annabelle tried to shrug herself free, but her feeble frame wouldn't allow it. "Oh, to hell with you! I don't *want* to relax. Do you know what this boy did? Do you know? His own sister hates him. And his poor mother..."

She relaxed, seemingly forgetting herself as quickly as she remembered.

Roach ambled away as the nurse helped Annabelle get settled. She joined him after a few minutes. There was an awkward tension between them.

"Ah, it might be best if you came back another day," she said, trying to be delicate.

Roach nodded with resignation. "Yeah, I think I probably should."

They began walking back toward reception.

"I've not seen her that agitated in a while," said Nurse Lane. "Seeing you must've been quite a shock to her."

Roach sighed. "Yeah. Sorry about that. I didn't mean to unsettle her."

Nurse Lane moved in front of him and stopped. "I'm sorry, William... but I have to ask. See, I'm not supposed to give out the contact information of next of kin that we have on file, even to other family members. Not unless you have a Power of Attorney or previous written consent." She glanced around. "I know you said it's urgent, and I want to help, but what she said back there... I don't want to get anyone in any trouble."

Roach gave a begrudging nod. "I appreciate that, and I wouldn't ask if it wasn't urgent. But I have to get in touch with my sister. Rosalyn, please..."

She let out a taut sigh, screwing her face up as she tried to decide what was best.

"Wait here, okay?" she said eventually.

She walked away, leaving him standing in the middle of the reception area. He looked around, restless. He glanced through the main doors, outside. It was mid-afternoon. Bright without being sunny. Mild without being cold. He subconsciously tugged at the collar of his sweater. It was fitted snugly to his torso. It wasn't as thick as he would've liked, but there was only so much use for an early spring wardrobe when he lived in the Mediterranean.

Only a few cars passed by. A couple were parked. Just a gray, Soccer Mom 4x4 and a black sedan. He was glad it was a quiet neighborhood. His mother deserved some peace and quiet.

"Here."

Roach turned around to see Nurse Lane holding out a piece of paper. He took it from her and glanced at it.

A Topeka address and phone number.

He nodded to her gratefully. "Thank you, Rosalyn. This means a lot to me."

She returned the gesture. "Honestly, you only have that because of how much your mom means to us. I think, deep down, she would want us to help you."

He smiled, lost for a moment in the idea there was still enough of his mother sitting in that chair to remember him for who he was, not what he had done.

"Listen," he began, "I saw how she got back there. If she ever remembers today, maybe it's best you don't tell her I was really here. I don't think it would do her any good."

Nurse Lane reluctantly nodded.

"See you around," he said, turning to leave.

As he reached the door, the nurse called after him.

"Hey."

He looked back to see her pointing at the piece of paper.

"I hope you find your sister and... y'know... that everything's okay," she said.

He smiled, gave a courteous nod, and left. He called an Uber outside, which arrived within a couple of minutes.

"Where to?" asked the driver as Roach slid across the back seat.

He let out a weary sigh. "Cheapest hotel in the city. Big day tomorrow. I should eat and sleep."

The driver nodded and smiled. "I know just the place. Have you there in no time, pal."

"Appreciate it."

The cab set off, leaving the care home in its rearview.

Two cars back, the black sedan followed.

14

April 21, 2020

The floor of the office was eerily calm. The silence was broken only by the occasional hum of a muted conversation, or by desk phones ringing, seemingly never to be answered.

The Topeka Times was the only major daily newspaper in the city. Its offices were located on the corner of 10th and Webster, overlooking Washburn Park. It was one of six newspapers, along with three major TV networks, that were owned by Media Corp, a subsidiary of Orion International. Working there was the dream of every journalism major in the state.

At a bank of desks in the far corner of the fifth floor, a woman stood, a phone receiver trapped between her ear and shoulder. She clicked her fingers repeatedly, attracting the attention of another woman sitting diagonally opposite her.

"Becky, line two," she said.

Rebecca Roachford looked up, seemingly dazed by the interruption. "Hmm?"

Her shoulder-length auburn hair fell across her face. She brushed it gracefully aside with her hand and tucked it behind her ear.

The woman placed her hand over the phone and glared at her.

"Line two!" she hissed impatiently.

Rebecca picked up her own phone and the call was transferred.

"Editorial. Can I help you?" she said professionally.

"Am I speaking to a Miss... Roachford?" said the voice.

"That's me."

Her tone was soft and friendly. Natural, not practiced. She had worked for the *Times* almost five years, and her innate ability to hold a conversation was useful in building up a network of sources.

She was also suspicious by nature—another quality that made her extremely good at her job. It wasn't uncommon to receive anonymous calls promising inside scoops on some juicy story. Capturing information from any call had become habit.

She reached for a pen and notepad, scribbling her notes. *Male. Calm.*

"I have a news story I think you would be interested in," he continued.

"Yeah?" She rolled her eyes. "Lay it on me."

"Ever heard of a private security firm called Tristar Security?"

Rebecca frowned. She recognized the name but wasn't sure where from.

She scribbled, *Tristar.*

"Let's assume I haven't," she said. "What about them?"

"They're an expensive security contractor, mostly compromised of mercenaries and ex-military. Known to have numerous VIP and celebrity clients."

"Okay. Doesn't sound all that newsworthy."

"They've also been engaged in illegal activity for years. Overseas operations. Arms deals. Espionage. Kidnappings. You name it. They cover it up with training drills and legitimate contract work."

"Uh-huh." She wrote in her notepad quickly. "And you have proof, presumably?"

"I do."

"What kind of proof?"

"All in good time, Miss Roachford. But I can tell you they recently assassinated four members of GlobaTech's peacekeeping force in Cambodia. They stole some proprietary weapons tech and covered it up to look like they were in the area protecting aid workers the whole time."

She stopped writing and looked up, eyes narrowed with surprise. "That's a specific claim, Mr...?"

"I'd prefer to remain anonymous for now, Miss Roachford. But yes, it's specific."

"Well, look, I'll need to speak to the chief editor, see if this is something we want to investigate further. Obviously, we'll need to see some proof of your claims. But I have to ask... why come to us? We're only in circulation in Kansas. If this story is as big as you say, why wouldn't you go to a national paper?"

"Because I wanted to give this to *you* personally. I just needed to talk to you about it first, see if you were tough enough for a good story."

"And?"

"And... I guess we'll see."

She didn't have the patience for games and detested people who took the cloak and dagger approach. It was rarely necessary and little more than a waste of time.

"Okay. Well... thank you for calling," she said, trying to remain professional. "Do you have a contact number I can get back to you on?"

"I do, but that won't be necessary."

Rebecca frowned, confused. "I'm sorry... how do you mean?"

"All in good time. Bye for now, Rebecca. I'm sure we'll be speaking again soon. Oh, and say hi to your brother for me."

The line clicked dead.

She slowly got to her feet, staring at the handset as if she had just seen a ghost. Her colleagues were quick to notice.

"Hey, Becky, are you okay?" asked the man beside her, an intern named Daniel.

She ignored him and looked over at her friend, Kristel, who had passed her the call. She was a few years older, with pale skin and short, spiky purple hair.

"Girl, what's wrong?" she asked, concerned.

"That guy, he just—"

"Hey, Becky!"

Becky looked over in the direction her name came from, still vacant with shock.

The receptionist, positioned on a small desk near the elevators, was waving. "That was security downstairs. You got a visitor."

She shook the cobwebs clear in her head. "Who?"

"Some guy. Says he's your brother."

Rebecca fell backward onto her chair as if hit by a train. Her jaw hung loose. Kristel dashed around the desk to her friend's side. They were close. She knew Rebecca well enough to know she hadn't seen or heard from her brother since she was a kid.

Rebecca turned to her. "What the hell is going on?"

Roach had arrived in Topeka a little after seven the previous night. He was tired and hungry and figured he had enough of a head start on Tristar that he could afford to take the night. A cheap hotel and two meals later, Roach felt alert and prepared once more.

It was late morning. Bright but a few degrees off being sunny. A strong breeze whipped through the city, around the corners of buildings and straight into anyone it could find. The change in climate had been severe, so his first stop had been an outdoor clothing store. He purchased a long-sleeved, red and brown plaid work shirt, a black body-warmer, and hiking boots.

Being unarmed was a concern, so he also bought a tactical hunting knife and leather sheath. The blade was six inches long, with a serrated edge along one side. The handle was carbon fiber, molded with a grip for easier handling.

He changed in the store and strapped the knife to his waist, high enough that the bodywarmer concealed it.

Roach didn't feel comfortable in the city. There were too many people. The last few days had made him paranoid. He couldn't help feeling he was on the edge of something far bigger than he was prepared for. He needed information. He needed answers.

He needed to protect his sister.

As he walked the busy streets, hands buried inside his

pockets, he tried to put the pieces together in his head. The problem he quickly realized was that he was missing far too many pieces to figure out the big picture, and that infuriated him.

Tristar wanted him dead. That much was obvious. He figured himself a loose end after the Cambodia fiasco last year, but it felt like more than that now. After the encounter in Corfu, it had become clear that One's primary objective was the flash drive. Getting him was just a bonus.

But was it a coincidence the flash drive had wound up in his hands?

He didn't know who had sent it to him, or why, but he knew the value of the information it contained. It listed every illegal operation Tristar had carried out. Every dubious client. And every contingency operation proposal... including the one to kidnap his sister to get to him. That drive could bury the entire company and send everyone who worked there to prison for a long time.

He needed to figure out what to do with it. He was a target anyway, but he could easily hide from them and start over somewhere. It was a big world, after all. But with the drive in his possession, he would be looking over his shoulder forever. He could handle himself, but it was his loved ones he was concerned with. This situation had made them targets too, and he couldn't allow that.

Roach stood across the street from the offices of the *Topeka Times*. He stared up at the modest building silhouetted against the morning sky. A small, proud smile crept onto his face.

"You done good, kiddo," he muttered to himself.

He crossed the street and headed inside through the revolving door. A security check-in desk stood before him. A walkway stretched off to the right, leading to the elevators. The guard looked up at him and nodded a courteous greeting. As he got to his feet, he revealed his overweight frame, previously hidden behind high, semicircular counter.

"Mornin'," he said as Roach neared the desk. "Help you?"

Roach cleared his throat, suddenly overcome with a wave of apprehension. "Yeah, I'm here to see Rebecca Roachford."

The guard reached for a sign-in book and placed it on the counter between them. "Name, time, and date in there. You got an appointment?"

Roach wrote a fake name in the book. "No, I'm her brother. I was in town and thought I'd say hi."

The guard looked surprised. "Huh. Never knew Becky had a brother." He scratched absently at the bristle covering his bloated jowls. "I'll call up for you. Take a seat. She'll be down in a moment."

Roach nodded his thanks and paced away nervously, trying not to focus on how long it had been since he saw her last.

It was an emotional reunion. While Roach did his best to stifle his personal feelings because of his true motives for being there, Rebecca wasn't as strong. She had run to him the moment their eyes met, thrown her arms around his neck, and burst into tears—each drop a cocktail of anguish, guilt, and happiness.

They were sitting across from each other in the coffee shop directly opposite her office. They managed to get a table by the window, overlooking the street, just before the lunchtime rush began. The place had gotten busier, but most people were taking their drinks and sandwiches out.

Roach sat back against the rigid seat, fidgeting to find comfort. Rebecca looked at him in awe, noting his imposing frame and stature.

In turn, he regarded her with more brotherly pride than he felt he deserved to have. The woman sitting opposite him was a world away from the young girl he last saw all those years ago. Her long hair fell over her face. She kept brushing it aside, and he noticed a spare hair tie around her wrist with a hair pin attached to it. He figured she didn't like it tied up unless it was necessary. Each time she tucked her hair behind her ear, it revealed her bright eyes, full of life and happiness.

"You look... really well," she said, smiling.

He smiled back. "You do too. All grown up."

They fell silent, then went to speak at the same time. They laughed and fell silent again.

Roach gestured to her. "Please."

Rebecca took a sip of her latte, took a deep breath, and said, "I'm sorry."

"What for?" he replied.

"Mom, she... When you went away, she was really hurt. Really angry. She refused to go and see you. We didn't even find out you had been released until years after."

"I know how she felt. I understand it, honestly."

"I still don't... I can't believe you did what they said."

He looked her dead in her eyes. "Good, because I didn't."

"So, if you didn't murder that guy, what really happened that night, Will? Please tell me."

Roach sighed. He knew he didn't have time for history lessons. But he also knew putting the past behind them for good would make what had to come next easier.

He took the chewing gum out of his mouth and stuck it under the table. Then he took a gulp of his own coffee, wincing a little at the minty aftertaste. "Christ, you must've been... what? About twelve? You remember I'd been doing a lot of overtime at the meat factory?"

She nodded. "Yeah. Mom had just had her shifts reduced at the diner, so you were bringing in some extra money, right?"

"That's right. I was working late one night. Easily past eleven when I left. I came out, started walking across the lot, and I heard this commotion. I followed the noise. It took me around back, away from everything. I saw three assholes beating down this older guy. I reckon he was in his fifties. What was I going to do? I couldn't just ignore it."

"So, you intervened?" she asked.

"Damn right, I did. Didn't even bother saying anything. I just waded in, fists swinging. Clocked the first guy pretty good. Second one pushed me against the side of the building. Third one moved in to finish me off. The old guy had run away. Must've gone straight for the nearest payphone to call 911. I pushed the second guy off me just in time to punch the third guy as he came in from my right. Right on his off switch." He pointed to corner of his mandible, just below his ear. "Out like a light before he hit the ground. Second guy panicked and disappeared."

Rebecca frowned. "Okay, so when did you..."

Roach sighed again. "I already had. The first guy I hit fell wrong. He landed on a three-inch concrete lip used to border the grass. Broke his neck. Died instantly."

"Oh my God." She placed a hand to her mouth, muffling her gasp. "But that's not murder, surely?"

"It is when the kid that dies is the son of the guy who owns the biggest casino in town. His father managed the single biggest source of income in all of Dodge City. He was also really good friends with the DA. I got five years for voluntary manslaughter. No chance of parole. And to save face for his piece of shit dead son, the story was released that I was the one robbing the old guy, and the son tried to be a hero and got killed."

"Will, this is... I can't believe Mom believed what the press said about you. I can't believe she made *me* believe it."

Her eyes glistened as they welled with tears.

Roach reached across the table and placed his hand on hers. The hair pin on her wrist poked against his finger. "Hey, it ain't your fault, kiddo. Okay? Our family was struggling. Dad wasn't around. I'd been in trouble at school for fighting and... failing to manage my temper." He gave a weak, embarrassed smile. "Not much of a stretch to think someone like me would try anything for some much-needed extra cash."

"But how could Mom not defend you? How could she give up on you like that?"

"Because she always saw our dad in me. You won't remember him. He left when you were little more than a baby. But I do. The nights he came home, steaming drunk after working all day, and took it out on Mom. I only ever saw him hit her once, but his anger was well documented."

"Will, I'm so sorry. If I'd known, I would've—"

He held a hand up and smiled. "It's the past, okay? All that matters is that I'm here now."

They fell silent again, finishing their coffees.

"Have you spoken to Mom at all?" she asked sheepishly.

"Not for a long time," he confessed. "But I flew in yesterday and called to see her."

"Really? How did it go?"

"About as well as you'd expect, I guess. In the few

moments that she actually recognized me, she started shouting I was a murderer to anyone who would listen."

"Oh, Jesus... I'm sorry."

"Nah, don't be. Truth be told, the main reason I went was to get your address. It's how I found you." He gestured across the street, to the office building. "You've done well for yourself. I'm proud of you, kid."

Rebecca blushed. "Thanks. So, not that I'm not happy to see you, but why come and find me now? Is something wrong?"

He smiled. "You're a natural reporter, all right."

They laughed together.

"Seriously, why now, Will?"

He didn't answer.

"Will? Are you okay?"

He wasn't okay. He was far from okay. Right now, he felt as close to afraid as he had in a long time. Not for himself but for his sister.

He was staring out the window. Across the street. Outside the entrance to Rebecca's office, two vehicles had just pulled in. One was a light gray minivan. It was inconspicuous, save for the five men in Tristar-issue riot gear that just climbed out of it.

The other was a black rental. Immediately, he knew he had seen it before. It was behind him when he left Millbrook Care Home yesterday. He cursed himself for being so sloppy. But there was no time for that now.

A woman climbed out of the rental. She looked up and down the street, then over at the group of men. She said something. Four of them quickly entered the office. The woman and the remaining man stayed outside by the vehicles, their backs to the coffee shop.

For now.

"Shit," he muttered.

"Okay, Will, you're starting to freak me out. What's going on?" She followed his gaze. "Who are they?"

Roach looked at her. His grave expression was laced with urgency. "They're the reason I'm here. We gotta go. Right now."

15

They walked hurriedly away from the coffee shop, away from the office, aiming for the biggest crowds as they navigated the busy sidewalk.

Roach had his hand around Rebecca's waist. It was half a gesture of protection, half to gently usher her forward.

"I don't understand," she said. "What's going on? Who were those people outside my office? Why are we running away?"

Roach checked back over his shoulder. The woman with the black rental hadn't looked around, which meant every second that passed was a crucial head start.

"It's a long story," he replied. "And this isn't the time to tell you. But those people back there... they're here for you."

Her pace involuntarily slowed. He felt resistance against his arm as he urged her onward.

"What do you mean?" she asked, her voice cracking. "What have I done?"

He was focused on the path ahead, trying to move as seamlessly as he could through the crowds. "You haven't done anything, kiddo. They want me, but they keep failing. So, they're trying to use you to get to me."

"You mean... kidnap me?"

"I do. Sorry."

"Oh my God..."

She began to hyperventilate. Roach stepped in front of her, placed his hands on her shoulders, and spun them both off to the side, into the doorway of a small department store.

"Hey, listen to me." He waited until she made eye contact. "I'm not going to let anything happen to you, okay? I promise. They're not going to get either of us. But you have to do as I say if we're going to get out of this safely, all right?"

Becky held his gaze. Her eyes misted over with tears. But she heard him. She understood.

"Good," he continued. "Now we need to get off the main streets. Somewhere they won't see us from their vehicles. Then I'll bring you up to speed, okay?"

She nodded vacantly. They stepped back out into the crowd, walking with a renewed urgency away from her office.

Jay took out her phone and dialed her boss. The squad had reappeared moments before, empty-handed. Their target had left roughly fifteen minutes before they had arrived. With her brother.

"Do you have her?" asked Crow when he answered the call.

Jay took a short breath, burying her frustration before responding. "No, sir. Roach got here first."

There was a pause.

"Goddammit!" yelled Crow. "Find them, you hear me?

Whatever it takes. Neutralize him and bring the sister to me."

"Should I not just bring them both?"

"No. We need to know what he's done with the flash drive. He's smart. We have to assume he has a contingency in place. Taking them both right now is a risk. If we just take the woman, we can use her more effectively as leverage. He'll lead us to the drive. Then we take him out."

"Yes, sir."

Jay hung up and stared at the expectant group of men. Each one was a highly trained Tristar operative. They were experienced, loyal, and deathly afraid of the woman everyone secretly called the Butterfly.

"What's the move, ma'am?" asked one of the team.

She threw him a look that could've turned him to stone. He took a small step back.

"The parameters of the operation haven't changed," she said tersely. "We capture the target and deliver her to the holding site as planned. If Roachford gets in the way, put him down."

"Is that a kill order, ma'am?" asked another.

"No. Crow wants him alive until we determine what he's done with the stolen intel. Just subdue him long enough to take his sister. Clear?"

There was a murmur of collective agreement.

"Move out," she said. "They can't have gotten far."

Jay climbed back inside her rental, made a U-turn, and nestled into the steady flow of midday traffic, trying not to let her frustrations get the best of her.

Roach and Rebecca had doubled back around in a wide arc. They were now approaching 10th Avenue from the opposite side. She had thought it was crazy to head toward the place they were running from, but Roach had assured her it was a sound tactic.

People tended to react to danger exactly the way she had. Her automatic response was to run away. It's also what the people chasing them expect them to do, which is why Roach said it was useful to head back to where they started. It was the last place anyone would look.

They crossed the street and headed down an alley between a restaurant and the pharmacy on the corner of 10th and MacVicar. A large dumpster stood against the outside wall of the restaurant. Another stood a little farther down, against the pharmacy. At the far end was a chain-link fence separating a patch of land yet to be developed.

They rested by the rear door of the restaurant. Rebecca squatted and leaned back against the wall, resting her arms on her knees. Her hands were shaking.

Roach paced back and forth in front of her, scanning the entrance of the alley, checking habitually for danger. It seemed clear, but he had no way of knowing for how long. They needed to get out of the city, which would buy some time for him to figure out the next move.

He looked down at his sister. She stared blankly at the ground in front of her. Her blank expression was a look he had seen many times before. Her entire world just got turned upside-down.

"How you are doing?" he asked.

Becky looked up at him, screwing her face in disbelief.

"Yeah, okay," he said. "Sorry."

"What the hell's going on?" she asked finally. "What do these people want with me? Who are they?"

He stopped pacing and crouched in front of her. "Six months ago, I woke up from a coma with no memory."

Her eyes popped wide. "You *what?*"

"I was left for dead by the people I used to work for. They came to finish the job, but I managed to escape. I got my memory back and have been hiding ever since."

"And what? They found you again?"

"Yeah. Someone sent me a flash drive with a ton of information on it, and they came asking for it back."

"What kind of information was on it?"

"The confidential, top secret kind. It was hacked from my old employer's systems. There was enough evidence of illegal activity to bury them forever. No idea who sent it to me or why, but now these people are after me for two reasons."

"How did you know they would come for me?"

"The operation was detailed on the drive. You were a contingency to get to me."

"Jesus Christ, Will." She shook her head. "Who the hell did you work for?"

"Tristar Security."

Rebecca leapt to her feet and backed away from him. She staggered as a wave of nausea washed over her.

Roach moved to help steady her, but she pushed him away.

"Becky, what is it?" he asked, concerned. "Are you okay?"

"This can't be happening to me..."

He rushed toward her, catching her in his arms as she fainted.

"Ah, shit." He lay her gently on the ground by one of the dumpsters, cradling her head and gently patting her cheek. "Come on, sis. This isn't the time. You have to wake up, okay?"

She stirred, moaning softly, and forced her eyes open.

"There you go, kiddo. Let's get you upright." He hoisted

her to her feet easily, allowing her to lean into his shoulder. He put a comforting arm around her. "We need to keep moving. We have to—"

He looked up to see three men standing in the entrance to the alley, blocking their access to the street. The retrieval squad sent for Rebecca.

She gazed up at Roach, saw his look of grave concern, then followed his eyeline. An involuntary shriek of panic escaped her lips. She clamped her hand over her mouth.

"Wait here," said Roach.

"What? Why? What are you going to do?" she asked.

He set his jaw and furrowed his brow. He let out a taut sigh of resignation. "I'm going to ask them real nice to leave us alone."

He walked away before she could say anything. He stopped halfway between her and them.

"Which one of you is in charge?" he asked the men.

The one in the middle stepped forward but said nothing.

Roach nodded to him. "You're here for me, right? Let her go and I'll come with you. I'm sure your boss would love to have a chat."

The man in the middle smiled. He was of similar height and build to Roach. A little shorter than the man to his left. A bit taller than the man to his right. The combat vest bearing Tristar's logo was a tight fit over his frame.

"We ain't here for you,' he said. "Not yet. The operation is to apprehend the woman. She has information critical to a classified Tristar assignment."

Roach tilted his head slightly. "We all know *that's* bullshit. You only wanted her to get to me. Well, here I am. No need to involve her anymore."

The man took another step forward. His colleagues

followed suit. "We'll be back for you when the time's right. For now, she's coming with us."

"What's your name?"

"I'm Davies. This is my operation."

"Okay, Davies. You lay a hand on her, I'll break it."

He smiled. "Please. Don't make this difficult."

"Take another step closer, I'll make this a crime scene."

Davies paced forward, smiling. No fear. No respect. Just the knowledge that the odds were three-on-one in his favor, and he had a gun strapped to his leg.

Roach didn't hesitate.

He strode toward him with violent purpose. Davies tried to react, but Roach's fist connected with his jaw before he could think. As he fell, Roach made a beeline for the nearest of the two remaining Tristar contractors. He knew their training. He knew their protocols.

He knew he was better.

He brought his leg up and down, stamping through the guy's kneecap without breaking stride, breaking his leg instantly. The guy yelled out in pain on his way to the ground, attracting the attention of the few people walking past. Some stopped and stared. Others ran, screaming.

Roach turned to the third man and grabbed his throat with one hand. He launched him against the wall, eating a couple of jabs as he moved in for the kill. He brought his right arm up, preparing to smash the point of his elbow down into the man's nose, but he never got chance. A dull impact on the back of his head dropped him to one knee, forcing him to relinquish the grip on his enemy's throat.

The moment he did, the man delivered a short knee to the side of his head, sending him sprawling. Roach hit the ground hard. Immediately, he tried to shake the fog clear. A fourth man, whom he surmised had appeared from somewhere down the street, stood over him, holding a pistol in his hand by the barrel. The butt shone with a layer of blood. He reached back, pressing his fingertips to the spot on his head where he got hit. When he looked at them, he saw crimson.

"Damn it," he muttered.

Roach pushed himself up on one knee again just as Davies walked over, having recovered from the blow to the face. He returned the favor with one of his own, sending Roach to the ground once more. Dust blew up in his eyes as his head connected with the unforgiving concrete.

A heavy boot pressed down on his spine, forcing him flat. His vision blurred. Sickness rose up in his stomach. His brain felt as if it was swirling inside, dizzy from the blow to the head.

He looked over at Rebecca. She was crouched into a ball, crying uncontrollably, no doubt more scared than she had ever been in her life.

There was a sound of an engine behind him. He rolled over, staring for a moment at the bright, neutral, late-spring sky. He let his head fall left, taking his gaze with it. He saw a minivan idle into view. The driver got out and moved around to the side door as a black rental pulled over in front of it, blocking the entrance to the alley.

"You two, help that asshole up," said Davies, pointing at their severely injured colleague. "Get him in the back of the van."

They obeyed, scooping the man up and hoisting him into the minivan with the help of the driver. They climbed in after him and slid the door shut. The driver got back in and started the engine.

Roach looked up at Davies, who had crouched beside

him. The barrel of his gun rested ominously close to his head.

"If you hurt her, I swear to God, I'll kill you," said Roach, struggling to get the words out.

"Sure you will, tough guy."

Davies stood and stepped over to Rebecca. He dragged her upright and pushed his gun against her side, holding her close to him.

He waited.

Roach struggled to roll over, then struggled even more to push himself up on all fours. He heard the clack of heels and glanced to his right in time to see a thick-soled combat boot moving quickly toward his body.

He grunted under the impact, rolling over on his back again and spitting up some blood.

Another face loomed over him. Female. Attractive. Emotionless.

Jay glared down at him. She placed a boot on his chest and applied enough pressure to keep him stationary.

"Take me," he said to her.

"No," she replied. "I wanted to kill you both, but that's not the order. Your sister comes with us until you're ready to cooperate."

"Fine." He coughed up a little more blood. "What do you want to know?"

"I want to know who you've discussed the content of the flash drive with. I want to know how many copies you've made. I want to know who gave it to you. And I want it back."

Roach understood the significance of what the drive contained. But he also knew if he handed it over, both he and Rebecca were as good as dead. The fact they didn't know what he had done with it was the only reason either of them would remain alive.

He smiled. "I bet you do. But I don't have it. Sorry. It's safe... and will remain that way as long as my sister and I stay alive."

Jay narrowed her eyes. She crouched beside him, placed a knee heavily on his body, and quickly frisked him. Nothing.

He looked at her and shrugged. "Told you."

She stood again. "And like I told *you*, asshole, until you're willing to cooperate, your sister will be in our custody."

Jay turned and signaled to Davies, who marched Rebecca over to her.

Rebecca looked at her with a mixture of fear and disdain as she wrestled against his grip.

Jay grabbed her face, squeezed her cheeks together with one hand, and leaned in close. "You better hope your big brother does the right thing soon. Otherwise, your stay will become increasingly unpleasant."

She shoved her face away and gestured to the rental.

"Throw her in the trunk," she said.

Rebecca screamed. "No! Let go of me!"

Roach looked on, dazed and helpless. Rebecca stared at him, silently pleading to help her. But he couldn't right now, and it killed him.

Jay looked down at Roach. "We'll see you soon."

He looked back at her, examining her face, her expressions. He saw no emotion in her dark eyes.

He lifted a hand and pointed to the circular scar on her forehead.

"Nice war wound," he said. "You hurt her, I'll make that seem like a papercut."

Jay said nothing. She simply brought her boot down hard on the side of his head and watched consciousness leave him. She turned and walked away without looking back.

Davies was standing by her car. "Target's secure, ma'am."

"Did you tape her mouth shut?"

He nodded.

"Oh, thank God," said Jay. "Last thing I want is her screaming the entire time."

"Yes, ma'am."

He climbed into the passenger side of the minivan, which drove away a moment later.

Jay glanced back at Roach, who remained motionless on the ground halfway down the alley. The faintest twitch of her lips betrayed her pleasure. She couldn't wait to kill him.

She got in her rental and set off after her team.

16

_____

April 22, 2020

Consciousness came to him like the memory of a bad dream. He frowned as he became aware of the artificial light penetrating his eyelids.

Roach slowly opened his eyes and looked around. He recognized the surroundings of a hospital immediately. Plain walls. A persistent low hum of chatter. A smell of disinfectant stung his nostrils.

It was any hospital, in any city, anywhere in the world.

At least I can remember why I'm here this time, he mused.

He lay on top of the sheets, still dressed as he had been in the alley. He felt relief that he still had his new clothes. He thrust his right hand inside the bodywarmer, feeling for the knife.

Nothing.

Crap.

He moved to shuffle up the bed, to sit upright against the pillows and gather his thoughts, but his movements were restricted. He looked down to see his left wrist handcuffed to the metal guard rail of the bed.

He frowned. "What the..."

The door opened and a nurse entered. She was young, maybe late twenties. She had the exuberance and the bounce in her step of someone who hadn't been in her profession long. Her light brown ponytail swished and swayed as she approached the end of the bed.

"Good morning," she said, beaming. "How are you feeling?"

Roach took a tired breath. "Like I just got the crap kicked out of me."

The nurse regarded him for a moment before allowing her smile to broaden into a polite laugh. "Not the official medical terminology, but... yes, basically."

"Where am I?" he asked.

"You're in the Topeka ER Hospital." She moved to his side and lifted his wrist to measure his pulse. "The good news is, there's no serious damage. The laceration on the back of your head is superficial. You'll have a headache for a day or two, but you shouldn't experience any symptoms of concussion."

He lifted his left arm, tugging gently on the handcuffs.

"I'm assuming there's some bad news relating to these?" he asked.

Her expression changed to one of sympathy. "Yeah, sorry. It's just a precaution until a police officer can take a statement. Standard procedure in these situations. I'm sure you have nothing to worry about."

Roach felt a tightening in his chest. More frustration than anger. More urgency than panic. He knew every second he wasted in that hospital put more distance between him and his sister. He couldn't allow that.

"Listen... Nurse, I understand you have protocols to follow, but I lost a six-on-one fight, okay? I'm not the one who needs to be handcuffed, and I don't have the time to talk to the police. Can you please get someone to remove these, so I can leave?"

Her smile remained unfazed, but her tone hardened. "Look, the police put them on. Only the police take them off. Until they take a statement from you, you wear the jewelry, okay?"

He was taken aback by her directness.

"My apologies," he began. "But I—"

"The officer is just down the hall. I'll let him know you're awake, and he'll be along in a few minutes to ask you some routine questions. Assuming you're—"

"I'm sorry, but I have to get out of here. Some real bad people have kidnapped my sister. I can't involve the police, or she's as good as dead. I can fix this, but you need to let me go. Please."

The nurse faltered momentarily. What he said sounded ridiculous, but there was something in his eyes. Something genuine. She had seen it many times during her time at the hospital. In patients. In visitors. In family.

It was love. Pure, desperate, unapologetic love.

She believed beyond a doubt this man's sister had been taken from him. He most likely went down trying to save her. But there was nothing she could do.

"I'm sorry," she said. "For what it's worth, I... I believe you. I honestly do. But the police are here, and they want to talk to you. I can't do anything about that."

Roach could see his way out of this wasn't through her. But he also knew he needed to get out of there without involving the police.

He looked at the nurse, examining her face. Her hair was

the same color as Rebecca's. He felt a pang of guilt for letting her be taken. He clenched his jaw as he argued inside his own mind over whether he could have done more to protect her.

His mind wandered. Then it refocused on something he had initially missed.

The nurse's hair.

He frowned. He looked at her hair again, then at her wrist.

He reached out, placing his hand on her forearm as she turned to leave.

"Wait, please." She looked down at his hand, then at him. He smiled. "Can you at least give me five minutes before you send the officer in here?"

She thought a moment, then nodded. "Five minutes."

She walked away, pulling her arm from beneath his hand as she did.

Roach watched her leave and close the door behind her, then looked at the hair pin he was now holding. He had seen a spare hair band around her wrist, just like Rebecca had. She had a hair pin hooked onto it, just like Rebecca had.

He bent and twisted and molded it into shape, then quickly picked the lock of the handcuffs. The high-pitched stuttering and grinding of gears as he loosened the mechanism sounded louder than it probably was in the mostly empty room.

Quickly and quietly, he got to his feet. He paused for a moment to make sure he had no trouble moving or standing.

He felt fine.

Roach moved to the door, turned the handle gently, and eased it open. He peered out, scanning the hallways. Away to the right, he saw the nurse talking to the police officer, whose back was to him. She stood slightly to the side, allowing her to see him, should she look that way.

He stepped out, backing away from the room, heading left. Toward the exit.

The nurse caught his eye. Roach held a finger to his lips and smiled, then turned and walked hurriedly away.

There was no time to waste.

Rebecca stared blankly ahead. Her hands were flat on the table. Her expression was vacant. Her blue eyes were dark and bloodshot; a combination of fatigue and fear was slowly chipping away at her humanity.

The room was cold. A gray floor and a gray ceiling were separated by dirty beige walls. She had noticed a security camera fixed above her in the corner. Davies stood beside the equally gray door, arms folded across his chest, silent and menacing.

She had no idea where she was, nor how long she had been there. Time had grown meaningless in the trunk of the woman's car. She recalled sleeping at one point, albeit not for long. However, it was probably closer to passing out than drifting off.

Her throat was dry. Her stomach growled from hunger. She needed the bathroom, and she needed her brother.

She turned slowly toward Davies. She tried to swallow, so words might come out easier.

"Can I please have a glass of water?" she asked.

He didn't respond. He looked at her impassively for a moment. His expression betrayed nothing.

She sighed with resignation and stared back down at the dull surface of the table.

Her hands were shaking.

A few minutes passed, then the door opened. A man walked in, holding a glass of water. Rebecca noted his nice suit and groomed looks.

He smiled as he approached the table and set the glass down in the middle. Then he took a seat opposite her, crossed his legs elegantly, and clasped his hands on his lap. He glanced at Davies, dismissing him with a curt nod. He waited until they were alone.

"Rebecca, my name is Brandon Crow. Do you know who I am?" he said.

She shook her head, flicking a glance at the water.

He noticed.

"Please, help yourself," he said. "You did ask for it."

She picked up the glass reluctantly, hesitating as she held it near her lips.

Crow smiled. "It's not poisoned, I promise. It's just water."

She looked down into the glass, then over at him. She held it out to him and nodded to it.

He shrugged. He took the glass, took a sip, and held it back out to her.

"See?" he said.

She grabbed the glass and gulped its contents, savoring the cool liquid as it flowed down her throat.

He continued. "Rebecca, I'm not here to hurt you. You have my word."

Rebecca glared at him through narrow eyes. Silent disbelief. Obvious disdain.

Crow laughed. "Wow. If looks could kill, eh? I can see

the family resemblance. Your brother always did have a hard time masking his displeasure."

"What do you want with me?" she asked quietly.

"Nothing whatsoever. But I *do* want your brother, and you being here is going to facilitate his cooperation."

"And where am I, exactly? Shouldn't I be allowed a phone call?"

"You're not under arrest, Miss Roachford, and we're not a law enforcement agency. We're not a government acronym, and we're not GlobaTech."

"Then you're holding me illegally and against my will, and I demand you let me go. You have no right to—"

Crow leaned forward and slammed his fist down hard on the table. The dull, metallic thud startled her. "I can do whatever the fuck I want! A fact you would do well to remember."

As quickly as his temper flared, it disappeared. He sat back again, composed. "Now you're here to help me get back something your brother stole from me."

Rebecca fought to flatten her hands on the table, to stop them shaking.

"W-what did he steal?" she asked.

"He has a flash drive containing sensitive information about my company. Given his past transgressions and their consequences, I believe he intends to use this information against us. Against me. Corporate espionage, Miss Roachford."

Rebecca smirked. "You obviously don't know my brother."

"I know him a lot better than you do. What's it been? Twenty years since you last saw him? More?"

"I know him well enough to know he doesn't have the capacity or the patience to care enough about corporate espionage. If you're so concerned about it, why didn't you just kidnap *him*?"

"I am perfectly well aware of what your brother can do. He's a smart, capable, and dangerous man. He's skilled. Focused. And sadly, he has a penchant for doing what he wants, not what he's told."

She frowned. "Really? Will?"

"Yes. And I should know—I spent a considerable amount of money training him. He's hidden the flash drive somewhere, and I have to assume he's put something in place whereby if anything happens to him, the contents of the drive are sent to someone else. Or, worst case, made public. Taking him wouldn't have made sense. Taking *you* does. That man needs incentive. He'll give us what we want because we have you."

Rebecca gazed vacantly at the space between her and the table. Her vision blurred as her mind screamed in a million different directions. A level of fear gripped her that she had never known before. Her world had been shattered in less than a day. It already felt like a lifetime ago she was in the office, sharing a laugh with her friend, lost in a world of news and—

Her eyes refocused. Her mind locked onto a singular thought.

The office. The phone call. The mystery man.

Tristar.

It couldn't have been a coincidence, could it? Was the evidence he mentioned the flash drive her brother had?

She fought to keep any emotion off her face. Maybe she knew more about this than anyone knew.

She looked over at Crow, who sat staring patiently.

"He'll come for you, y'know?" she said, feeling some confidence return to her voice.

Crow smiled. Arrogant and cocky. "No, my dear, he won't. He doesn't know where you are. Whereas I know exactly where he is, which is how I'll get in touch with him for a little chat."

He got to his feet, signaling the end of the conversation. The sound of his chair scraping across the floor echoed around the room.

"Hopefully, you won't be here too long," he said. "But I'll make sure you're comfortable. Just hope your brother cooperates. Otherwise, comfort will be a luxury you're no longer afforded."

He left the room. As he stepped out into the hall, Jay pushed off the wall she had been leaning against, fell in step beside him, and the pair walked away.

"Are you sure this will work?" she asked him firmly.

"Yes," he replied. "We have her now, and she's all he has left."

Roach entered the coffee shop opposite the *Topeka Times*'s office. It was mid-morning. No rush. Minimal lines. Plenty of seating available.

He ignored the counter and headed straight for the table where he and Rebecca had sat the previous day. A young couple were sitting there now, holding hands across the table, sharing a laugh.

The woman had her back to him. The man looked up as Roach stopped beside their table.

He didn't have the time or the patience for pleasantries. He crouched and reached under the table.

"Hey!" shouted the woman, prompting people sitting nearby to look over.

"What the hell is your problem?" asked the man, clambering to his feet.

Roach ignored them. He placed his hand flat against the underside of the table, moving it blindly. He found the chewing gum he had stuck there yesterday.

And the flash drive it was holding in place.

He stood and smiled apologetically at the woman. "Sorry. I needed this."

The man stepped toward him, one hand balled into a fist, the other pointing an accusatory finger at Roach's face.

"You perverted bastard!" he yelled. "Where the hell do you get off, groping a woman like that? Huh? I'm calling the police. You're lucky I don't beat the crap out of you for—"

Roach grabbed his finger and pushed it back against the joint. The man dropped to his knees, yelping and wincing.

He leaned forward, looking down into the man's eyes. "Shh."

He let go and left before anyone else decided to get involved. He thrust the drive into his pocket and headed away from Rebecca's office, toward the alley where he was left yesterday.

He needed to find his sister and didn't know where else to start.

17

Roach stood facing the alley from across the street. He dug his hands into the pockets of his bodywarmer as the wind whipped by. In his hand, he held onto the flash drive, twirling it absently.

Crime scene tape cordoned off the alley, but there were no police standing guard. Still, he didn't want to draw attention to himself by heading back down there. He just wanted to see where everything went down yesterday, hoping it would spark some inspiration and help him figure out his next move.

He had no idea where his sister had been taken. No way of tracking the vehicles or the people inside them. No one to ask for help.

"Did you see what happened?" asked a man's voice beside him.

Startled, he turned to see who had managed to stand so close without him noticing, but then he felt a hard pressure in his back. The cold steel of the gun barrel penetrated his clothing, causing a small shiver on his spine.

"Keep looking ahead, Billy," said the voice.

It was familiar, and it took him a moment to place where from.

"You," said Roach.

"Me," came the reply. A smile clearly affected the tone.

"You're getting sloppy. I saw you in Corfu, outside the bar."

"Yeah, you did. You also dismissed it immediately. I know that because I was still watching, and you didn't see me the second time."

Roach huffed. "Right."

"Oh, and if you think I didn't make damn sure you saw me, then *you're* the one getting sloppy, old friend."

"Are we still friends?"

The pressure from the gun barrel increased. Roach winced.

"If you think I've forgotten what you did to me, you're dumber than you look. But you know me, Billy. I'm a big picture kind of guy. Let's go."

"Where?"

"Wherever I tell you." The man used the gun barrel to gesture him left. "Move."

The pair set off walking, rounding a corner onto a quieter street. They stopped beside a parked car. It was a Dodge Challenger SXT with a matte black finish. It looked fresh off the production line. The man moved in front, holding the gun close to him but keeping it aimed steadily at Roach's body.

Zach Goddard.

Roach quickly looked him up and down. He hadn't changed much since they had last met. His head was shaved now, but he still wore the same mean stare and cocky smile. He was dressed like the star of a seventies cop show, complete with bootcut jeans and a fitted jacket.

"What's it been, Zach?" asked Roach. "Thirteen years?"

"Fourteen," said Goddard. "But who's counting?"

"You, apparently."

"What can I say? I've got a good memory."

"When did you get out?"

"Couple of years ago. Time off for good behavior."

"And it took you this long to find me?

"Billy, please. I found you in the first week after my release. Did you forget how good I am at what I do?"

"Okay. So, why come for me now? I'm guessing it's not a coincidence."

"Opportunity, old friend... opportunity." He reached into his pocket and tossed Roach a set of car keys. "Now get in. You're driving."

"Where are we going?"

Goddard moved around the hood, keeping the gun trained on Roach.

"We're taking a little road trip," he said. "We got a lot of catching up to do."

They cruised along I-35 as the bright morning faded into a gray afternoon. Despite being held at gunpoint, Roach was enjoying the drive. The Challenger was a nice car—powerful, easy to handle, and a smooth, comfortable ride.

They were almost an hour into their journey. Few words had been exchanged, aside from vague directions by Goddard.

"You going to tell me what this is about?" asked Roach, breaking the silence.

"This is about you ratting me out to the feds," said Goddard sharply.

"I figured that much."

"I watched your back for six years inside. I got you connected when we got out. And that's how you repay me? By informing on me and my people to the goddamn FBI? I ought to shoot you right now."

Roach shrugged, not taking his eyes off the road. "We'll probably crash if you did. I'm doing eighty."

"That's funny. You want to know what else is funny? Someone I used to consider a friend is being hunted by a private security firm who just kidnapped his sister, and he has no clue what to do about it."

Roach looked over, fixing Goddard with an icy stare.

Goddard smiled. "You might want to look at the road. You're doing eighty... you wouldn't want to crash."

Roach let out an impatient sigh and refocused on the interstate.

"You're so far down the rabbit hole, your world is pitch-black," continued Goddard. "And you have no idea what you're mixed up in."

"And you do?"

"Of course I do. I wouldn't be here otherwise. Opportunity, remember?"

"Zach, if anything happens to her, I'm going to hold you just as accountable as Tristar. Start talking."

"Patience, Billy. Patience. It's a long drive. First, I want answers. And maybe an apology."

Roach rolled his eyes. "I'm not in the mood for your games."

"Well, that's just tough, isn't it? Why did you give me up to the FBI?"

"Because I didn't have a choice."

Goddard jammed the gun into his temple, pressing hard enough to force Roach's head away. The vehicle swerved a little.

"Do you mind?" asked Roach.

Goddard sat back. "You chose to be a backstabbing piece of shit. No one made you."

"Yes, they did. I know you looked out for me inside. You helped me smarten up, showed me how the world really worked. Taught me how to protect myself. Hooked me up with work when we got out. But that was a bad deal, Zach. The first job that asshole boss of yours set us up with was a bust. You remember? We went to collect his debt from that club..."

Goddard nodded. "Yeah, and there were, like, thirty guys in there waiting for us. I remember."

"Exactly. We barely made it out of there. We split up and ran, but that place was being watched by an undercover FBI team. They picked me up before I reached the end of the block."

"Then you should've kept quiet. You didn't have to talk. You didn't have to give us all up. Give me up."

"They already knew you and your boss. They knew me. They knew about my family. They knew everything. I only agreed to work for you because I needed the money to support my mom and sister. They were going to throw me back in prison, which would've left them with nothing. But they offered me a deal to deliver you and everyone else in exchange for immunity. You were a good friend, Zach, but my family will always come first."

Goddard absently nodded. "Huh. So, I'm not getting an apology?"

"You don't start telling me what the hell's going on and why you're involved, you'll be getting your face rearranged. I don't care how fast I'm driving."

He smiled. "You always did like to get straight to the point, didn't you?"

"I want to know what the hell's going on."

"I'm not going to lie to you, *Roach*. I don't care about your family or your FBI-sponsored sob story. Getting sent back to prison ruined me. Got me into some deep shit with some bad people. It made my life hell, and I hold you accountable. I hate you for that, and I want you dead."

"Okay..."

"But the game being played here is bigger than either of us, so I'm shelving my issues for now." He clicked the gun's safety on and waved it at Roach. "Peace offering. Now promise you won't crash on purpose while we talk?"

"Depends on what you say."

Goddard shifted in his seat. He took a moment to stare out at the world as it whizzed past them.

"This is about Cambodia," he said finally.

Roach sighed impatiently. "I know that. It's why they want me dead—because I survived the first time they tried to tie up their loose ends."

"Wrong. This isn't about you. Well, it is a little bit. But mostly, it's about Tristar and that warehouse."

"Enlighten me."

"The crates you acquired were filled with proprietary technology that had a range of uses, from weaponry to computers to transportation."

"And you know that *how?*"

"Because information is my trade. It's how I also know that you didn't beat GlobaTech to the punch that day."

"What do you mean? We extracted the crates before they could."

"Always rushing to use all those farm boy muscles of yours except the one that matters, aren't you? GlobaTech wasn't there to steal those crates, Billy..."

He fell silent for a long moment. The impact of Goddard's revelation hit him like a freight train.

"We killed them for nothing," he said quietly.

"Yes. The technology had been stolen *from* Tristar. Some low-level guerilla outfit in the area saw an opportunity and took it. However, because the goods were recovered by Thai forces along the border, it caused a diplomatic issue when the driver stealing them headed back to Cambodia. GlobaTech were called in to act as peacekeepers while the proper authorities figured out who was allowed to do what."

"Why was my unit sent in, then?"

"Because GlobaTech didn't know what the crates really contained, and Tristar couldn't run the risk of them finding out. Your mission was to secure your company's property and take out anyone who got in your way. But GlobaTech wasn't there for the reasons you thought. So, no, you didn't have to kill them. They were innocent and ignorant. You could've just waited for them to leave, then packed up your shit and disappeared. No harm, no foul."

"Okay, so what does that have to do with my old team tracking me down? With me being a loose end. How is it connected?"

"It never was. You were in the wind after your recovery. They had no idea where you were and had swept the whole thing under the rug. But then GlobaTech got you involved."

"GlobaTech? How?"

"Because they're a million times better at this than Tristar is. Brandon Crow likes to think he's God's gift to mercenaries and espionage, but the truth is they will always be a low-budget GlobaTech Industries. See, after Cambodia, Tristar made GlobaTech's radar. The boys at the Big G didn't like being attacked by piss-ant wannabes for no reason. Especially with them being so busy with, y'know, rebuilding and policing the world and whatnot. They're no strangers to doing things off the books either, so they hacked Tristar's systems and stole a bunch of classified material, hoping to find evidence of wrongdoing. As we know, they hit the motherlode. But they couldn't use what they had to involve the authorities because it was obtained illegally. So..."

"...they sent it to me?"

"They did. It took them little effort to track you down. They figured, if they gave that information to a disgruntled former employee, he might just do with it the one thing they couldn't—use it against Tristar."

"Hell of a risk though, wasn't it? How did they know I would get involved?"

"Because they saw everything on that drive. It was a million-to-one coincidence, but you were still a loose end and Tristar had an *unofficial* official contingency plan for taking you out, should you ever resurface. GlobaTech knew you would see it. They knew you would fight, if for no other reason than to protect your sister."

Roach's grip tightened on the wheel, draining the color from his knuckles. He weaved through some slower moving traffic, then hit the gas.

"I don't like being played," he said.

"Difficult to avoid when you're in the middle of the big game," replied Goddard.

"How did One and the team find me? And why were you in Corfu?"

Goddard chuckled. "You just answered your own question there, Billy."

"You?"

"Me."

Without warning, Roach's arm shot out, and he grabbed Goddard by the throat. He felt both hands clawing at his wrist, but he never took his eyes off the road, wrestling with the wheel to stay straight. "You gave me up to Tristar? You put my sister in danger? I'll kill you!"

"Take it easy," said Goddard, choking as he struggled against the grip. "Let me... explain."

Roach let him go and put both hands back on the wheel. "Make it good, or I'm pulling over and leaving you dying at the side of the interstate."

Goddard massaged his neck. "I made contact with Brandon Crow and told him where you were."

"Admitting it doesn't help you as much as you might think."

"I knew Tristar still wanted you dead. Word still travels in our world."

"Oh, yeah? And which world is that?"

"Mercenaries, assassins, brokers of information... underground entrepreneurs. I have contacts. I have resources. I have money. I pieced everything together, watched from a distance, and made my move when my information had the highest price tag. I gave him your location to earn his trust."

"And now that you have that?"

"Once I realized the flash drive was in play as well, it was too good of an opportunity to pass up. I intend to drop the bombshell that I know who gave you the flash drive, and for the right price, I would tell him how to get it back."

"Why are you telling me all this?"

"Because there's an even bigger picture I'm trying to put together. I don't know what it all means yet, but I reckon what's on that drive will help fill in the gaps."

Roach fell silent, running through everything in his head.

"You're playing both sides, trying to get rich," he stated after a couple of minutes.

"I am. Crow believes I'm helping him because I want you dead."

"Are you?"

"I'm helping him because his bank account has a substantial balance. Me and you aren't square by a long shot, Billy, but right now you're a convenience, not a grudge."

"You're going to make Crow pay to find out who hacked them and gave me the data. And he will, whatever you ask for. He trusts you because you served me up to him on a silver platter."

"Correct."

"Okay. And you're helping *me* because..."

"Because Tristar and their issues are nothing but a stepping stone to something bigger. For me to stay in the game, I need that flash drive."

"You want me to give it to you when all this is over?"

"You're finally caught up. Congratulations."

"Jesus... you're something else, you know that?"

"Thanks."

"Not a compliment. Besides, I couldn't care less about whatever game you're playing. Unless you can tell me where my sister is, there's no reason I shouldn't kill you right now."

"I could find out where she's being held, but frankly, I've done enough for you already. I have more important things to do."

Roach turned and glared at him. He knew how intimidating he could look if he needed to. "Zach..."

"Which is why I brought you along for the road trip. Keeping heading north on the 35, to Des Moines."

"Why? Is Rebecca in Iowa?"

"No, but there's a quaint little dive bar you might want to

visit. A hangout for independent contractors and general low lives. It's your best chance of finding a lead."

"But she was taken back in Topeka..."

"Yes, but Tristar's an international company. They're unlikely to limit themselves to the state of Kansas just to make your life easier."

"Fine."

"You can drop me off just outside the city limits. I'll let you keep the car. Hell, you can even keep my gun too. I'll leave it in the glovebox for you."

They shot past a sign announcing Des Moines was a little under two hundred miles away.

"Why are you helping me?" asked Roach.

"I'm not," said Goddard with a casual shrug. "Have you not been paying attention? I'm helping *me*. It just so happens that right now that means helping you a little too. In twelve hours, it will mean helping Tristar."

Roach couldn't resist a small smile. "Well, at least you're honest."

"Best way to be, Billy. Without our word, there's nothing separating us from the animals."

"Yeah, right."

"So, listen. What have you done with that flash drive? Have you made copies of it, sent it to a newspaper... what?"

"Why?

"I told you what it's worth. I told you why I want it. Things like this only remain valuable when they're unique. If everyone has a copy, the original becomes worthless, which doesn't work out so well for me."

Roach sighed. "I haven't done anything with it. I looked at it and immediately wished I hadn't. I don't care, all right? This is your game, not mine. I just want my sister back and to be left alone."

Goddard frowned. "So, you're not going to use it to go after Tristar, like GlobaTech wanted?"

"No. I don't care what Tristar are up to anymore. I honestly don't care who it affects. So long as it isn't me and mine, it's not my problem. I just want to be left alone."

Goddard smiled and nodded. "That's fair enough, Billy. That's fair enough."

He reached for the radio, settling for the default station. He turned the volume up enough to make it obvious the conversation was over.

Roach took a deep breath. That suited him fine.

He was done talking.

18

Night had fallen by the time Roach reached Des Moines. He parked the Challenger in a public lot that was still half-full. It wasn't exactly an inconspicuous car, but he figured it was easier to hide it among other vehicles.

He believed most of what Goddard had told him, but that didn't mean he trusted him. He had no idea who or what was waiting for him in the bar. It was best to stay hidden as long as he could.

He took the gun Goddard had left him out of the glovebox and tucked it at the back of his waist. Then he walked away from the lot, taking a left onto a main street. The traffic was light and steady. The sidewalks were busy without being crowded. That suited Roach just fine. He needed space and time to think.

Des Moines had a strange climate. Roach remembered it from the last time he passed through. It had been around the same time of year, and he recalled it feeling as if someone had flicked the switch on a city-wide thermostat. Toward the end of March, the temperature was still low, rarely venturing above forty degrees. Yet, by the second week of April, it was pushing sixty.

The air was still tonight. An uneasy calm blanketed the city, wrapping itself around him as he strolled past a strip of stores. He glanced idly in the windows as he walked by, looking at the various displays. A combination of street-lamps and the bright half-moon provided ample lighting. He saw his faded reflection staring back at him. From his hunched shoulders, he could tell he was tired. He had barely slept or eaten in the last thirty-six hours, although it felt like much longer. He straightened, cracking his neck and rolling his shoulders. He resolved that he would find a motel for the night and head wherever he needed to in the morning.

Roach passed the next large window and slowed to check himself again. To make sure he looked alert, ready. In the reflection, he caught a glimpse of a figure stopped, leaning just inside an entrance a couple of hundred yards behind. They stuck out because the few other people around were walking.

In a sea of movement, it's the stillness that cannot hide.

Whoever it was wore a baseball cap tugged low and an oversized sweater. He dismissed them and walked on, crossing at a red light and continuing along the opposite side of the street. It was busier on this side, but if he had interpreted Goddard's directions correctly, he was heading in the right direction to find the bar.

A small group of young women were walking toward him, laughing between themselves. Roach twisted slightly to let them by but still managed to accidentally bump into one of them. The woman turned to look at him vacantly. He looked back and held up an apologetic hand.

"Sorry," he said.

She ignored him and turned back to her friends.

He noticed the figure in the baseball cap and sweater walking half a block behind him, staring down at the ground.

Roach made a mental note and carried on. His paranoia was in overdrive right now. Roach was an unwilling pawn in a game where he barely understood the rules, and that infuriated him beyond measure. He had been trying not to think about Rebecca, but he was beginning to struggle. He was seeing danger everywhere as a result.

He knew it was the right move to let her go. She would be safe so long as he had the flash drive. But that didn't make his choice any easier to live with. He hated that he wasn't able to protect her.

So, now he had to save her. The only problem was, he didn't know where to start. He hoped the bar Goddard had mentioned would yield some results. Despite not dealing with the seedier side of his former occupation, he was aware it existed. People he knew during his time with Tristar took private work on the side, to make some extra cash. Anything from personal security to beat-downs on behalf of some low-life gangster. There was always money to be made.

He would need to tread carefully. If what Goddard had said was true, then as far as Tristar was concerned, he was a wanted man. That meant people might see him as an opportunity to make some of that extra cash.

Similarly, the woman who had taken him out, with the butterfly tattoo and the scar, was quite distinctive. There's a chance someone could know how to get in touch with her. Maybe even track her down.

Roach turned a corner, using the opportunity to casually glance behind him. No sign of the baseball cap and sweater.

He rolled his eyes and smiled to himself.

Paranoid.

Goddard walked at an even pace along the highway, heading toward the junction where it met East Main Street and entered the small city of St. Charles, roughly thirty miles south of Des Moines. Roach had let him out a couple of miles north, and he was walking back, enjoying the crisp night air.

As the highway dipped and snaked along its path, the lights of the city filled the sky before him. He took out his cell phone and hit redial. It was answered after one ring.

"Well?" asked Brandon Crow.

"Worked like a charm, just like I said it would," replied Goddard. "He should be in that bar within the hour."

"Can you trust your contacts?"

"As much as I trust anybody. I've worked with them before. They've never given me a reason not to work with them again."

"Good. I'm looking forward to having a chat with our mutual acquaintance."

"I hope you haven't forgotten our agreement, Mr. Crow."

"Of course not. I'm a man of my word."

"Uh-huh."

"Think what you want of me, but one thing I'm not is a liar."

"Whatever you say, Brandon. Has the price been agreed?"

"It has. Five million dollars for the identity of the hackers responsible for that drive being in Roach's possession."

"Excellent. Once you have what you need from him, you

kill him. Send me proof, along with the money, and you'll have your information."

"Your information better be worth it."

"It is, don't worry. And as a caveat, I'll tell you right now that he has the only copy. He doesn't have a contingency plan in place. He doesn't have a goddamn clue what he's doing. So, you have even less to worry about."

"And you know this... how?"

Goddard shrugged. "He told me."

"And why on Earth would he do that?"

"Because I asked him."

Crow sighed, losing patience. "Well, obviously. But why would he trust you enough to tell you that?"

Goddard paused, measuring his next words.

Finally, he said, "Because me and him go way back."

Crow laughed. "I *knew* it! I knew this was personal for you. Tell me, how did Mr. Roachford screw up *your* life?"

"Okay. I was Roach's cellmate back in the day. I'm sure you have ways of looking me up if you want to know anything else. After we both got out, he struck a deal with the FBI—chose the family that abandoned him over me, the friend that didn't. I got sent back inside for over a decade; he got a cushy gig working for you."

"Huh. I know he's a ruthless sonofabitch, but I never had him pegged as a rat."

"What can I say? Some people will surprise you."

"Fair enough. He's as good as dead. Will a picture suffice?"

Goddard smiled. "Sure. I'll pin it to my refrigerator beside my report card."

Crow ignored the quip. "Do you have any preference as to what happens to his sister?"

Goddard thought for a moment, then shrugged to

himself. "No. Do whatever you want. Me and my money will be long gone. Not my business what happens after that."

There was a pause.

"It wasn't easy, y'know?" said Crow. "Getting your deal agreed by the board."

Goddard smiled. "I'm sure a man with your natural charisma and talent for bullshitting made light work of it."

"I stuck my neck out because your intel on Corfu played out. But make no mistake. If you're playing me... I'm not someone you want as an enemy."

"Brandon, if I were playing you, you wouldn't know until the game was over."

He hung up. He took the SIM card out of the handset and snapped it in two. Then he tossed the phone in a nearby trashcan.

Goddard walked on, entering the city limits of St. Charles, whistling a tune that had been stuck in his head for a few days that he couldn't seem to shake.

Roach stood outside the bar. Its entrance was halfway along a dark alley, haphazardly built into the side of what appeared to be an abandoned warehouse or storage unit.

The Double Tap.

Subtle, he thought with a half-smile.

A single doorman stood outside, leaning casually against the wall, a cigarette pinched between two fingers. He blew out a slow stream of smoke and turned as Roach neared the door.

"This the right place for a drink around here?" he asked, trying to sound pleasant.

The doorman eyed him up and down, caring little for discretion.

Eventually, he shrugged. "You can definitely get a drink inside. Whether or not you're in the right place remains to be seen."

Roach nodded, ignoring the skepticism, and pushed open the door. As he stepped inside, he was hit by a wave of stale air, musty and damp. A quiet rumble of chatter emanated from the end of the short corridor he found himself in. He followed the noise and headed down a small flight of stairs, then veered right. He found a set of double swing doors. They were painted with a mural that gave the illusion he was looking into an Old West bar over saloon doors.

He pushed his way inside, where the sound of subdued conversations grew louder in an instant. It was a simple, wide-open space, with a bar counter running half the length of the far wall. The scattered tables, chairs, and booths were all full.

Roach cast a quick eye over the crowd, trying not to linger on any one person or table for too long. It was an assorted mix of people. Some, he thought, looked as if they belonged in bars exactly like this one. Others surprised him by looking as out of place as he felt.

The lighting was artificial and poor. There was no music in the background, unless it was too low to be heard over the chaotic ambience. Two pool tables stood in opposite corners across from the entrance, both surrounded by a small group of men and women.

Roach headed for the bar. The best place to spark conversation.

He made it halfway before the noise all but disappeared, like flicking a switch. Roach did his best to ignore it. He knew it was for him. It happened in any bar in the world when a stranger walked into a place only frequented by locals. The curiosity. The disbelief anyone would have the audacity to enter their own personal drinking domain.

Roach understood this was a tough crowd in a hostile environment, but if Goddard were right, this was his best— and perhaps *only*—chance to get a lead on Rebecca before it was too late.

He approached the bar and leaned on its scratched, faded surface. He nodded to the bartender, who had watched him all the way from the entrance. He walked over to Roach, a towel draped over one shoulder, pacing like he had all the time in the world. He stopped in front of him and rested both his tattooed hands on the bar. He didn't say anything. Just stared.

Roach straightened. "Can I get a beer?"

The bartender didn't move. Didn't speak.

"You speak English?" asked Roach. His tone had an impatient edge but remained on the diplomatic side of confrontational.

The bartender held his gaze for a long moment, then turned away without a word. He bent to reach into a low refrigerator, then turned back a few seconds later, holding a bottle of beer. He placed it forcefully down in front of Roach and gestured to it.

Roach looked at it. The cap was still on.

He looked up at the bartender. "You going to open it, or is it purely for decoration?"

The bartender's mouth curled into a slight smile. He produced a bottle opener and flipped the top off. Then he nodded once and turned away to serve another patron.

Roach took a grateful gulp.

Acceptance.

He apparently passed the test. The chatter resumed, growing in intensity until it reached its previous volume.

Roach turned and leaned back on the bar, holding the bottle loose in one hand. Now he could observe properly. There was less scrutiny and therefore more freedom. No one paid him any heed. He was just another face in a crowd of people who asked no questions.

It took him two minutes to pick out the loose-fitting sweater and baseball cap, sitting alone in a dark corner, back to the wall, watching everything.

Watching him.

Paranoia, my ass, he thought.

He pushed himself away from the bar, fixing to approach the mystery figure and ask why they were clearly following him. But he didn't get chance.

"Hey, are you Roachford?"

Confused, he turned to see the bartender standing there, holding a cordless landline handset in his hand.

Roach remained impassive. Calm.

"Who's asking?" he said.

The bartender held out the handset without a word. Roach took it reluctantly. He placed it to his ear and turned to look back at the bar.

"Who is this?" he asked.

"Hello, Mr. Roachford," said the voice, which he recognized immediately.

"Brandon Crow."

"It's been a long time, Billy. How've you been?"

"Cut the small talk, you sonofabitch. Where's my sister?"

"You first, Billy. Where's my flash drive?"

"In my pocket. Come and get it."

"Now, now, Billy. This is a business call. You should exercise some restraint and diplomacy. That's the key to achieving the result you want."

"What I want is to rip your head clean off your shoulders."

Crow laughed. "So short-sighted. There's a bigger game being played here, Billy. You're just a pawn. A bit part. If you're lucky, you'll get out of this alive. You and your lovely sister. I had no idea she was so pretty."

Roach felt every muscle fiber in his body tense. "If so much as a hair on her head is out of place when I find her, I swear to God, I'll punch a hole right in the middle of your chest and pull out your heart."

"Well, as lovely as that sounds, I think you're getting ahead of yourself. I have something you want, and you have something I want. This is the part where we make a deal. Tell me, who have you shown the flash drive to?"

Roach thought for a moment. "Just the three people who have copies. You give me my sister back and let us both go, I'll destroy them all and we call it even."

"Hmm. See, I think you're lying. You're not very good at this, are you?"

"And why do you think that, asshole? What makes you think that wasn't the first thing I did when I saw what was on it?"

"Simple, Mr. Roachford. Because it wasn't."

They fell silent. Crow was right; he wasn't good at this. He had never been one for diplomacy. Perhaps if he were, his life would have played out differently.

The path not traveled.

He found himself in a momentary daydream, watching himself engaged in possibly one of the most crucial conversations of his life. Then he realized something. Crow called the bar's landline.

"How did you know I was here?" he asked.

"I wondered how long it would take you, Billy," replied Crow condescendingly.

Suddenly, everything made sense.

Goddard.

Roach rolled his eyes. "He's playing you. You know that, right?"

"Who? Your friend? Yes, he told me the story he intended telling you to get you to Des Moines. I'll admit, he's an infuriating little bastard..."

"Correct."

"But he's effective. He finally told me who he was and why he was helping us find you. When I have that flash drive and you're disposed of, he will be paid a significant sum of money to tell me how you came to have it in the first place."

Roach did his best to think how his next words would play out, but his impulsivity quickly took over.

"I can save you some money, if you're interested," he said.

"Meaning?"

"Meaning he told me who sent me the drive. Same people who hacked you. You're being played just as much as me, Brandon."

If that got any reaction, he hid it well.

"Did he really?" said Crow. "Well, he conveniently omitted that small detail from his plan. Please, enlighten me."

"What, are you kidding? You were going to pay Goddard a fortune for that information. You give me my sister and promise to leave us alone, and maybe I'll tell you for free."

Crow laughed again. "Poor Billy. Still think you're in a position to negotiate. Now I know you have the drive with you, and that it's the only copy, I'm thinking I'll just take it and kill you now. Then I'll move your sister up to my penthouse. Have me a grand old time."

Roach's grip tightened on the phone. He fought to stay focused. "You're welcome to come here and try, asshole."

"Oh, Billy... I don't need to. There are plenty of people eager to help, if the money's right."

Right then, a cacophony of beeps and rings filled the air, drowning out the overlapping conversations. Distracted and confused, Roach looked around. One by one, almost everyone around him reached for their phones. He saw them look at the screens. He saw them all turn to stare directly at him.

"You think we're both being played by your old friend, Billy?" said Crow. "Maybe you're right. But I can tell you one thing. You are *definitely* being played more than me. Which is why you're standing in a bar right now surrounded by mercenaries and PMCs looking to make some extra cash. And as luck would have it, they just received an offer of a considerable amount of money in exchange for bringing the flash drive, along with your corpse, straight to me. Do have fun."

The line went dead.

Roach stared at the receiver for a moment, then looked up to see a roomful of people looking at him like they were starving, and he was the main course.

He took a deep breath. "Well... shit."

19

Roach had never backed down from a fight in his life, and he wasn't about to start now. But he wasn't stupid. One-, two-, even three-on-one, he would always bet on himself to come out on top. But sixty-on-one?

He eyed the exit across the room.

He needed to get out of there.

Now.

Roach turned to look at the man sitting nearest to him at the bar. He appeared older than most others in there. His face was creased like old leather. His mouth was a permanent hard line of disinterest. His eyes had seen more than their fair share of the world.

He was holding a phone. The screen was illuminated.

Roach nodded to it. "How much?"

The man's expression never changed.

"Hundred grand," he replied with the voice of a nicotine addict.

Roach held the man's gaze and asked, "Do I need to worry about you?"

The man stared for a moment. Then he shut his phone off, pocketed it, and shook his head.

"I'm too old for whatever shit you're in the middle of, son." He spun in his seat, nodding to the increasingly hostile crowd. "But I gotta tell ya... I reckon you're about to have a real bad night."

Roach looked out. His eyes narrowed. "Yeah... I reckon you're probably right."

"You want some advice?"

"Sure."

"Take out the first four that come for you. Kill the fifth. The rest will likely let you go."

Roach looked at him. "Kill the fifth?"

The man shrugged. "Yeah. Build up to it. Makes more of a statement."

"Right."

"You'll be fine." The old man smirked, looking him up and down. "What are you? Six-two? Six-three? Maybe two-twenty? You're built like a collegiate linebacker. You'll be fine."

Roach smirked back. "I admire your optimism, if nothing else."

He rested the phone and his near-empty bottle on the bar beside him and casually brushed his hand against the flash drive in his pocket for reassurance. He left it lingering by his side, ready to whip out the handgun tucked in his waistband if he needed to.

A last resort.

He took a breath, steeled himself, and stepped forward.

A scraping of tables and chairs resonated around him as people got to their feet, reacting to his movement.

Roach stood still, scanning the crowd.

Two men stepped forward, seemingly nominating themselves to claim the prize. Both were similar in stature and build. One was dressed like a biker, complete with long hair and leather waistcoat. The other wore a football jersey and loose-fitting pants. They moved directly in front of Roach, putting their bodies between him and the exit.

Roach eyed them both in turn. He figured the biker was the more senior of the two, so he addressed him.

"I'm walking out that door," he said. "Whatever Brandon Crow's offering you to stop me isn't worth it. Move."

Neither man flinched.

Nor did Roach.

An instant stalemate.

He knew he was at a disadvantage. He needed to make a statement. To prove a point. To convince everyone in that bar he wasn't to be messed with.

Not an easy task. But as an image of his sister being tortured flashed into his mind, he remembered it didn't matter how difficult his evening was about to get.

He needed to leave.

"Last chance," he said. "Move or be moved."

No reaction.

He took another taut breath. "Okay. Have it your way."

Roach took a half-step back, keeping his back foot resting on the ball, rather than the heel. The biker stepped forward to close him down.

Roach shifted his weight forward and pushed off his back foot. He dropped his head slightly so that the curve of his skull, above the brow, connected just below the bridge of the biker's nose.

No one ever suspected a headbutt. They hurt the person delivering them, so most people assume no one would risk throwing one. But while they left a noticeable, pulsing pain in the attacker's head, the damage inflicted when thrown properly was vastly more significant. That was the case of the biker, who was unconscious before he hit the floor; his nose was split open, misshapen, and bleeding profusely.

The surrounding crowd reacted, though remained nothing more than quietly surprised.

Roach took another half-step back, clenching his jaw as he forced himself to ignore the pain in his head.

The man in the football jersey moved next. He rushed toward him, quickly closing the small gap between them. Roach shuffled to the side and jabbed a sharp elbow into the man's temple as he drew level. The movement was minimal but devastating. Unprepared, the man crashed to the floor, his head connecting with the surface of the bar on the way down.

Roach watched to make sure he was out cold, then turned his attention back to the crowd. While still hostile and clearly motivated, they seemed a little more skeptical now. A few looks of uncertainty. Some exchanged glances. Restless shifting of weight.

He knew he had to expend as little energy as possible, while at the same time making enough of a statement to buy him the respect he needed to walk out of there.

"Anyone else? Because I got places to be," he said.

Three men shuffled into position on his right, fanning around to form a tight quarter-circle in front of him. All were of similar height. One had a significantly larger gut than the other two. It poked out from under his T-shirt, hanging over his belt. But all three looked useful in a fight.

The one nearest to Roach produced a flick knife. He stepped toward him, holding it with the blade pointing forward.

Without looking, Roach reached behind him for his beer bottle. He grabbed it by the long neck and swung it around as if aiming to hit a home run. It connected with the side of the man's head, breaking just below his grip.

Glass bottles didn't usually break like in the movies. The glass was a little thinner where the neck formed, but the rest of it was thick. Getting hit with one would feel like being hit with a brick, but the bottle would stay in one piece. However, such was the ferocity of Roach's swing, it shattered on impact. Pieces jutted out from the side of the man's head as he lay on the floor, blood cascading from the wounds.

Roach was done waiting around. He had no issue with the escalating severity of his violence, but that didn't mean he was happy for it to continue. He needed to put an end to this before—

He grunted as he felt a dull impact across his shoulders. He dropped the broken bottle neck and stumbled forward into the crowd. He glanced back to see the old man holding his bar stool, smirking.

"Sonofabitch..." muttered Roach.

He straightened and moved back, winding up a strong right, with the intention of making sure the old man landed in a heap a few days later.

He never got to swing it.

A pair of hands grabbed his forearm, spinning him around instead. The man with the large gut smiled at Roach, revealing broken and rotting teeth, then delivered a headbutt.

Roach gritted his teeth as he countered it, prepared for how much it would hurt. By dropping his own head, he protected his nose—his own target, moments earlier—and exposed the thick bone above his brow.

The contact was dull and flush. Both men staggered back. The man fell over a table behind him, and Roach tumbled to the floor.

Disoriented, he crawled toward the bar, seeking to use it for balance as he attempted to get back to his feet. He blinked hard to clear the fog, but the world was spinning, and his head throbbed beyond measure.

A stiff kick buried itself in his rib, sending him rolling away. He looked to see the remaining guy from the group of three bearing down on him. His hands fumbled in the gloom for something he could use to hoist himself upright. They wrapped around the broken bottle neck.

The man bent forward, grabbed two handfuls of Roach's bodywarmer, and pulled him up. As he did, Roach turned sharply into him and thrust the jagged edge of the bottle into the man's throat, just beneath the chin. It sliced through his vocal cords like they were made of butter. He fell back, clutching at the wound. Blood spewed out, soaking his hands and body.

Roach pulled himself upright and found his footing. His head pulsed with pain. His back, shoulders, and ribs all ached from their respective blows. He took a long, deep breath as looked at the carnage he had managed to create. Bodies were strewn across the floor to his right. Two large pools of blood merged together as they expanded out from the injured parties.

Roach studied each one in turn. Quickly and expertly. Three were out cold. One was alive but struggling with the blood loss from his head wound. The last man was dead.

He turned to look at the old man who had attacked him from behind and shrugged.

"Kill the fifth," Roach muttered between staggered breaths.

He brushed his hand over the flash drive in his pocket.

Still there. Still in one piece.

He sighed with relief and set off walking slowly over to

the exit. More patrons moved to block his path, staring challengingly. Some folded their arms over their chests.

Roach counted eleven in front of him and maybe thirty more to his left, spread out across the entire bar area. There was nowhere to go to his right—just walls and bodies.

"Oh, come on..." he whispered.

He saw movement to his left, out the corner of his eye. There was someone else within arm's length.

Enough was enough.

Roach lunged left, grabbing the man that was there. He dragged him in front of him and pulled the gun from his back. Roach pressed the barrel to the side the guy's throat, holding him in place with his hand wrapped around his neck. He shuffled behind him.

"All right, look. The piece of shit who put the contract out on me has kidnapped my sister. I'm going to get her back. Maybe kill him while I'm at it. I don't have a problem with anyone here, but I will end you if you get in my way. Starting with *this* guy." He pushed the gun harder against his flesh. "Let me leave, and you'll never see me again."

One of the men in front of him stepped forward, separating himself from the pack. His hair was long and disheveled, with gray streaks running from root to tip. The handlebar mustache was the same. A dark, sleeveless denim waistcoat revealed wiry arms covered in tattoos. The man towered over everyone else, easily seven feet tall.

Roach looked up at him. "Listen, Lurch, I got enough reasons to start shooting already. Do yourself a favor and back up before you give me another one. I have no issue with putting a bullet in you."

The giant took another step forward, smiling.

Roach rolled his eyes. "Fine."

He quickly took aim at the man's knee and fired. The

gunshot was deafening in the enclosed, underground space. But the man remained upright.

Roach frowned. No blood. No bullet wound.

"What the..."

He took aim again, this time at the man's chest, and fired two more times.

Gunshots. No impact.

For a split-second longer than a blink, he closed his eyes as the scale of this set-up became painfully clear.

The gun was loaded with blanks.

"Zach, I swear to God, I'm going to pull your lungs out through your mouth and stomp on them," he muttered.

The tension in the room relaxed as everyone realized the gun was useless. In the moment of calm that followed, Roach glanced around the room. He happened upon the booth in the dark corner at the back. The large sweater and baseball cap had gone.

The image of his sister faded into view in his mind. Even the idea that she was in danger was all the incentive he would ever need. He had to leave here, and he was prepared to die trying.

Without warning, he slammed the pistol into the side of the head of the man he had been using a shield. It connected on the point of the jaw, knocking him unconscious. He let the man's body drop and leveled the gun at the giant before him. He emptied the magazine as he ran toward him, knowing it would do little except cause a distraction.

Instinctively, the man flinched. When the hammer thumped down on an empty chamber, Roach threw the gun at him and dropped his shoulder, plowing into him. As he connected with his midsection, he reached around and grabbed the backs of the giant's legs, taking him down. The momentum carried them both through the table behind them.

They landed hard. The giant took the brunt of the impact, along with Roach's body weight, which crashed down on him at the same time.

Roach bounced back to his feet and kicked the guy in the head like he was punting a forty-yard field goal. He felt something give beneath his boot. He didn't care to waste time seeing what it was. All that mattered was that the big guy wasn't moving.

He stumbled back against the far wall, catching his breath. In the same moment he realized he was standing no more than ten feet from the exit, he felt a sudden, white-hot pain in his arm. He turned to see a short woman in a sweat-soaked camo top holding a combat knife. His shirt was torn and soaked with blood.

A combination of shock and adrenaline prevented the pain from registering, but Roach knew that wouldn't work a second time. He lunged forward, delivering a short, stiff jab to the woman's face. She rocked back and dropped to one knee. The knife flew from her grip as she clutched her nose.

Roach turned back to the exit, only to catch an incoming punch from the left. He felt his cheek split from the contact, and he took a couple of steps back to compensate. He re-focused in time to see another guy throwing a big follow-up. Roach ducked under it and jabbed his elbow into the man's ribs, momentarily knocking the wind from him. He then shoved him to create some distance and threw a punch of his own, connecting squarely with the man's throat. The man's eyes bulged as he gasped and careened away. Roach followed it up with a stiff uppercut to the jaw, which sent the man flying backward into a nest of tables.

Roach took the opportunity, turned, and bolted for the

exit. He thrust open the doors, then turned on his heels to slam them closed again once he was through. There was a fire axe hung on the wall at the foot of the small staircase. He yanked it from its clasps and jammed it through the door handles. It wouldn't hold everyone in there forever, but it would buy him enough time to get to safety.

He ran up the stairs and burst through the door at the top and out into the alley. The doorman turned, surprised. Without breaking stride, Roach rushed past him, smashing his forearm into the doorman's face as he did. He sprinted around the corner and didn't stop running until he was back on the street that led to the parking lot where he had left the Challenger. No one had pursued him from the bar.

Roach slowed to a walk as he crossed the street, fighting to catch his breath. He passed the stores with the large windows again and couldn't help but glance at his own reflection. Even in the late evening luminance, he could see he looked like hell.

The streets were quiet now. The sidewalks even moreso.

Which is why the large sweater and baseball cap that was keeping pace roughly half a block behind him stood out in the reflection.

This town... seriously, thought Roach.

He didn't falter. He kept walking until he saw the lot up ahead. Just before it was another alley between two takeout joints. At a casual pace, he turned into it. The moment he was hidden from view, he pinned himself to the wall and waited, camouflaged by the shadows.

A solid minute passed. Then the figure in the large sweater and baseball cap turned into the alley. Whoever it was, they were much shorter than him. But they had undoubtedly been tailing him since he arrived in Des

Moines, and after the night he had just had, he wanted answers.

He burst out of the darkness, grabbing them with both hands—one around the throat, one on the shoulder. He spun them around and slammed them against the wall.

"Who the hell are you, and why are you following me?" When they didn't answer, he slapped his palm against the wall in frustration. "Answer me!"

He ripped the cap from their head, revealing a striking woman with dark eyes and dark hair. She looked back at him defiantly.

He frowned. "What the hell? Who are you?"

The woman smiled, but it wasn't friendly. "My name's Julie Fisher. I work for GlobaTech Industries, and I'm here to help you."

He failed to hide his surprise. "GlobaTech? Christ, this night just keeps getting better. I saw you in that bar back there. If you're here to help me, why did you sit back and let me get my ass handed to me by half of Iowa?"

She brushed his hands away and shrugged. "Whatever that was back there wasn't my problem. I'm here to help you with the things that *are* my problem."

"Look, Julie Fisher, this has been a bad night in a worse week, and I'm not in the mood for whatever the hell this is. Turn around and go back to wherever you came from. I'm not interested in getting any deeper into this than I already am."

"Yeah, well, I'm afraid I can't do that. We need to talk. I don't care how bad of a night you're having. One way or the other, we will do."

Roach narrowed his eyes. "Are you serious? Listen, lady. I don't care how good GlobaTech thinks it is. It'll take a lot more than you to get me to do anything. You made a big mistake coming for me on your own."

She smiled as he felt the cold, unforgiving steel of a gun barrel press against the base of his skull. His gaze dropped with defeat.

"She's not on her own, dickhead," boomed a voice from behind.

He turned slowly to see a mountain of a man aiming a pistol directly at his head with unwavering accuracy. He was a few inches taller than him and twice as wide. The guy looked like he could bench press a tank.

Roach stepped away and held his hands up slightly, signaling his resignation.

Julie moved to the man's side. "This is my colleague, Jericho. I reckon he's the only person around here whose lack of patience rivals yours. However, *his* gun isn't loaded with blanks. Now how about we go have that talk, hmm?"

20

Brandon Crow paced back and forth in front of his desk with concern etched onto his chiseled face. The panoramic view of downtown New York was lit up by the nighttime rush. Seemingly endless streams of red and orange lights illuminated the world outside.

It had been an hour since his conversation with Roach. An hour since the communique had been sent out to the network of contractors. He had heard nothing, which worried him.

Worse still, he was told to expect a call from the board any moment. It was the only reason he was still in the office so late in the evening. He wanted a seat at that table one day, and if he didn't get that drive back and eliminate Roach soon, he could kiss that idea goodbye.

Crow took out his cell phone and selected a contact from his list. The call was answered after two rings.

"What's happening?" he asked.

Over a thousand miles away, behind the wheel of her black rental, Jay blasted along a near-deserted highway. Her phone was on speaker, and the faint hum of the radio was audible in the background.

"I don't know," she replied hurriedly.

"What do you mean, you don't know? Where the hell are you?"

"I'm heading back to New York. After you put the contract out on Roachford, it all went to shit. He fought his way out of there, sir."

"Are you kidding me? How?"

Jay sighed. "It was... he was a force of nature. I've never seen anything like it. I was standing at the back. He didn't see me. I snuck out before he managed to escape, but I saw him leave at full speed. He looked like shit, but he was alive."

Crow looked around his office, as if searching for something to direct his sudden wave of fury toward.

"Goddammit!" He slammed his fist down on his desk, making a nearby pen leap into the air. "Why didn't you go after him?"

"Because I'm pretty certain he was being followed."

"By who?"

"Unclear. But two of them cornered him in an alley not far from his car. I took off before they spotted me."

Crow massaged the bridge of his nose between his finger and thumb. He couldn't think straight. He was distracted by how this new development would be received by his superiors.

"Fine. Get back here as soon as you can," he said finally. "But I want you to pick up Goddard on your way. We traced his last call, so we have his position. I'll send you the coordinates."

"You think he sold us out?" asked Jay.

"I think he's playing both sides and can't be trusted. I'm done with his games. I want him here."

"Okay. What about Roachford?"

"From what you've said, he's someone's else problem for now. But we have his sister. It's only a matter of time before he makes contact. He wants to ride off into the sunset and be left alone with his family. He doesn't care about us or the drive. He'll hand it over if he thinks he can walk away."

"Can he?"

"Walk away? Of course not. Once I have that drive, I'll kill him and his sister myself. No loose ends."

The door to his office opened, and his secretary hovered in the threshold, trying to catch his attention. She looked tired and was struggling to hide her displeasure at being in work so late. Her expression softened when Crow looked over. She tapped her wrist to indicate the time, then pointed to the large TV screen mounted on the wall opposite his desk and nodded.

He nodded back. She left, closing the door behind her.

"I've got another call," he said to Jay. "Bring Goddard back here."

"What if he doesn't want to?" she asked.

Crow shrugged. "Make him."

He hung up, reached for a remote on his desk, and clicked the screen into life.

What appeared was a live feed of a conference room. Seven people sat around an oval table made of mahogany, with the camera at one end. Six men, one woman. Three sat on either side with one at the head, facing the camera. Behind them, just visible in the camera's periphery, was a wall of screen, linked together to show one image. It was a dark blue background with a silver logo spinning and bouncing slowly around, like a screensaver.

Crow straightened, pushed his shoulders back, and puffed his chest out. He adjusted his tie.

"Gentlemen, madam... good evening," he said as confidently as possible.

The man at the head of the table leaned forward in his seat, resting one elbow on the table. Thick smoke from the cigar he was holding whispered into the air next to him.

"Brandon. We appreciate you making the time at such a late hour."

"Of course, sir. Always a pleasure."

The man rested back in his seat and took a long drag of his cigar. "Brandon, it's come to our attention you have yet to recover the confidential information you allowed to be taken from your company. This is... troubling."

Crow smiled defensively. "Sir, I can assure you that won't be a concern for long. I'm overseeing the efforts to retrieve it personally."

The man nodded to a younger man sitting on his left, who slid a thin folder across to the table to him. He opened it.

"And what of your former asset? The one who has this information..." He glanced at the file. "Roachford."

"He will be handled in due course, sir, naturally."

"Tread carefully, Brandon. You have been given great freedom to run Tristar, but that doesn't mean you have carte blanche with impunity. We are visible at all times. You are not, and you should always act with the intention of staying that way."

"I understand, sir. I do."

The man leaned forward again, pointing his cigar at the camera.

"Tell that to the Greek authorities!" he barked. "Tell that to the Topeka PD!"

Crow felt himself shrink away from the screen. His shoulders slumped as he perched on the edge of his desk, folding his arms across his chest. He said nothing.

The man on the screen relaxed. "If this situation is getting away from you, we can find someone else to resolve it."

Crow stood. "That won't be necessary, sir. I promise the situation is in hand. I guarantee Roachford will be taken care of and the drive recovered within twenty-four hours."

"Good," replied the man sternly. "We are at a critical stage right now. Scrutiny is at its peak. If any of Tristar's operations are linked back to us, it could jeopardize everything we've worked for. That cannot be allowed to happen, Brandon. Understand that we will take steps to ensure our protection."

Crow nodded, fighting to control the melting pot of emotions he felt. "Of course. I would expect nothing less. You have my word, gentlemen... madam. Give me a day. I will give you peace of mind."

"One day, Brandon. Then we will fix this for you."

The feed cut off, switching to display the same dark blue screensaver.

Crow took a long, deep breath as he reached for the remote. He aimed it toward the TV, then paused to stare at the silver logo of Orion International before clicking it off. He then turned and launched the remote at the adjacent wall, accompanied by a guttural roar of frustration. His anger bubbled to the surface, and he stood breathing heavily, staring at the broken remote on the floor of his office.

21

Julie Fisher slid across the seat in the booth opposite Roach, precariously carrying three coffees. She pushed one over to him, then passed the other one to Jericho, who had squeezed himself into a chair beside them.

They had pulled in at a truck stop just outside the city limits, southbound on the I-35. It was anonymous and typical. Given it was almost midnight, the place was quiet. Only a couple of vehicles were in the lot outside. There was only one other customer inside too, which meant they likely belonged to the skeleton staff working the counter and kitchen.

Roach tried to relax. He glanced over at Jericho as he took a grateful sip of coffee. The gun was visible on his lap, aiming at him. He maintained a hard, unblinking stare. In the improved lighting of the diner, the sheer size of the man was more evident. Roach was no slouch, but Jericho dwarfed him. The long-sleeved tee he wore appeared three sizes too small, though he guessed it probably wasn't.

Roach turned his attention to Julie, who was sitting opposite and regarding him quietly with a bemused look on her face. She was attractive, he thought. A pretty, yet world-weary face. Hair that suggested some effort, despite her line of work not requiring anyway.

He took another sip of coffee and sighed.

"So, is someone going to tell me what this is about?" he asked.

"In a minute," replied Julie.

He rolled his eyes.

"Got somewhere else you need to be?" Jericho challenged.

Roach turned to him. "Yeah, actually. I need to go and rescue my sister. Maybe kill the people who took her." He looked back at Julie. "Though I suspect you already knew that."

She nodded silently.

"Look, it's been a long day," he continued. "I'm tired, I just fought my way through a small army of mercenaries, and I'm no closer to finding my sister. So, how about we skip all this cloak and dagger shit and get to the point."

Julie smiled. "I saw you in that bar back there. That was impressive."

Roach shrugged. "That was necessary. I just want to be left alone, but if someone comes for me, I'll end them."

She held his gaze. "My friend here doesn't think I should trust you. Is he right?"

Roach looked over at Jericho. "Don't think I'm trustworthy, huh?"

Jericho shook his head but said nothing.

"Well, I don't care what you think. And for the record, you keep giving me that stink-eye from over there, me and you are going to have a problem."

Jericho smiled. "Oh, no..."

Roach tensed in his seat and balled his hand into a tight fist.

Julie held up a hand. "All right, knock it off, both of you."

Jericho looked at her. "What did I do?"

"You antagonized him. What did I say to you on the way here?"

"Don't antagonize him..."

"Oh, good. I wasn't speaking Japanese, then? Just... sit there and be quiet."

Roach failed to suppress a smile.

"And you," said Julie, turning her attention to him. "You would do well to remember we're here as friends."

"Friends with guns pointed at me," he countered.

"Friends with well-justified trust issues. And as fun as it was watching you rampage your way through a bar full of assholes, it would be wise not to provoke someone who could pull your arms out of their sockets."

Roach glanced at Jericho, who was smiling. He looked back at Julie. "Whatever. Just tell me what the hell is going on."

She sat back in her seat, cradling the warm cup of coffee with both hands.

"This all started in Cambodia," she said. "We've been watching Tristar ever since, trying to piece together whatever they're up to."

"Why does GlobaTech care what a mid-level security contractor is doing? Haven't you got enough to do?"

"We care because they killed a team of our guys in that warehouse over some crates of tech. We care because a few days after that, they killed six more and stole sixteen million dollars in cash from a shipping container we helped seize in Nova Scotia."

Roach frowned. "They did? I didn't know that. I'm sorry."

"So, you don't know why?"

He shook his head. "I was in a coma at the time."

"Convenient," muttered Jericho.

"Not really," said Roach, turning to him. "It messed up my plans for the fall..."

Julie sighed. "Enough. William, we know what happened to you in Thailand. At the hospital. You were lucky to escape."

"I had help. A doctor there gave his life to get me out."

"I'm sorry for that. Truly, I am. You managed to stay off the grid for a long time. In your condition, that was impressive."

"Not impressive enough, apparently."

"Well, you stayed hidden from most people."

"But not you?"

She smiled. "We're not most people."

"Right. The almighty GlobaTech. So, why involve me? I wasn't bothering anyone in Corfu."

"Our investigation into the Cambodia incident led us to you pretty quickly. You weren't *that* hard to track down— sorry. But we *did* leave you alone. We knew what had happened to you, and despite your part in everything, we didn't feel it was our place to go after you."

"And yet..."

She smiled sympathetically. "But in the six months that followed, we discovered more and more questionable things about Tristar. Worrying things."

"Such as?"

"That's a conversation for another time. Suffice to say, they concerned us enough that we decided to... obtain more delicate information on them, to confirm our suspicions."

"The flash drive?"

"That's right. The information we copied from their servers proved valuable but ultimately useless, given how we came to have it."

"Yeah, I imagine corporate espionage isn't among the list of services you advertise as offering."

"It was pure coincidence we chose to involve you. We had placed you on a watchlist, so when we saw you and your sister mentioned on that drive, it made sense to approach you. See if you would be willing to help."

Roach took a sip of his coffee. He stared at the window beside him, looking half outside, half at his own reflection. "See, I already know how Tristar found me. But I also know it had nothing to do with the flash drive. They knew I had it, but when they came for me, they had no way of knowing if I had looked at it. Which I hadn't, for the record. Yet, when they took my sister, it was because they were threatened by what they assumed I knew, having seen the drive. So, how did they know?"

Julie and Jericho exchanged a glance. Roach saw it. It was tense. Uncertain.

She cleared her throat. "We think Tristar hid a virus of some kind among the data we stole."

Roach frowned. "Why would they sabotage their own data?"

"No, not a bad virus. It was a failsafe. Should their systems ever be compromised, whoever stole the data would unknowingly also steal the virus, which would give Tristar a back door into the hacker's own systems. They could then see if certain information had been accessed."

Roach shifted in his seat and took a breath. "So, you're telling me that when I looked at the contents of the drive, I basically sent them a message saying I had done as much, along with exactly where I was?"

She nodded. "Basically, yes. Once they knew you had seen what was on the drive, their issue with you became about more than just loose ends. That was when they took your sister."

He sat for a moment, staring at the table until his vision glossed over, piecing the last few days of his life together. When he looked back up at Julie, his expression had hardened.

"My sister's life is in danger because of you," he said.

Julie held his gaze. Her lips pursed into an apologetic line. "Indirectly and inadvertently... yes, it is. I'm sorry for that."

Roach leapt to his feet before either of them could react. Jericho was first to stand, holding his gun low, out of sight of the staff who had looked over at the disturbance.

Roach pointed to him. "We're done. Try to follow me, I'll kill you."

He marched toward the door without looking back, although he heard the commotion of movement behind him. He pushed the door open and stepped out into the cold night air. He hunched against the steady wind as he headed toward his car.

He heard hurried steps behind him. He glanced back to see Julie running after him.

"William, wait," she said. "Just hear us out. Please."

He turned, forcing her to stop a few feet away. "No. Rebecca's life is in danger because of *your* actions. You chose to involve me. I didn't ask for this. I never wanted any of this. I just want to be left alone. I just want to forget..."

Jericho caught up and stopped beside her, his gun still held low.

"Maybe you should've thought about that before you shot our guys," he said.

Roach sighed heavily and turned away. He looked up at the dark sky for a moment, then turned back. "I didn't kill your people, okay?"

"What do you mean?" asked Julie.

"Why do you think my own team shot me and left me for dead in that goddamn warehouse? I refused to engage with your team. Something about it didn't sit right with me. Those damn principles of mine didn't get me very far though, did they? So, no, my sister being kidnapped doesn't make us even, you juiced-up sonofabitch!"

A tense silence fell on the three of them. The wind rushed around the triangle they formed as they stood beside Roach's car.

Eventually, Julie stepped forward and placed a hand on Roach's arm. "I'm sorry."

He brushed her away. "I don't want your apologies. I want my sister. I want this to be done with."

"We know where you sister's being held," announced Jericho.

Roach looked at him. "How?"

Jericho smiled. "We're GlobaTech, remember? We're good at this."

"You really should've opened with that. Could've avoided the godawful coffee and unnecessary conversation."

"We needed to know if we can trust you," said Julie. "And I think we can. So, we'll tell you where she is, if you do something for us first."

He rolled his eyes. "What?"

"Give us something... anything on Tristar that might help us. How they operate, the type of work they're doing, key employees... anything."

"Are you not able to figure all that out for yourself? I thought you guys were good."

Julie shrugged. "We are. But we're also visible, and much of what we do is public record. We have to tread carefully."

Roach thought for a moment. He didn't feel like they were trying to play him. That had been happening a lot recently, so he knew it when he saw it. But he wasn't sure what he could give them that would be of use.

Eventually, he said, "I don't know much besides what's on that drive, and I barely understood half of what I saw. I certainly wasn't privy to anything when I worked for them. But I know one thing—if there's anything going on that's not legit, Brandon Crow will be involved."

"Who's he?" asked Jericho.

"He's the Head of Logistics. He's also the piece of shit holding my sister captive and the man who put the bullseye on my back."

"That's perfect. Thank you," said Julie. "We'll begin quietly investigating him, see if we can tie him to anything we already know."

"He has a woman who works for him too. Crazy-looking. A real piece of work. Got a butterfly tattooed on her neck."

"Appreciate it," said Jericho. "Your sister is being held beneath Tristar's head office in New York. It looks like they have a number of sublevels they use for God-knows-what."

Roach nodded. "Thanks. Although, that's not much use to me. Do you have any idea how many Tristar personnel will be on site? So, unless you two want to stick around and help..."

"We would if we could," said Julie. "But they won't know you're coming, so the element of surprise will help. Besides, I thought you liked long odds."

She smiled, which Roach returned.

"I just play the cards I'm dealt," he said.

Jericho reached into his jacket pocket and produced a key card, which he held out for Roach to take. "Maybe this will help."

Roach took it and examined it. It was for a hotel in New York.

"I could use a shower and some sleep, I guess," he said, a little confused. "But how does this—"

Julie nodded to it. "You'll find a care package on the bed. A black sports bag, courtesy of our boss."

"Call it a gesture of goodwill," added Jericho.

Roach waved the card gratefully, then slid it into his own pocket. "Thanks. Although, I might need more than a fake mustache and a janitor's uniform to get inside that place."

Julie and Jericho exchanged a knowing smile.

"Trust me," she said. "We're pretty good at handing out gift bags."

Roach nodded. "Fair enough. Listen... I'm sorry for the losses you've suffered."

"Thanks," said Jericho.

"Understand, once I have Becky safe, she and I are gone. This isn't my fight."

Julie held out a business card. "That's fair. But if you change your mind, call us, okay?"

Roach turned and moved around to the driver's side of the Challenger. He looked back at them over the roof. "I'd offer you both a ride somewhere, but I still don't like you all that much."

"We're good," said Julie, smiling.

"One last thing," said Jericho. "What do you intend doing with the information on that drive, once you have your sister?"

Roach leaned on the Challenger, clasping his hands.

"Nothing. Once I have Becky, you can either have it back, or I'll destroy it. Whatever gets me a clean break."

Julie and Jericho exchanged a quick look. Roach noted the disappointment on their faces.

"That's your call," said Julie. "If you're happy to return it when all this is over, we'll leave you in peace."

Roach nodded and patted the roof of the car a couple of times as an unspoken farewell. He ducked inside, gunned the engine, and pulled out of the lot without looking back. Within minutes, he was back on the interstate, the needle pushing ninety.

"I'm coming, Becky," he said quietly. "And I swear to God, hell's coming with me."

22

Dawn was still an hour away. Slivers of pink decorated the dark horizon. The moon was obscured by low clouds that threatened another gloomy day.

Jay drove in silence. She allowed her mind to wander, having little to focus on around her. She cruised at a steady, anonymous speed along the quiet interstate, as she had done for the last six hours.

Beside her, Goddard was still unconscious.

As instructed, on her journey back from Des Moines to New York, she had detoured to his last known location following his call with Crow. It was late, and it was a small town. He had likely intended to stay for the night. Perhaps he had arranged transport for the morning. She would never know. With only three motels to choose from, it didn't take her long to find him. It took even less time to get him in the car.

He hadn't wanted to come, which was understandable,

given his position. He was smart. It wasn't part of his plan. But it was part of hers, which is why he was out cold beside her.

A low groan made her look over. Goddard stirred in his seat. His eyes rolled as they tried to open. The swelling around his cheekbone had settled into a yellowing contusion, and he winced as enough consciousness washed over him to make him aware of the pain.

He looked down to see his wrists and ankles bound together with plastic ties.

"Where are we?" he asked groggily.

Jay sighed.

"Don't start talking, or I'll put you to sleep again," she replied bluntly.

Goddard shuffled in his seat, half-turning to look at her. "You're not really a people person, are you?"

She shot him a cold stare but remained silent.

"Can you at least tell me where we're going?" he asked.

She sighed again. "Mr. Crow requests your presence in New York."

"Ah," he said, smiling. "He does, does he? Well, I hope it's to discuss our deal. Frankly, he could've just invited me to come. No need for such unpleasantness."

"Mr. Crow has run out of patience. When we get there, you'll tell him exactly what Roach has done with the flash drive and who gave it to him."

"Of course. In exchange for my pre-agreed fee, naturally."

She looked across at him. "In exchange for keeping a hold of your breathing privileges."

"Oh." He glanced out the window. "What is it with people nowadays not appreciating the fine art of negotiation? It's always straight down to the threats. This used to be a gentlemen's game."

Jay didn't respond.

"People seem to forget that information is currency in today's world," continued Goddard. "Social media. The news. Even politics. It's all centered around the value of information and the skill comes from knowing when to cash in."

"Mr. Crow doesn't need to play your game," she countered. "He doesn't need to spend any money. He can simply make you tell him what he needs to know, and he'll kill you if you don't. How's that for skill?"

"Honestly... you people. Savages. It's like watching someone try to perform surgery with a sledgehammer. No finesse, no technique, just brute force and to hell with the mess you leave behind. Am I right?"

"You can stop talking now."

"The information I have is valuable. You can't blame me for trying to negotiate a fair price for it."

Jay shook her head. "Information is only worth what someone is prepared to pay for it. Whatever nugget you're betting your life on is worth jack right now."

"What makes you think the identity of your hacker is the only nugget I have?"

She shrugged. "That's all you were selling. Mr. Crow is unlikely to care about whatever else you think is important."

Goddard smiled. "Is that so? I wonder what Brandon Crow would think if he learned who *you* really are?"

She glared at him, scowling with both concern and confusion. "What the hell are you talking about? I've served him loyally for years."

"Yes, you have. But you and I both know the skeletons in

your closet, don't we, my dear? What you've done... where you came from... who you used to—"

Jay snapped her arm to the side, grabbing his throat with an iron grip. Her nails pressed into the thin flesh, drawing pinpricks of blood.

"Who I am and who I worked for before he found me is none of his concern," she said firmly. "Nor is it any of yours. I don't know what you *think* you know or who you think I am, and I honestly don't care. Utter a word of it and I'll rip your tongue out."

Goddard nodded quickly, desperate for her to relinquish her grip. After a moment, she did. He gasped for air as she refocused on the straight road ahead.

Once he had regained his composure, he looked over at Jay again. He noted her profile—defined and strong. In another life, she would be considered beautiful. But her perpetually harsh expression and the mild scarring on her brow made it hard to see past the exterior she clearly relished being on show. She was notoriously formidable as Crow's right-hand woman. It had taken Goddard a while to piece together all there was to know about the Butterfly, right down to the origin of the eponymous tattoo.

He took a tired breath and stared ahead, calculating all the odds of his current predicament.

Perhaps that information would be more valuable at a later date. For now, he knew he must focus on finding a new sales pitch for the details of where Roach's flash drive came from. He was under no illusions that Brandon Crow intended asking nicely.

When Rebecca awoke, she found herself in a windowless holding cell. There were no bars. The floor and ceiling were tiled. The three walls were smooth brick. In front of her was a pane of thick glass, split to function like a sliding door. A strip running down the right side was frosted, where the unappealing steel toilet stood, offering a modicum of privacy. The bed was against the opposite wall, with no such luxury. It was bolted to the floor.

She had been wearing the same clothes for two days. She had been given water and basic meals, but she hadn't showered, which made her feel uncomfortable. She had been escorted to the cell shortly after her conversion with Brandon Crow yesterday. She hadn't moved since.

Rebecca spent most of the time crying. She was more afraid than she could ever remember being in her life. She was cold and alone, and with each second that ticked by, she became more convinced she was going to die.

But on occasion, her innate sense of logic prevailed, granting her a brief reprieve from her situation by focusing her mind on why this was happening to her.

You can take the girl out of the newsroom...

She worked on the assumption she was at a location owned by Tristar Security. She had no idea where, but she took Crow for someone important, which meant it was likely she was at their head office.

She knew almost nothing about them. However, she was certain they didn't have the authority or jurisdiction to keep her locked up against her will. That meant whatever they were up to wasn't legal. It wouldn't be the first time that a seemingly legitimate company did things it shouldn't behind closed doors, but this was different. The way she had been taken, out in the open like that, was borderline reckless.

Rebecca paced around her cell, biting her nails and muttering to herself as she pieced together the story in her head as best she could. Usually, the same ritual was carried out wearing pajamas and drinking a glass of red wine.

"Tristar aren't stupid," she whispered to herself. "Which means they must be protected or exempt from prosecution in some way. No other explanation for being so brazen. What did that guy say to me on the phone? That he had evidence they were up to no good? Did he mean this flash drive Will has? Who was he? How did he know about it? And how did Will get the flash drive? What's on it? How is Will going to find me? What can he do, even if he did?"

She held her head and growled to the ceiling.

"What's the matter?" said a voice from outside. "Time of the month?"

Rebecca spun around, startled. Davies stood outside her cell, staring at her. She noted the sleazy grin and the narrowed eyes that flicked up and down. She didn't need to be a mind reader to know what he was thinking.

She shuddered as gooseflesh ran up her arms but fought to compose herself.

She threw him a look of disgust. "If it were Shark Week, trust me, I wouldn't be this nice to you. Now go screw yourself, asshole."

Davies laughed. "Y'know, I was thinking. You might be here a while. That brother of yours is just as dumb as he looks. Maybe you and I should get to know each other a little better. How about I come back later and keep you company?"

Rebecca flipped him the finger. "How about you go and play with something poisonous, you cretin."

His expression darkened. He slammed his hand on the

glass, making her jump. "Watch your mouth, you little bitch, or I'll watch it for you."

She retreated back to her bed, sitting and leaning back against the wall. She brought her knees to her chest and hugged them for comfort.

Davies's sickening smile returned. "Yeah, that's what I thought. I'll be seeing you, sweetheart."

He walked away, out of view.

Rebecca let out a deep sigh, not realizing she had been holding her breath. She clutched her knees tighter and buried her face between them.

Time passed immeasurably. She stared at the bedding between her feet, transfixed on the subtle pattern until it began dancing in front of her eyes. Then a commotion from outside her cell dragged her back to reality. She looked up as the woman with the butterfly tattoo walked into view, followed a moment later by Davies and another Tristar employee. They were escorting a third man. She watched intently as they threw their latest prisoner into an identical cell opposite hers, directly across the corridor. He seemed shaken, distant. She noticed bruising on his face.

Her gaze drifted. The woman was staring at her with dark, sunken, emotionless eyes. Rebecca yelped with surprise, then immediately clasped her hands over her mouth, as if trying to force the sound back inside her.

The woman held her gaze for what felt like an eternity. Then she looked back at the new prisoner as she walked away, disappearing from view a moment later. The other man followed. Davies was the last to move, smiling menacingly at her as he did.

A door closed somewhere out of sight, a short distance away. Silence fell like an overnight blanket of snow at winter. Cold and all-encompassing.

Rebecca looked over at the new arrival. He smiled and waved from his bed. She frowned, confused by such a normal reaction, given their mutual predicament. She waved back half-heartedly.

"Are these things soundproof?" he asked.

She raised an eyebrow. "Yes."

He went to speak but caught himself. He smiled and pointed. "Ah, very good... that's funny. I can see the resemblance."

She shook her head. "What do you mean?"

He smiled back. "I mean, you're just like your brother. He doesn't have a sense of humor either."

Rebecca tilted her head, lost in a sudden thought.

That voice.

"You're the one who called me, aren't you?" she asked. "About Tristar. You know my brother."

He nodded. "I am. Nice to finally meet you, Rebecca. And yes, I have the... pleasure of your brother's acquaintance."

"Why did you call me? What do you know?"

He stood and moved toward the glass doors of his own cell. "I know that good information isn't cheap."

Rebecca rolled her eyes. "Whatever. Who are you?"

"Zach Goddard. I was your brother's cellmate back in the day. He and I have some unfinished business."

"Where's Will? Is he..."

She trailed off, not wanting to ask a question she was unprepared to have answered.

Goddard laughed. "Oh, he's alive. Don't worry, Rebecca. I mean, they wouldn't have brought me here if he wasn't."

"Please tell me what's going on. Why this is happening to me. To Will. If you know anything..."

"Oh, honeybunch, I know everything. I know what

Brandon Crow knows. I know what your brother knows. I also know what neither of them know."

Her face contorted with disbelief. "What? Just... stop talking in backward riddles and tell me straight. What the hell is going on?"

Goddard laughed and returned to his bed. He made himself comfortable, fluffing the pillow behind him and wrapping the thin bedding around him.

"May as well make yourself at home, dear," he said, smiling. "We might be here a while. I guess I can tell you a few stories to pass the time."

23

Roach pulled over outside the hotel. He killed the Challenger's engine and sat for a moment in the alien silence. The car was a dream to drive, but after hearing the primal roar from beneath the hood for the best part of a day, to experience quiet again was an overdue blessing.

He drummed his fingers idly on the wheel; the leather was still damp with palm sweat. He had spent the entire journey trying to decide whether or not he could trust GlobaTech. He had arrived at the conclusion that he probably couldn't. Not completely. But he had to admit they were upfront with him from the start, and so far, they seemed like they genuinely want to help him. Like Julie had said, they operated under intense public scrutiny. Maybe they thought he could do what they couldn't.

The idea of that frustrated him. Roach had turned his back on his old life, on everything that he had done, only to wind up doing the same damn thing for somebody else. He took out the room key Jericho had given him, examining it. He twirled it around with his fingers.

Was he on the side of the angels now? Or had he just found himself another demon to work for?

Roach took a deep breath and exhaled heavily.

"Screw it," he said as he climbed out of the car.

A quick, habitual glance up and down the busy street satisfied his immediate concerns of being followed. As was the case on most streets in New York City, traffic was perpetually crawling. It made it easier for him to spot a tail.

He headed toward the steps leading up to the hotel entrance, weaving his way through the stream of pedestrians that flowed against him.

The building stood tall and proud, dominating half a block in the West Village. Roach leaned back, craning his neck to stare skyward. It was high enough that it looked as if it were falling.

He was greeted by a warm gust of air when he stepped inside. Pillars of marble lined the spacious reception area. Porters and maids dashed around in smart uniforms. Everything around him seemed accentuated by gold.

Roach stopped for a moment, composing himself against the unavoidable feeling of discomfort. He was a simple man. He had grown up with little more than what he worked for. He was unaccustomed to luxury and felt out of place around it.

He glanced at the keycard. Room 615.

Sixth floor, I guess, he thought.

Minutes later, he was standing outside the door to room 615. He slid the keycard into the slot, then removed it gently, triggering the lock. He gripped the handle.

The idea he might be walking into a trap had occurred to him more than once. He was unarmed and exhausted. Hardly prepared for another fight. But he knew he had little choice. This was the only way he stood a chance of getting his sister back safely.

Roach pushed the door open and burst into the room.

It was luxuriously basic. A high-quality version of a standard hotel room.

It was also empty, save for a black sports bag resting on the bed. It looked about as out of place as anything could be.

Letting the door swing shut behind him, Roach walked over to the bed and sat beside the bag. He placed a hand on it but quickly became distracted by how soft and comfortable the bed felt. A couple of minutes later, he lay flat on his back, feet still on the floor, sleeping like the dead.

The world was black beyond darkness. Total emptiness surrounded him. Two parallel lines of low flame stretched out before him. They were the only indication there was any direction to follow.

The wind billowed around him, carrying with it the haunting cries of a thousand tortured souls.

Ahead of him, in the far distance, was a lone pinprick of white light. It was as if someone had pierced the veil of purgatory that covered his world. Behind him, he saw nothing but a void staring back.

He walked toward the light, ignoring the cold and the screams that surrounded him. He focused on nothing except the lines of fire that guided him.

He no longer felt trapped. No longer felt restricted. There were no walls anymore. No prison. No judgment. He felt freedom for the first time since his condemnation. The only thing that still plagued him, that still tainted his newfound liberation, was seeing how far away he was from the end. No matter how hard he battled, how far he traveled, that light always appeared unattainable. It was as if someone stayed ahead of him, keeping pace, pushing it forever out of reach.

As he walked, he began to see shapes appear beside him, beyond the confines of the flaming trail. Almost like shadows within shadows. Like whispers of smoke, gradually forming something identifiable. He mostly ignored it. Occasionally, he glanced to his side, tracking the progress of his companion.

Eventually, he saw the gaunt frame of the young boy who frequently plagued his nightmares. In the flickering light of the fire, he could see dirt on his face. In his hand, the boy cradled a cockroach. He stroked its hardened exterior with the tip of his finger, as if nurturing a beloved pet.

He took a deep breath, feeling strong and proud. He had always fought to escape, to ultimately follow the boy toward the next stage of his journey. But this time, he took the lead. He determined the journey and the destination. The boy followed, quiet and obedient.

The path he was on was exactly where he should be heading, though what waited for him at the end remained a mystery.

Ahead of him, the light went out.

Momentarily fazed, his footsteps slowed but never stopped. Beside him, the boy did the same.

He squinted into the nothingness that now lay before him. As his eyes adjusted, he began to see another shape in the darkness, flanked by the occasional flickers of light.

That was when he realized the light hadn't gone out. Someone, or something, was in front of it, obscuring his vision of his journey's end. The back-and-forth movement that revealed slivers of distant luminance suggested that whatever lay before him was running toward him. Whatever final obstacle he had to overcome was rushing to meet him and would be there soon.

The wind died, muting the hollering of lost souls. The flickering flames that defined his path settled.

He clenched his fists, focused his gaze on the approaching unknown, and quickened his pace. He hadn't come this far or fought this hard to be stopped now. Not when he was so close to his journey being over.

Beside him, the boy's image dissipated like dust in the wind.

Whatever was coming for him was in for the fight of its life.

Roach gasped as his eyes snapped open. He bolted upright on the bed, silently cursing himself for falling asleep.

He checked his watch, sighing heavily when he saw almost four hours had elapsed.

He stood and unzipped the bag next to him, pulling the sides apart to see inside.

"Holy crap..." he muttered.

His eyes remained wide with disbelief as he began emptying the contents onto the bed.

Two handguns, an assault rifle, and a shotgun, along with all the ammunition he would ever need.

All GlobaTech issue. Top of the line.

A bunch of grenades. Smoke, flashbangs, fragmentation, white phosphorous... something for every occasion.

A knife. Streamlined and deadly. Much better than the one he lost in Topeka.

A bulletproof vest. Tactical holsters and clothing.

And a laptop.

Roach frowned, not expecting to see a computer among everything else.

He booted it up as he moved over to the desk, affixed to the wall opposite the bed. A simple chair stood in front of it.

He sat down and stared at the home screen for a long moment. No programs or apps were installed, other than a web browser.

He opened it up and searched for a map of New York. He zoomed in on East 23rd and 3rd.

Tristar Security's main office building.

Jericho had told him that's where his sister was being held. He was familiar with the building. It had been years since he was there last, but he doubted much had changed. The main entrance on street level looked normal. The first few floors were mainly offices used for genuine clients and briefings.

The further up one went, the worse it became.

The upper echelons of the company who occupied those floors were the subject of constant gossip and hearsay among the contractors who worked for Tristar. The suits in charge were treated like they were bogey-men. Roach knew that Tristar's security personnel were split evenly into two groups—legitimate contractors looking to do an honest day's work and cut-throat merce-naries who leapt on every opportunity to do whatever Tristar wanted, legal or otherwise, so long as the money was good.

Roach had personally suspected the latter group was privy to more than the former. He had taken the job to do legitimate work. It was something he enjoyed. His work got noticed, and he was assigned to a unit that did more ques-tionable things. Orders were light on description. Clients were anonymous.

He didn't last long.

And now he was faced with the unenviable task of breaking into a facility that was crawling with mercenaries who wouldn't hesitate to kill him and his sister. He had no idea where Rebecca actually was, and he knew he wouldn't have the freedom to explore.

Roach got to his feet and began pacing the room, hands clasped behind him, lost in thought.

The only thing that made sense to him was to try and get to Brandon Crow, then negotiate with him the way Goddard intended to do. It would mean selling GlobaTech down the river, but he didn't owe *them* anything. Sure, they gave him the goodie bag, but they were also the reason he was in this mess in the first place. The reason his sister was in danger.

Assuming she was even still alive...

Roach shook the thought from his head.

His pacing slowed to an idle wander around the room. He put his hands in his pockets and shifted his gaze from the ceiling to the floor. He felt his shoulders slump.

He had nothing. No idea how he could possibly—

He took his hand from his pocket and looked at the flash drive he was holding.

That's it!

Roach stormed over to the laptop and slotted it into a USB port on the side. He navigated to the file directory.

What had Julie said? Tristar could track the location of the drive by monitoring who accessed it. He needed to look through everything again anyway, to see if there was something crucial he might have missed. If Julie were right, doing so would lead Tristar right to him.

That might be just the opportunity he needed.

24

The bitter chill from the bricks penetrated the thin pillow at Rebecca's back. She sat huddled beneath the equally ineffective blanket, staring blankly ahead as Goddard finished recounting the story of how he and her brother had met.

"And I hadn't seen him since," concluded Goddard. "Until a few days ago, anyway. Sorry to be the bearer of bad news there, darlin'."

She looked up at him, confused. "How do you mean?"

He shrugged. "Well, finding out your brother turned his back on his friends, ratted them out to the feds, then went working for such a morally ambiguous company like Tristar... can't be easy to hear."

Rebecca got to her feet and padded over to the glass door, wrapped in her blanket. She leaned close, as if it would in some way reduce the distance between their respective cells. "Did you even listen to your own story? God, you're an asshole."

Goddard leapt to his feet defensively. "Hey, what did I do? I'm just telling it like it is."

"Exactly. If everything happened how you say it did,

then it certainly doesn't make my brother look bad. He told me about going to prison. I believe him when he says what happened. When it comes to the FBI, he chose his family over a criminal. Something he had every right not to do, given we had basically abandoned him. He did something honorable in an otherwise dishonorable situation. No one can tell me he's a bad person."

Goddard scoffed. "You're just biased."

She rolled her eyes and gave an exasperated gesture with her hands. "What the hell do you expect? You tried to make someone look bad to their *family!* Even if you were right, I'm not going to agree with you, am I?"

"You're only here because of him. You're just too blind to see it."

"And why are *you* here, exactly?" she asked, folding her arms across her chest defiantly.

Before he could answer, a door opened farther along the corridor, just out of their sight line. Multiple footsteps sounded out. A moment later, Jay appeared, followed by four security personnel, including Davies.

She stopped just before the cells and looked at each of them in turn.

"Let's go," she said.

"W-where?" asked Rebecca.

"Wherever I tell you," replied Jay.

The men split into two teams. Each pair moved to a cell and opened it. Goddard and Rebecca were ushered out and immediately flanked. Davies stood on Rebecca's left, leering at her.

"Hey, beautiful," he said. "Given any thought to my offer?"

She turned and stared at him with revulsion. "Yes, and

when I stop throwing up in my mouth, I'll give you my answer."

His expression changed in an instant. She saw the flash of anger in his eyes. "You better remember who you're talking to, you little—"

He was cut off abruptly as he walked into Jay, whom he hadn't noticed had moved in front of him and stopped. He looked at her with a mixture of surprise and concern.

"Mr. Crow wants to see her," she said to him. "She's valuable to us, at least until we've dealt with her asshole brother. I see you looking at her that way again, or hear your perverse bantering, I'll rip your balls off and make you choke on them. Are we clear?"

He nodded, his cheeks flushing with anger and embarrassment.

Jay looked at Rebecca, who had lost all color in her face.

"T-thank you," said Rebecca.

Jay shook her head. "Don't thank me. Just pray you remain valuable to us. The minute you're not, I'll kill you myself."

The group set off walking again.

Goddard tried to make eye contact with Rebecca, but there were too many bodies in the way.

He liked her. She was his type of person. No bullshit. Not afraid to say what she thought. He wasn't kidding when he said he saw the family resemblance.

It was a shame she likely wouldn't make it out of this.

The four men frog-marched Goddard and Rebecca out of the elevator, following Jay into the corridor. The floor wasn't as busy as the lower levels; it consisted mostly of large boardrooms, which were currently unoccupied.

They walked through a set of double doors into a small vestibule. A couple of chairs stood against the wall to the right, like a waiting room. To the left was an L-shaped desk. Brandon Crow's secretary sat behind it, looking flustered and uneasy.

Jay ignored her and knocked once on the inner door. She waited a polite few seconds, then opened it and stepped into Crow's office. He was sitting behind his desk, reading a report on his laptop. He looked up at the new arrivals.

"Ah, perfect timing," he said, flashing his best politician's smile.

He gestured to the chairs across from him. Rebecca and Goddard were thrust unceremoniously into them. Both squinted and glanced away from the influx of light now blinding them from outside, courtesy of the large window dominating the room.

The four men spread out across the office. Davies stood by the door. The other three formed a loose semicircle in the opposite corner.

Jay moved to Crow's side and clasped her hands casually behind her back.

"So glad you could join me," said Crow. He looked first at Rebecca, then rested his gaze on Goddard. His charming demeanor quickly changed. "Who gave Roachford the drive?"

Goddard shifted uncomfortably in his chair. A thin film of sweat glistened on his forehead.

"What about our deal?" he asked, trying to keep the concern and growing fear from his voice.

Crow shrugged. "It wasn't working for me. So, I'm thinking we should make a new deal. See, our mutual acquaintance knows you set him up in Des Moines. He wasn't happy about it."

Goddard looked shamefully at Rebecca. He instantly felt her glare burning a hole into the side of his head.

"You did *what?*" she asked.

"I lured him into a trap, so these guys could get their drive back. Sent him to a bar with fifty-plus mercenaries all looking to collect a bounty on him. I'm sorry. I... I like you. You don't deserve to be caught up in all this. But the truth is your brother is likely dead." He turned to Crow. "And your flash drive should be on its way here by now, surely? I'm still of use to you. I still have—"

Crow held his hand up.

"Let me stop you right there, Mr. Goddard," he said, firmly. "First of all, that incessant prick isn't dead. He managed to escape from that bar, which means he still has the drive and is still going to come for her." He pointed at Rebecca. "But I would also wager he'll jump at the chance to get his hands on you, so here's my new deal. You tell me how he got that drive, and we'll protect you from him."

"My brother's still alive?" asked Rebecca. Conflicting emotions pulled her in every direction. Relief, anger, sadness, frustration... fear.

"He is," confirmed Crow. "And if I were a betting man, I imagine he knows where *you* are by now, which means it won't be long before he gets in touch to negotiate."

"What assurances do I have that you won't just kill me?" said Goddard.

"None," replied Crow, shrugging. "But the prospect of squaring things with you is going to be a useful tool when dealing with Roachford, so for now, you're useful to me. But if you don't tell me who hacked our systems, that will change."

The tension in the room was palpable. Behind them, the security personnel restlessly shifted their weight back and forth. They exchanged uncertain glances, expecting an order to kill at any moment.

Rebecca didn't know what to think or do. She had never felt so out of her depth before. She barely understood what was happening. She was relieved her brother was alive. However, she remained unsure about whether she would see him again.

Goddard wiped the perspiration from his brow as he struggled to keep his heart rate under control. The situation was getting away from him. Panic was trying to set in. He stared at Crow, who calmly stared back. Crow sat comfortably in his chair, relaxed, exuding the confidence that came with the unwavering knowledge he was in complete control.

Eventually, Goddard exhaled heavily with resignation. He momentarily closed his eyes.

"Fine," said Goddard. "It was—"

The door to the office burst open, almost hitting Davies.

An analyst stumbled in, out of breath and disheveled. "Sir, I'm... I'm sorry, but... you wanted to know if..."

Crow glared at him. "What?"

The analyst swallowed hard, taking deep breaths. "Sir, the flash drive. Someone's just accessed the drive again. The confidential files. The reports on—"

"Is it him?"

"No way of knowing for sure, but as far as we can ascertain, he hasn't given it to anyone."

"Where is he?"

"That's the thing, sir. He's... he's here. In New York."

Crow leapt to his feet. "What? Where?"

"In a hotel roughly twelve blocks northeast of here. Room 615."

Crow turned to Jay, who had already straightened to attention. "Go get him."

Without a word, Jay strode purposefully out of the office, almost knocking the analyst off his feet on her way past.

Crow stood with his back to the room, staring gravely out at the sprawling city below him. He had been right. Roachford clearly *did* know where his sister was. He had to admit, it was a bold move coming to New York.

He knew he needed to be ready for anything. He cursed himself for perhaps underestimating the man. He thought back to what Jay saw in Des Moines. She wasn't afraid, but she had described what happened almost with admiration. She respected the man's abilities, and he respected her opinion, which meant he had to prepare for every eventuality from this point on. There was too much at stake for this to be allowed to go on much longer.

It wasn't just Tristar's reputation, either. It was his own neck on the line.

He had to be ready.

Crow turned and looked at Rebecca. Her eyes had the wide, glazed look of perpetual fear. She simply accepted everything going on around her because the logical part of her brain was still denying any of it was real. He had seen the look a thousand times before, on the faces of all the other people killed on his orders.

Crow smiled at her. "This will all be over soon, my dear. I promise."

25

_____

Jay rode the elevator to the sixth floor of the hotel, enjoying the silence. It helped her control the noise within her own mind. Helped her focus. In this state of violent meditation, she had always been able to channel the rage that flowed through her. She used her body as a conduit, allowing her to unleash that rage as a controlled weapon.

She had done that for as long as she could remember.

With a soft ping, the doors glided open. Jay stepped out into the corridor and drew the gun from her back. She screwed the suppressor in place as she walked, unhurried and calm, toward room 615.

She turned a corner, following the wall signs to her destination. There was a maid's cart ahead, standing beside an open door. She slowed her pace as she neared it. She hid the gun behind her and peered inside. She saw a pair of legs and hips bent over a bed, tucking a fresh, white sheet in place.

A glance up and down the corridor confirmed she was alone.

She walked into the room. Her footsteps were light and

silent. The maid straightened and turned when Jay was less than three feet from her. She wasn't a young woman. The lines on her face suggested early fifties. Little time had been spent on stopping her olive skin and dark hair from betraying her years.

The maid's dark eyes grew wide. Jay thrust her hand forward, clamped it over the maid's mouth, then gracefully moved around her. She pressed her body close the maid's back, then produced the silenced gun and pressed it to her temple.

"If you make a noise, this room will need more than fresh bedding. Am I clear?" Jay's voice was nothing more than a gentle whisper, which made what she said even more unsettling.

The maid nodded urgently, humming a muted *mm-hmm* into Jay's palm.

Jay slowly released her grip, allowing the maid to step away. She shuffled back, terrified, and stumbled into the bed. She fell onto it heavily, the springs audibly popping under the impact.

With the gun aimed steadily at the maid's face, Jay asked, "Do you have a keycard that opens every room?"

The maid nodded again.

Jay circled the barrel of her gun impatiently. "Can I have it?"

With a trembling hand, the maid unclipped it from her waistband and held it out to her. Jay took it.

"See? That wasn't so hard, was it?" said Jay, smiling.

Then she pulled the trigger. The bullet fired with a muted *pffft*, effortlessly drilling a small, neat hole into the maid's forehead. The pillows and headboard behind her were instantly covered by the spray of thick blood.

Jay left the room, pushing the cart inside before shutting

the door. She continued along the hall, passing four more doors on her right before stopping outside room 615.

With a deep, steady breath, she used the newly acquired keycard to unlock the door. She held her gun close to her chest and wrapped her hand gently around the handle. She pushed the door open, an inch at a time, careful not to irritate any hinges in need of oil.

The room was dark and quiet. As Jay moved inside, she saw the curtains were closed, blocking out the daylight almost completely. The door to the bathroom stood open on her right. A small closet with a single sliding door was built into the wall on her left. The room ahead opened out and expanded out of sight to the right. With the light of the corridor outside still shining in over her shoulder, she could see the faint outline of a bed, a desk, and a wall-mounted TV.

As she drew level with the bathroom, she snapped her body to the right, taking steady aim inside, checking the corners and behind the door for signs of life.

Nothing.

Jay continued on into the room. The outer wall of the bathroom formed the corner where the room expanded away. She pressed herself against it, her gun held low, ready. She neared the edge and saw a bag standing open on the bed.

She stepped out, her body tense, her aim steady.

Nothing.

Just the bed, a side table with a lamp on it, and a painting hung on the wall. She looked around and realized the room wasn't as big as she had thought. She relaxed and lowered her gun.

A moment later, she tensed again as the barrel of a gun rested against the back of her head.

"Drop it," said a voice.

She tossed her gun to the floor. A light flicked on in the room. She was shoved forward, toward the bed. She turned to see Roach aiming a gun at her, having clearly just emerged from inside the closet.

Jay stared at him impassively.

"How many of you are there?" he asked her.

"Just me," she replied.

"Bullshit."

She shrugged. "I'm usually all they need for a standard retrieval."

"If I were anybody else, I'd be insulted."

"If you were anybody else, you'd be dead already." She looked him up and down. "What are you wearing?"

He had donned the full tactical outfit GlobaTech had included in their care package, complete with bulletproof vest, ammo belts, and weapon holsters.

He smiled. "Oh, this? Just a little gift from some friends."

Her expression faltered. Her eyes narrowed and her brow creased as the cogs inside her head turned.

Roach recognized doubt when he saw it.

"It was them," said Jay. "GlobaTech hacked Tristar?"

"They did," he said. "I'll admit, I kinda wish they hadn't. I much preferred it when everyone just left me alone. But... here we are."

"What are you going to do?"

"I'm going to get my sister back, then disappear."

"Just like that, huh?"

He nodded. "Just like that."

Jay smiled. Just a subtle curl of her lips to show bemusement. She edged forward a couple of inches.

"You know why I'm here, right?" she asked.

Roach shrugged. "Probably to take me back to Tristar

HQ, drag me in front of Brandon Crow, and threaten me until I give you the flash drive. At which point, you'll shoot me and my sister in the head."

Her smile broadened. "What makes you think she's not dead already?"

"If she were, they wouldn't have sent you."

She moved another inch closer. "You think?"

"That flash drive has you running scared, even moreso because it's in the hands of someone who has a grudge against you. Rebecca's the only leverage you have on me. This right here... it's part of the game, right? If you were simply wiping the board clean, Crow would've sent a sledge-hammer, not a scalpel."

"And here's me thinking you were just a dumb grunt."

"Sorry to disappoint."

She moved closer. Slowly. Roach noticed and stepped to meet her, placing the barrel of his gun on her forehead.

"I haven't forgotten you took my sister and left me half-dead in an alley. I owe you."

Jay held her hands out to the side, grinning wider. Her eyes sparked with life. "I'm right here, William. Give me your best shot."

He said nothing. He didn't move. His finger rested gently on the trigger.

"Come on," she insisted. "I saw you in Des Moines, you know. In that bar. I was there. Saw the whole goddamn thing."

Roach tilted his head slightly. "Then you know it's unwise to test me."

"I've not seen fighting like that in a long time. It was—"

"Necessary."

"Beautiful."

The comment caught Roach by surprise. His arm

relaxed in the confusion. The barrel slipped no more than a millimeter.

It was all Jay needed.

She lashed her hand out, knocking the gun from his grip. She immediately followed it up with another strike, an open palm to Roach's jaw.

He staggered back, colliding with the side of the closet. He regained his focus in time to deflect a third blow to his face. Jay's punch hit his shoulder as he side-stepped left. He threw a punch of his own, which connected heavily with the side of her head. The impact made his knuckles throb. She stumbled back. He stepped away and went to reclaim his weapon.

With a guttural shriek, like a war cry, Jay leaped toward him. Roach saw the attack and braced himself, catching her by her throat as she wrapped her legs around his waist. She twisted and thrashed in his grip, delivering short blows to his head and body.

He winced at a painful breath. Her thighs tightened around him with inhuman strength. He tried to hold her torso at arm's length, all the while squeezing her throat in an attempt to weaken her. Her attacks, while lacking in power, were becoming increasingly difficult to weather.

Roach rushed forward, releasing his hold of her as he slammed her into the wall. She grunted as the wind was punched from her lungs, but it did nothing to weaken the hold her legs had on his midsection.

He stepped back and rushed forward again, slamming her a second time into the wall. Again, he remained locked between her thighs. As the impact shook her, Jay smiled, allowing the air to escape her lungs in a moan.

Their faces were close. Their lips closer. Their eyes locked.

She saw the unbridled fury in his. He stared back into the sick pleasure in hers.

"Is that all you got?" she asked. Her voice was low and seductive.

Before he could respond, Jay snapped her head forward, butting the side of his nose. The blow dazed him, and he felt himself falling backward. Instinctively, he grabbed both her thighs and spun around. She landed hard on the bed. He landed on top of her, still trapped. He did his best to straighten, but his movements were restricted.

Jay sat up and grabbed the back of his head. She pulled his body down on top of her, allowing her to restrengthen the clinch she had him in.

Roach snarled through gritted teeth as more air was forced from his lungs. Deep breaths were becoming constricted. He began to jab at her thighs with both hands, delivering short hooks to both sides, trying to weaken the muscles.

She pulled him into her body, closing the distance between them, which made it harder for him to throw effective punches.

He lifted his head and stared into her eyes. They were wild, alive with an inexplicable mix of adrenaline and pleasure.

Jay laughed. She arched her back, then her neck, as if writhing in ecstasy. Doing so allowed for better positioning with her legs. She felt the pressure ease on her quads as her legs shifted up to just below his ribcage, resulting in more damage and less work.

Roach was beginning to feel lightheaded. Breathing was becoming worryingly difficult to do. He glanced to his right and saw the vase-like bedside lamp, just out of reach. He planted his feet and steadied his legs. He felt pain in his lower back as he stood, bent over the bed, his body forced to a ninety-degree angle by the grip Jay maintained on his head.

He grabbed her hips tightly, wrestling for leverage.

Jay screamed again, the pleasure of the fight overwhelming her.

"That's it!" she yelled. "I want your best. I want the man I saw in the bar. Fight me, you bastard!"

Roach roared through the exertion as he lifted her up and whipped around into the wall behind him for a third time. Finally, her thighs relented. He fell against her, forcing his body weight into her as much as he could while battling his own exhaustion.

Their lips were millimeters apart. Both were breathing heavily. Her eyes still sparked with life.

"Can you feel that?" Jay whispered. "That rush. That energy. The thrill of the fight. You only ever truly know someone by connecting with them physically. By fighting them."

"You're... you're insane," replied Roach.

"And you're in denial. The way you fight—you love the conflict. The brutality. The sheer... honesty of it all." She searched his eyes. "Tell me I'm wrong. Tell me you weren't born for this. Tell me you don't *crave* this."

He held her gaze. Both of them were locked in a moment of intense and pure violence. Her persistent smile was unnerving, but her words struck a chord he never knew he wanted played. He had no doubt he was in a fight for his life. She was formidable. Not the strongest opponent he had ever faced but one of the most skilled. Certainly, one of the most outright violent. Her apparent thirst for the fight made her all the more dangerous.

But he couldn't deny he felt it too. The rush of adrenaline. The satisfaction from each shot he landed filled a hole inside him that would otherwise remain empty. The conflict within him fueled his rage. The desire for peace only ever truly felt satiated by the violence needed to achieve it.

Despite everything, in that frozen moment, he stared into the eyes of one of the few people who ever truly understood him. And that scared him.

Feeling the heavy beat of life in each other's chests, their lips met. Gentle at first, then harder. The intensity grew. Their hands still urgently sought each other, but the efforts to hurt subsided in a twisted moment of inexplicable passion.

Jay moved her head away and sank her teeth into his bottom lip, drawing blood. Roach snapped back into the moment. The reason for being there outweighed his own fractured turmoil.

He flung her around, breaking completely free of her grip as he pushed her away onto the bed. Her momentum allowed her to bounce straight back to her feet, but when she did, he reached for the bedside lamp and smashed it against the side of her head.

The sound of it breaking filled the room. She dropped to the floor like a stone in water.

He rested back against the wall, sucking in deep, desperate breaths.

"You... crazy... bitch," he managed.

She pushed herself up on all fours, spitting blood onto the carpet. She crawled over to the desk and used it to pull herself up.

"We're... we're the same," she said. "If we fought together, we would be... we'd be unbeatable."

"What is this? Is Crow trying to recruit me now?"

"No. I am."

She dashed forward, stepping up onto the bed and launching herself off it toward him.

"Oh, shit!" he hissed, moving to catch her again.

This time, she landed higher. Her legs wrapped around his head. He held her lower back and buttocks, trying to find his footing, but he never got chance. She fell back onto the bed, clutching at the back of his head again. Her thighs crushed the sides of his head. She brought her left ankle up and hooked the crook of her right knee over it, locking in a tight triangle choke. Using her hands to help keep his head in place, she twisted her lower body, forcing him to roll over onto his side.

He couldn't breathe. He felt his cheeks flushing with blood. His mouth was pinned against her groin. No way to move. No way to breathe. His only saving grace was that his arms were free. Had one of them been trapped inside the grip, he would have been dead already.

Jay arched her back again. Her breaths came in loud moans, releasing frustration, anger, and pleasure in equal amounts. She began raining down blows to his head. Elbows, mostly. One after the other. An unrelenting assault that gained both speed and intensity with each shot, accompanied by the animalistic screams of exertion.

Roach fumbled blindly with flailing arms as he felt his brow split open from a well-placed elbow. An immediate waterfall of warmth gushed free.

He was running out of time.

He couldn't reach her face or throat. He began to throw desperate, hooked punches to her sides, driving his fist into her body in an effort to stop her. He felt her begin to slow with each punch he threw. He lost count of how many he had hit her with, but his own energy was almost completely drained.

He connected with what he was certain would be his final attack. His knuckles pushed hard against her skin, burying into her side, striking the liver. His arms dropped. His body relaxed. Her shots kept coming.

Until they didn't.

A lifetime of moments after feeling him go limp, Jay was hit by a wave of agony and nausea. She relinquished her hold on him and rolled off the bed. She dropped onto all fours and vomited on the carpet.

Roach slid to the floor on the opposite side of the bed, lying in the shattered remains of the bedside lamp, blood gushing down his face. His breaths were ragged, but he was conscious.

Jay crawled across the floor. Her previously discarded gun lay just ahead.

Roach stirred, trying to turn onto his side. The first step to standing. He was disoriented and blinded by pain. Each breath felt like a knife in his chest. Warm blood continued to flow down his face, obscuring his vision. Its coppery taste coated his lips. Using a hand, then a leg, then another hand, he slowly clawed his way back to a vertical base. He wiped a hand over his face before pressing it against the wall for balance, leaving a crimson palm print.

He looked over at Jay. Her arm was outstretched, inches away from her gun.

Roach stumbled toward her, diving to reach the weapon before she did. He landed heavily on her back, his weight stunning the air from her lungs. He reached up and grabbed her wrists with his hands, pinning her down as she twisted and wrestled beneath him. He fought against her, eventually pulling her arms apart, circling them both out to the sides. His head rested beside hers. His mouth rested close to her ear.

"I *will* kill you," he grunted. "This is... over. Do you hear me?"

Her breathing came in sporadic, primal growls. Her struggling lessened under his weight. Then, using every ounce of strength she had left, Jay bucked with her hips, thrusting her backside up into him, forcing him to roll off her. In a flash, she was on her feet. He was a split-second behind her. They both straightened and turned to face each other at the same time. The side of her head was soaked with blood, matting her hair flat. She still wore the maniacal, perverse smile on her face; her teeth shone against the dark red that covered half of her face.

Jay threw a wild right. Roach rocked away from it, blocking it with his arm before grabbing her. He spun her around and held her close to him, restricting her movements. She reached up and behind her, frantically scratching for purchase as his arm tightened around her neck.

He fought her hand away, but in doing so, allowed a little distance between their bloodied and bruised bodies. She spun around and placed both hands on the sides of his head, her thumbs pressing into his eyes. He screwed them tightly shut and jabbed her in the stomach. The moment she let go, he placed a hand on the side of her head and yelled out as he thrust her into the mounted TV screen.

The glass exploded from the impact. Shards shredded her face and neck. He slammed her with such force, he felt the moment her head connected with the wall behind the screen. He stepped away and let her body snake awkwardly to the floor. He watched as the spark in her eyes died out, consumed by a crimson mask.

Roach stared for almost a full minute to make sure she didn't move. Then he sat heavily on the bed and wiped a hand over his face to remove some of the blood from around his eyes.

"Man, that was weird," he said quietly.

He slowly got to his feet. He grabbed a towel from the bathroom and cleaned up his face as best he could. He picked up the bag and headed for the door. He glanced back at Jay, but she hadn't moved.

As he reached for the handle, there was a loud knock from outside, which startled him.

"Excuse me, sir?" said a firm voice. "Is everything okay? We've had some complaints of a disturbance and excessive... noises."

He yanked the door open and stared at the man and woman in front of him. He wore a suit. A slim build and a young face. She was dressed as a maid. Overweight. A little older.

The man was taken aback by Roach's sudden appearance in the doorway.

"Oh my God! Are you all right?" he asked.

"Never better," said Roach sharply.

He pushed past them and headed toward the elevators.

Behind him, the woman screamed. A moment later, as he was turning the corner, he heard the man say, "She's still alive. Call 911."

He sighed a frustrated breath.

There was no time to lose.

26

Roach stood in front of the steps that led to the entrance of Tristar's headquarters. Almost an hour had elapsed since he left the hotel. He had patched himself up as best he could in the car. Band-Aids covered the worst of the lacerations on his face. The handful of painkillers he took would take care of everything else, at least temporarily.

The sea of people hurriedly navigating the streets gave him a wide berth, as if avoiding a quarantine zone or an uncovered manhole.

He wasn't complaining. Nor was he surprised.

Just behind him, the Challenger was haphazardly parked, mounting the curb. He was standing next to it, looking fresh off a battlefield—scarred and bloody, dressed in combat gear, and holding an open black sports bag.

It was an intimidating sight.

Strapped to both thighs were pistols, secured in their holsters. Roach had opted to leave the assault rifle in the car. The shotgun rested inside the bag, along with the selection of grenades he didn't have room for on his tactical vest.

On any other street, people would have been fleeing in

all directions, screaming. But it wasn't uncommon to see armed and armored personnel moving in and out of this particular building, so no one paid him much heed.

That being said, what he was about to do was neither quiet nor discreet. He had been fortunate so far that no sirens had followed him from the hotel.

He suspected that was about to change.

With his gaze locked with laser focus on the doors ahead, Roach climbed the stairs. They leveled out into a walkway that wound itself around two sides of the building on a ninety-degree angle, bordered by plant boxes. A few people walked along, seemingly in no rush to be anywhere.

Roach ignored them and pushed open the doors. There was an audible suction noise, and he felt the resistance of a hermetic seal relenting. A cool breeze greeted him as he stepped inside, carrying with it the smell of a lavender-scented cleaning product.

The open space covered almost the full width of the building, with two main corridors leading away from it up ahead. The one to the right led out of sight, but a nearby sign indicated a fire exit and storeroom lay ahead. The left led to a wide staircase with glass sides that climbed to the next floor, where a bank of elevators serviced the rest of the building.

A host of indoor plants and artificial trees dominated the reception area. Built into the left wall was a security station, currently occupied by two Tristar guards dressed in matching uniforms. Separating the corridors from the entrance were two gateway metal detectors and a barrier gate operated by keycards.

Roach headed straight for the barriers. The security guards hustled out from behind their desk to cut him off, signaling for him to stop.

"Hey, hold it right there!" shouted one of them. He was a tall, thin man whose employment was likely more of a token gesture than anything else.

His hand hovered over his own pistol, holstered to his belt. His colleague did the same.

Roach stopped and looked at them both in turn.

He had made it this far. He knew Rebecca was in the building. He knew Brandon Crow was too. This was when his involvement ended. When Tristar cut their losses and left him and his family in peace. Nothing was going to stop that. Not after everything he had been through to get here.

As far as he was concerned, anyone in a Tristar uniform was an enemy. A threat that must be neutralized. Leave nothing to chance.

Roach glanced up at the security camera mounted on the wall, overlooking the foyer, then flicked the bag up out of his grip, plunging his hand inside it as he did. When the bag dropped to the floor, he pulled the shotgun free and chambered a round with a loud, distinctive double-crunch.

"Oh, shit!" yelled the tall, thin guard. "Call for backup. Do it now, before—"

The shot was thunderous. It echoed all around, ringing in Roach's ears. The kick of the shot thumped back against his shoulder. The cartridge punched a hole in the guard's chest the size of a plate.

Before the other guard could react, Roach snapped the shotgun to him and fired. The guard flew backward, colliding awkwardly with the side of the security station and landing in a crumpled, bloody heap.

He looked up at the camera again, then vaulted the barrier, skirted around the metal detector, and headed for the stairs.

"I'm coming, Rebecca," he said quietly. "I'm coming."

. . .

Crow paced back and forth behind his desk, his cell phone held up to his ear. Rebecca and Goddard watched him like they were watching a tennis match. He was tense. Agitated.

He clicked the phone off and tossed it onto his desk. It clattered noisily.

"Goddammit," he hissed.

By the door, Davies stiffened and adjusted his grip on his gun.

"There a problem, sir?" he asked.

"Jay's not answering her cell phone," he replied. "She should've been back by now with that asshole in tow."

"I'm sure it's nothing to worry about, sir. Jay's as tough as they come."

"Never underestimate a desperate man," said Crow, pointing a cautionary finger. He took out his own gun from his desk drawer and moved around to stand in front of Goddard. He chambered a round and rested the barrel down on the top of his head. "Tell me who hacked our systems. Tell me who gave the data to Roachford. Tell me now, or I'll shoot you."

Goddard shuffled in his seat, anxiously and unsuccessfully trying to move his head from the firing line.

"What about our deal?"

"Oh, screw your deal! I no longer have the time to play your games."

"Wait, wait, wait! Just... give me a second here, okay? You're going about this all wrong."

Crow smiled. "Am I really? I know Roachford has this information as well, and I think it's safe to assume he would gladly share it in exchange for his sister's life."

Goddard laughed nervously. "You know what they say

about assumption's parenting skills. Think about it, Brandon. *How* does our mutual friend know?"

Crow wavered slightly. He stepped back to sit on the edge of his desk. His gun was still trained on Goddard, albeit casually.

"He only knows what I told him," Goddard continued. "And I told him whatever I needed to get him into that bar in Des Moines for you. I'm not an idiot. Information is my currency, remember? Why would I tell our mutual enemy everything for free when I was going to be paid a fortune to tell you?"

"What are you saying?"

"I'm saying, if you kill me now, all you'll be told by Billy is the bullshit *I* told *him*. You want to know who really hacked you and involved him, then you need me alive."

Rebecca had heard enough. She had listened patiently to the conversation, silently grateful the gun wasn't aimed at her, but she couldn't stand to hear another word about how her brother had been set up. She prayed he was trying to figure out how to save her. He deserved better than this.

She lurched to the side, reaching for Goddard.

"You sonofabitch!" she shouted.

Before she could stand, a heavy hand clamped down on her shoulder, forcing her into the chair. She looked around to see the unforgiving stare of a Tristar operative, who wagged his finger slowly at her.

Her heart raced in her chest. She gripped the arms of the chair until the color drained from her knuckles.

Crow looked on, bemused.

"It seems that temper is a family thing," he said, then redirected his attention back to Goddard. "If you're lying to me, you're dead. There's too much riding on this."

Goddard relaxed into his seat and breathed a sigh of relief when Crow placed the gun on the desk.

Just as Crow sat back in his own chair, the door opened. His secretary marched in, flustered.

"Sir..." she said hesitantly.

Crow looked over, frustrated. "What is it?"

"Sir, there's been a security breach in the lobby. There... there are casualties."

"What!" He leapt to his feet, seized the remote, and turned on the TV. "Put the security feed through. Now!"

The secretary disappeared, and a moment later, footage played on the screen. The Tristar men looked over. Rebecca and Goddard turned in their seats, curious. Crow glared angrily as he watched Roach storm in through the entrance and kill two men with shotgun blasts.

"Oh my God!" shouted Rebecca, shocked but unable to hide the elation in her voice that her brother was here.

Goddard turned back around and slid down in his seat, placing a hand to his forehead. "Oh, crap..."

Crow paused the screen on an image of Roach staring directly into the camera and flipping his middle finger at it. He pointed and looked over at Davies.

"Find that sonofabitch right now," he barked. "Find him and bring him to me alive."

He looked at the screen again, picked up his gun, and fired a round into it. The glass exploded amid sparks and screams from Rebecca, who jumped in her seat.

The other Tristar personnel shifted uneasily where they stood, exchanging concerned glances. Whatever fight this was, it had been brought to their doorstep.

27

Roach climbed the stairs to the upper floor—a mezzanine bordered by waist-high frosted glass that branched off to various corridors and offices. The bank of elevators stood to his right, central, overlooking the reception area below.

There was no sign of life. The two shotgun blasts likely sent people on the nearby floors scattering for safety beneath their desks.

Roach understood that a lot of the people in the building were innocent. They were office workers cranking out a nine-to-five to pay the bills. But he also knew there were two kinds of employees in this building: admin staff and contractors.

He knew he had to treat anyone dressed in Tristar gear as a threat. Maybe that wasn't fair to the handful of genuine security personnel there. He knew there were some—he used to be one of them. The people who followed orders, did their job, completed their contracts... and didn't ask questions. That didn't mean they were complicit in whatever Brandon Crow and the rest of the Tristar upper echelons were really up to. Unfortunately for them, he was in the unenviable position of not having the luxury to make that distinction.

Not today.

Today, he had to do a bad thing for a good reason, and he could live with that.

Roach moved over to the elevators and hit the call button. His plan was to start at the top and work his way down. He figured Crow's offices would be up there somewhere. Worst case was that Rebecca was still being held somewhere on the basement levels. If necessary, he would have to navigate the entire building to get to her, using Crow as a human shield. It was far from ideal, but he would do whatever it took to get his sister back.

He looked at the shotgun in his hand.

Whatever it took.

He stared at the panel between the two sets of elevator doors. There was no whirring of motors. No straining of cables. Nothing.

He jabbed at the call button again.

"Come on, you piece of shit," he muttered.

He sighed heavily with impatience at the exact moment a loud alarm began to sound. It was deafening, and he winced as the noise assaulted his ears. The piercing wail peaked and troughed, clearly notifying the entire building of his presence.

Roach looked around, instantly alert. To his right was nothing but a wall with a cheap piece of art hanging on it. To his left were two corridors. One stretched out ahead of him, and the other disappeared to the right, down the side of the elevators. He glanced below, over the glass railings. No sign of movement. Just the two bodies he had left there moments earlier.

Guess I should find the stairs, he thought.

As he turned, gunshots rang out, pinging the railing next to him. He looked up and saw three Tristar security contractors at the end of the corridor ahead of him. Two were standing, with the other on one knee between them, all taking aim with their handguns.

Roach ducked low, zig-zagging his way toward them. He fired a shotgun round in their direction before slamming his back to the wall just around the corner. From where he was, the elevators were at his eleven o'clock, the second corridor at his nine o'clock, and the stairs down to the entrance directly in front of him.

He glanced along the second corridor. It appeared to be a dead end. There was a green, illuminated sign for the bathroom on the left wall.

He peeked around the corner. Another gunshot punched into the wall just in front of him. He moved back. He had managed to see the positions of the contractors. Two had begun moving along the corridor toward him. One had remained at the far end, likely to provide cover.

He looked down at his tactical vest. He unclipped a flashbang grenade and pulled the pin. He let it cook in his hand for two seconds, then threw it blindly around the corner.

"Grenade!" he heard someone yell.

Roach glanced away as it detonated, screwing his eyes tightly shut. The high-pitched whine threatened the building's alarm for dominance.

He spun out of cover, dropping to one knee. There was no sign of the guy at the far end, but the other two were standing still, their hands over their ears, their faces contorted with discomfort.

Roach leveled the shotgun and fired two quick blasts, hitting both men dead center. They dropped unceremoniously to the floor, their bodies shredded. He stood and moved quickly and carefully forward, the gun trained, waiting for another target.

The third man jumped out from cover on the left. Roach was ready and reacted faster, firing without hesitation. Because of the close proximity, the blast took the man off his feet, punching him into the wall behind. He landed sitting down, his head hanging lifelessly to the side, a thick trail of blood in his wake.

Roach quickly scanned both directions. To the left was another dead end. To the right were some offices and a set of double doors leading to the stairs.

He looked back at the carnage he had left. Three dead bodies in a river of blood. His ears were still ringing, but he couldn't tell if that was from the alarm or the flashbang. Not that it mattered.

He headed for the stairs.

There was little time to waste. That alarm would likely attract the attention of more than just the people inside the building.

The stairwell was wide, with two staircases winding up between floors. The walls were pale and devoid of decoration. Roach had made it up five floors without any contact and had yet to see any security cameras along the way.

He hadn't spent much time there during his tenure with Tristar. The layout had changed a lot since his last visit too. He had certainly never heard the alarm, either as a drill or otherwise. He assumed everyone who worked there understood the protocol should they ever hear it, which would explain why it was so quiet.

It also made his mission a little easier. The chances

were, anyone he *did* see would be under orders to apprehend or kill him, which made it simpler to identify targets.

The stairwell wrapped itself around a column of space, allowing him to see all the way to the top. He sighed as he leaned out slightly over the handrail, staring up at the daunting amount of real estate between him and the top floor.

Then he heard movement.

Roach stopped and pinned himself to the outer wall, away from the edge and out of sight. He listened intently. The rhythmic thumping of grouped footsteps echoed both above and below him. It was impossible to tell how many people were in each group.

He thumbed a fresh set of cartridges into the magazine tube of the shotgun as he considered his options. A sign on the wall next to him indicated he was approaching the sixth floor. He could maybe make it up one more level, but that ran the risk of having to engage in a firefight in a tight stairwell with no exits, which was suicide.

He edged forward, risking a look up and down to see where the approaching Tristar contractors were. As he leaned out, a burst of gunfire rattled out around him. He dove back out of sight.

His decision had been made for him.

Roach quickened his pace and burst through the doors onto the sixth floor. He stepped into a small vestibule with another set of doors to the left and right. The wall ahead of him was glass. It was tinted and thick, offering a view of the streets below. He glanced down. There was a cordon around the entrance, trapping his Challenger inside it. A crowd of people had gathered around the outskirts.

The alarm had clearly done its job.

He looked back and forth before heading left. He

pushed through the doors and came out into a wide, open-plan office space, filled with cubicles defined by a maze of dividers that stood approximately four feet tall. At the far end, in the left corner, was a fire exit.

Roach moved forward, glancing in all directions. The floor space expanded away to his left. He figured it spread all the way around, forming a wide U-shape that bordered the stairwell. He approached the corner and peeked around. He could see the elevators in the middle of the near wall.

A wave of stifled whimpers rippled across the floor, barely audible over the persistent alarm. The tops of people's heads were partially visible in places as everyone crouched for safety by their desks, most likely scared out of their minds.

He looked back at the fire exit. He hoped that led to a maintenance stairwell of some kind. That was his only logical option for navigating around the approaching onslaught of Tristar's internal army.

He strode purposefully toward the nearest cubicle. A man and a woman were sitting on the floor inside it, their arms wrapped around their heads, visibly shaking. Roach winced with reluctance at involving anyone else, but he needed information.

"Hey, look at me," he said to the woman.

The woman slowly lifted her head and stared at him with bloodshot eyes. Tears streamed down her face.

"I'm not going to hurt you, all right?" said Roach. "I'm not going to hurt anyone unless they shoot at me first. I just need you to tell me which floor Brandon Crow's office is on."

Next to her, the man shuffled to his left, putting a little distance between them. He had thick, greasy hair and designer stubble. Roach watched him in his periphery and saw him try to discreetly draw his legs up beneath him, ready to spring up.

He turned to him and aimed the shotgun at his face.

"Are we going to have a problem?" asked Roach.

The man stopped moving. The color drained from his face.

"L-leave us alone, please," he spluttered.

Roach rolled his eyes. "I just said I'm not here to hurt you. Brandon Crow has kidnapped my sister, and every contractor on site is out to kill me because I'm trying to get her back. I'm not the bad guy, but you need to understand I will drop whoever tries to stop me. One way or the other. Now where's his office?"

"Is... is that true?" asked the woman.

Roach looked at her. "Sadly, yes. Tristar isn't what you think it is. They're corrupt and into some seriously illegal shit. I'm just trying to keep my family safe."

The man beside her pounced to his feet, lunging with both hands for the shotgun. He grabbed the gun and began twisting it, trying to wrench it from Roach's grip.

Roach saw him move a second too late but quickly recovered. He easily pushed the man away to create some distance between them. With both hands holding the shotgun like a baton, he thrust the stock forward, swinging right to left, swift and accurate. It smashed into the man's head and sent him sprawling to the floor, unconscious before he landed.

The woman shrieked with fear, her whole body shaking.

"I warned him," said Roach without remorse. "Now where is Crow's office?"

She extended her arm, pointing with a shaking finger toward the elevators.

"The n-n-ninth floor," she said. "Please, d-don't kill me."

"Thank you. And I won't. Just... stay down, okay? This will all be over soon."

He stepped forward. In that same moment, a small group of Tristar guards rounded the corner. Everyone froze as Roach locked eyes with Davies.

"You..." he snarled.

Davies smiled. Cocky and confident. "Me. You're done, you little prick."

"Not yet, I'm not."

"Mr. Crow wants you alive." Davies cracked his neck. Three guards moved from behind him and fanned out beside the elevators. "He didn't say anything about you being conscious though."

Roach rolled his shoulders, loosening his neck muscles. He tightened his grip on the shotgun, which he held by the stock in one hand, finger hovering over the trigger.

"I'm assuming there's more of you out there?" he said.

Davies raised his eyebrow, bemused. "You think I need more than four guns to take you down?"

Roach nodded. "A *lot* more."

"Think highly of yourself, don't you? Your sister has that same attitude. Such an annoying family trait. I'm looking forward to teaching her some manners when all this is over. You know... before we dump her body at the side of the interstate somewhere."

He smiled again, almost daring Roach to react.

There was an air of palpable tension all around. Even the workers who were hiding held their breath, riveted. Seconds felt like hours as they ticked by.

Then Roach reacted.

He charged forward like a raging bull, his eyes locked on Davies. He blindly fired the shotgun to his left, aiming in the general direction of the three men who had formed a semicircle there. He knew with a shotgun, especially at close- to mid-range, accuracy wasn't a priority. As long as he aimed at the right compass point, he was likely going to get close to a target.

The shot thundered out around the office, prompting screams and panicked movements all around. Davies hadn't moved. He hadn't had time. Roach covered the ground between them quickly, and he swung the shotgun like a five iron as he bore down on him. The stock arched through the air, down and up again at speed, smashing into Davies's hand.

He dropped his handgun as three of his fingers shattered beneath the impact. He yelled out in pain. Roach kept coming. He dropped his shoulder and plowed through him like a linebacker, with enough force to take him off his feet.

The moment his feet left the floor, Roach spun around, leveling the shotgun again. He saw one man was already down. Another had caught some of the first shot and was inching closer to him on one knee, clutching at a wound on his side that was gushing blood. The third ducked away inside a cubicle as Roach fired. He fired and hit the wounded man in the chest. His body lurched backward, torn apart from the blast.

Roach knew he couldn't risk firing on the third man yet. He turned back to see Davies staggering back outside the office area, toward the stairs.

"Where are you going, asshole?" asked Roach as he stalked after him.

He grabbed a handful of his tactical vest and threw him into the doors that led to the stairwell. Davies crashed through them. As they swung open, Roach caught a glimpse of the six men waiting on the stairs.

His eyes widened with surprise.

Without thinking or even looking, he unclipped a grenade from his vest, pulled the pin, and tossed it through the gap as the door swung shut. He looked at the pin hooked onto his finger, then down at the space on his tactical harness.

He realized what he had thrown.

"Oh, f... rag!" he yelled out.

Roach dove to his right as the grenade exploded. The blast tore through the doors and part of the wall. The shockwave caught him mid-air and hurled him back into the office area. He landed hard on his shoulder. The shotgun flew from his grip.

He grunted as he rolled with the momentum, landing awkwardly on his back, breathing heavily. He stared up at the ceiling for a moment, running through a mental checklist to make sure he was still alive and had everything attached. Then he looked back out into the corridor. The glass had cracked and spiderwebbed all over from the explosion but hadn't shattered.

Blast-proof, Roach figured.

He had seen it before. The outside of the glass was covered in a sheet of strengthened, adhesive sheeting, so when the glass fragmented, it was contained, preventing any external fallout. It made sense that a company like Tristar would have it in place.

He dragged himself upright and looked over at the nearest cubicles to him.

"Everyone okay?" he asked.

He was answered by shocked stares and vacant nods.

A gunshot rang out. A split-second later, he was punched in the chest by the bullet. He collapsed, landing hard once again. He gasped for breath, wheezing and wincing. The bullet had hit the protective vest he was wearing, which had stopped it dead. But the impact still felt like a freight train to the ribs, and the stabbing sensation he felt as he took a breath suggested at least a couple may be broken.

Roach lifted his head to see the third man bearing down on him, his gun trained steadily on him with both hands, finger outside the trigger guard. He was too disoriented to move. His arms were out to the sides. He was flat on his back like he had been crucified.

The man had him beat.

"Mr. Crow will be pleased when I bring you to him," he sneered.

Roach scoffed. "I'm sure he will. Hell, you might get a promotion. Check on the stairs. I think a few jobs have opened up."

"Always got something to say, haven't you, Roachford? Maybe I should shoot you again, just to shut you up."

"Whatever, asshole. Just... give me a minute."

He winced as he fought to regulate his breathing and calm his rapid heartbeat. To relax and focus.

There was a dull thud. The noise confused him. He lifted his head to see the Tristar guard staring with disgust at a young woman crouched in one of the nearby cubicles. At his feet, a stapler lay on the floor. A trickle of blood ran down his face from his hairline.

"Bitch, are you out of your mind?" he shouted.

Roach watched as the woman tried to back away, seemingly not realizing she was pinned into her cubicle. Her hair was matted to her cheeks by tears.

"Y-you leave him alone," she managed. "He said he's just trying to s-save his sister. You should let him. D-don't be cruel!"

Roach couldn't suppress a small smile, touched by the

sentiment of support from a total stranger who had no reason to trust him.

The distraction was all he needed.

He lashed out with his foot, connecting squarely with the guard's knee, forcing him to buckle beneath his own weight. Roach then twisted his hips to the right, opened his legs like a pair of scissors, and closed them again on the guard's ankles, toppling him over.

The guard landed hard, face-first on the worn, faded carpet. Roach raised his arm and slammed the back of his fist down hard on the base of the guard's skull, at the nape of the neck. The impact smashed his nose into the floor, stunning him a second time. Roach scrambled to his feet and delivered a soccer kick to the side of the guard's head, knocking him out cold.

He retrieved his shotgun, then scooped to pick up the stapler. He held it out to the woman, who took it, looking confused. Roach thought she looked unsure that she had done the right thing.

He smiled at her. "Thank you. That was a brave thing you did."

She nodded hesitantly and managed to smile back.

"J-just promise me you're the good guy," she said.

Roach held her gaze. His mouth formed a thin line, complementing his grave, almost regrettable expression.

"I've done a lot of bad things," he said. "But I've never hurt anyone who didn't have it coming."

She slowly, cautiously, got to her feet, resting on the side of the cubicle for balance. She sniffed back more tears and emotion.

"These men who worked here... did they have it coming?" she asked innocently.

Roach nodded. "Yes. They did."

She nodded back, as if accepting his answer. "Then good luck. I hope you get your sister back."

Roach smiled. "Thank you."

"Mr. Crow... he's an evil man, you know. The people who work here are terrified of him."

He crunched his shotgun to chamber a round, startling her. He lifted it up, resting the barrel back on his shoulder. "Well, after today, there won't be anything left to be afraid of. I promise."

She smiled weakly and moved over to her colleague beside her. The other woman, who looked older, wrapped her arms around her.

He was done here. There was no sign of any other guards. Most of the workers had opted to stay huddled inside their cubicles.

Roach turned and headed out into the corridor. He pushed the doors open and stepped out into the stairwell. The walls and floor were covered in blood, like someone had put red paint in a jet wash. Body parts were strewn across the stairs.

He looked around, unfazed but no less repulsed.

"Grim," he muttered.

He stepped over an arm and continued up the stairs to the ninth floor.

28

Rebecca looked on as Crow paced back and forth behind his desk, seemingly growing more frustrated and anxious with each minute that passed. Every now and then, he paused to stare accusingly at his phone, wondering why neither Jay nor Davies had called him.

She gripped the arms of her chair, tense and afraid, sitting as if she were restrained and unable to stand, despite the fact she wasn't. Behind her, the three guards formed a line across the width of the office. She could feel their restless energy, like they were caged dogs waiting for their master to give them permission to feed.

Goddard sat beside her, watching her as discreetly as he could. She was angry at him for betraying her brother. He could understand that. As much as he hated to admit it, he could also understand why Roach made the decision he did all those years ago, choosing his family over him when the FBI came calling. It didn't change the fact he resented him for it, but seeing Rebecca now, caught up in all this, afraid and in danger... he understood.

"The hell are you looking at?" said Rebecca, spitting her words out with impressive venom.

Goddard's vision refocused, and he held her gaze for a long moment. A small smile betrayed him as he looked away.

"What?" she persisted. "Reminiscing over how much of a backstabbing piece of crap you are?"

He smiled again, wider this time. He looked back at her. "No. I'm smiling at you."

She looked disgusted. "Why?"

"Honestly? Because you genuinely impress me. Here you are, in grave danger, in a situation so far removed from your normal life, you probably can't comprehend just how close you are to death. You're lost in your own fear, yet... the moment you realize you have something to hate, you forget to be scared. That hatred gives you strength, and that makes me think you might just survive this. Believe it or not, I really hope you do."

Rebecca stared at him, stunned by his answer and confused by his sentiment.

Eventually, she said, "Well, I guess I should thank you."

He frowned. "For what?"

"Giving me something to hate. Now don't talk to me again. Your voice makes me sick."

Her response felt like a gut punch, but he respected her request and fell silent.

They both went back to staring straight ahead. They saw Crow standing there, arms folded across his chest, watching them with a look of revulsion on his face.

"For the love of God..." he muttered. He picked up his gun once more and aimed it at Goddard. "You two are just nauseating. Time's up, Mr. Goddard. Who hacked Tristar?

Who gave Roachford the flash drive? Tell me now, or I'll shoot you."

Goddard swallowed hard as fear's icy hand wrapped itself around his chest, crushing the breath from his lungs. He had no more cards left to play. Crow was desperate and ruthless. No way could he negotiate more time for himself. But he knew if he told him, he was as good as dead. That information was the only thing keeping him alive. Roach knew everything too, and he wasn't sure if Crow had bought his bluff earlier.

He took a deep breath.

"Okay, I'll tell you. Just... promise me you'll let us go. Both of us."

Rebecca looked over at him, uncertain of his motives.

"I don't think you fully grasp the gravity of this situation," replied Crow. "Whether I like it or not, I have to deliver a satisfactory resolution to this shit-show like my life depends on it. Because it does. So, your lives are less than meaningless to me. You tell me what I need to know, or I kill you and have this same conversation with *her* brother."

"What good will that do?" asked Rebecca. She gestured to Goddard. "This asshole already told you my brother doesn't know anything. That he fed him lies to manipulate him. He has nothing to tell you."

Crow shrugged. "Then I'll kill him. Either way, this all goes away."

"You sure about that?" said Goddard.

"Yes. He dies, the knowledge of whatever he saw on the drive goes with him. Problem solved. Whoever gave him the drive clearly can't do anything with it themselves. Otherwise, they would've done. I want answers, but I'll settle for this just being over."

Goddard hesitated, glancing over at Rebecca. He knew if

he talked now, they were both dead. If he didn't talk, he was definitely dead, and she probably would be at some point shortly after.

He wanted revenge on Roach so badly for his betrayal, no matter his reasoning. He wanted the payday he had spent months working toward, orchestrating this game, manipulating all the pieces on the board.

But it was all for nothing.

He sighed with resignation.

"Fine," he said. "You were hacked by—"

The door to Crow's office burst open, banging loudly against the wall. Everyone in the room turned to see Roach standing there, shotgun in hand, bloodied and bruised.

"Will!" shouted Rebecca, unable to contain her excitement and relief.

But her words didn't register. Time froze as Roach scanned the room. Crow was standing directly ahead, pointing a weapon at Goddard, who was sitting opposite him. Beside Goddard was his sister, who looked like she had been through the roughest couple of days of her life. Her eyes were bloodstained, and her face was dirty with dried tears. Behind her stood three men in Tristar uniforms, weapons held loosely in their hands.

The shotgun was useless here.

Time resumed its normal pace. Roach dropped the shotgun and drew the gun holstered on his right. He fired three shots in quick succession. His aim was lethally accurate and uncompromising. All three guards dropped to the floor with dull thuds, bullet holes dominating what remained of their faces.

Roach snapped his aim to Crow at the same moment Crow took aim at him.

"Been a long time, Billy," said Crow, smiling.

"Not long enough," replied Roach.

"So, what happens now?"

"That's easy. Me and my sister walk out of here." He turned to Rebecca. "Becky, let's go."

"Ah-ah-ah, not so fast," said Crow. "We have much to discuss, you and I."

"We really don't."

"Oh, but we do. You see, Mr. Goddard here told me that everything he said to you about that flash drive was a lie. Which means whatever leverage you think you have here is worthless." He took a long, satisfying breath. "You have been a pain in my ass for a long time, Billy. I should shoot you right now and be done with it."

Roach shrugged. His aim never wavered.

"Yeah, you should. But you won't."

"And why's that?"

"Because he didn't lie to me."

Crow's face dropped. The confidence slipped from his expression. "What?"

Roach looked at Goddard. "You're so full of shit, it's actually impressive."

Goddard smiled. "Thanks."

Roach returned the gesture, but it wasn't friendly. "Not a compliment."

"Enough!" yelled Crow. "This ends right now. This *has* to end right now."

"You're sounding desperate, Brandon. That's not like you."

"Shut up! Who gave you the drive? Tell me!"

"The same people who asked me to help them take you down. GlobaTech."

The color drained from Crow's face. His aim faltered an

inch. He took a step back, reeling. "GlobaTech? That's not possible. That can't be. How?"

"They've had their eye on you ever since Cambodia. Ever since you gave the order to my teammates to kill me. And speaking of which, you're going to tell me where One is. I owe that sonofabitch."

Crow shook his head vacantly. "He's already dead. You're welcome."

"Oh." Roach failed to hide his disappointment but quickly recovered. "Well, that saves me a bullet, I guess."

"GlobaTech hacked us," sighed Crow.

"They did. Seems you and Tristar have found yourselves a large blip on an even larger radar. Good luck with that."

"This changes everything..." Crow murmured. He gazed at the surface of his desk, his eyes flicking back and forth as if reading something quickly. The cogs turned inside his head.

"It changes nothing for me," said Roach. "We're done. You'll call off your hunt and leave me in peace. I get so much as a bad feeling anyone from Tristar is within a hundred miles of me or my family, I will level this entire building, I swear to God."

Crow snapped out of his trance, jumped to his feet, and aimed his gun at Roach again.

"You just became incredibly valuable," he said. "So, I'm afraid you and your sister aren't going anywhere."

Both men stood like statues, their aims steady and their eyes locked. Stalemate.

Crow was grinning. The evil in his smile touched his dark eyes. Roach's expression lacked any emotion, even hate. All that was etched on his steely face was determination and the unequivocal certainty that he would do what he had to do in order to survive. Nothing more. Nothing less.

Movement in his periphery distracted him. He let his eyes wander to the right in time to see Goddard launching his chair toward him.

He registered what was happening in an instant. He stepped back and ducked to avoid the impact of the chair. It sailed past him, smashing loudly into the door and tumbling to the floor.

The distraction was all Goddard needed. He quickly moved to one of the dead guards behind him, drew their sidearm, and lunged for Rebecca. He dragged out of her seat by her hair, pulling her close to him. As her body pressed back against his, he adjusted his grip and wrapped his arm tightly around her neck, holding her in place. He rested the barrel of the gun against her temple.

Roach moved like lightning, drawing his second handgun with his left hand. He aimed it at Crow. The other jerked right, settling its aim on Goddard.

Another stalemate. A three-way stand-off.

"New deal," said Goddard. "I get out of here, and your sister lives."

29

"Let her go," said Roach firmly. "If you don't, I'll kill you."

Goddard scoffed. "You're not that good of a shot."

"Try me."

Rebecca whimpered. Her attempts to struggle free were futile.

Roach stared at her. "Becky? Becky, look at me."

She did, through eyes misty with tears. Her lips quivered with fear.

"You're going to be okay," he said. "I promise you."

"Don't listen to him, Becky," hissed Goddard. "He'll leave you here to save his own ass, just like always."

Before he could say anything, Roach saw Crow shift his weight slightly out the corner of his eye. He looked over, reaffirming his aim.

"Don't think I've forgotten about you, you sonofabitch," he said.

Crow continued his maniacal grin. "Face it, *Roach*. It's over. Give me the drive, and I promise you won't suffer. It'll be a quick, clean kill. A warrior's death."

Roach failed to suppress his eyes rolling. "Shut your mouth, Brandon."

"Hey!" interjected Goddard. "We ain't done talking, asshole."

Roach looked over at him. "Yes, we are. You still got a problem with me after all these years, fine—take it up with me. Leave my sister out of it."

"Oh, I do, Billy. I really do. But now isn't the time. You and me, we're on the same side here, okay? We both want the same thing. We both want to get out of here. We both want your lovely sister to see another sunrise."

Roach shook his head. "We are not on the same side. I'm going to kill you, Zach. No drama. No negotiations. I'm just going to straight-up kill you."

"You owe me!" yelled Goddard, incensed.

"How d'you figure that?"

"If it wasn't for me, you would've been arrested in Corfu a week ago! You would've been exposed there and then, and Tristar would've found you a lot sooner. They would've killed you in your holding cell."

Roach frowned. "What are you talking about?"

"That drunken idiot you threw through the window. He was going to report you to the cops for assault."

Roach thought for a moment, recalling the incident. "Who? Eddie?"

"I didn't know his name, but I killed him. For you. To protect you."

"Jesus, you're insane..."

"You were the centerpiece of my game. Don't you see that? I had to protect you until it was time to kill you. Otherwise, none of this would've worked."

Roach's eyes narrowed. "Have you not been paying

attention? What part of all this makes you think your plan worked, exactly?"

Goddard went to speak but caught his own words before he could. He looked back and forth between Roach and Crow, forcing the gun harder and harder against Rebecca's head in frustration. Finally, he let out a growl of anger through gritted teeth.

Rebecca didn't know what was going to happen next, but she knew she didn't want to die. Not like this. Not because of him. She stamped down as hard as she could on Goddard's foot. The impromptu attack surprised him, and he yelled out in pain. In that moment of distraction, she dropped into a crouch, freeing herself from his grip. A heartbeat later, a gunshot rang out around the office.

The sound trailed off over the next few seconds, dragging behind it the eventual silence that would take hold of the scene.

Rebecca looked up, having had her arms wrapped around her head, in time to see Goddard fall backward like a felled tree. His eyes were wide and lifeless. She straightened as he hit the floor and looked over at Roach. A thin whisp of smoke danced from the barrel of his gun. The hardened glare of his unblinking gaze was matched only by the tight line formed by his lips, clamped together to imprison any emotion he might have felt in that moment.

Then she saw Crow move.

"Will, look out!" she shouted.

Roach turned as Crow pulled his own trigger. The bullet punched through Roach's shoulder. The impact spun him counterclockwise, knocking him off-balance.

As he moved, Roach fired one of his own guns. The shot caught Crow on the top of his leg, just below the hip. He immediately buckled underneath his own weight and tumbled to the floor. His gun flew from his grasp. He clutched desperately at his wound, which had already begun leaking blood all over his expensive suit.

Roach staggered back into the wall, using it for balance. Rebecca rushed over to him. She reached out to steady him and placed a hand over his shoulder.

"Jesus, Will, are you okay?" she asked, trying to stifle her tears.

"I'm fine," he replied, grimacing. "Just... give me a minute."

Roach pushed himself upright and moved slowly over to the desk. He stepped around it, looking down at Crow as he tried feebly to shuffle over to his gun. Roach kicked it away, placed his own guns on the surface of the desk, then reached down and grabbed two handfuls of Crow's suit jacket. He hoisted him up, grunting from the pain in his shoulder caused by the exertion. He dropped Crow awkwardly in his chair, then picked up his guns and stepped away.

Crow was breathing heavily. He smiled, mostly to mask his own agony.

"You think this is over?" he asked.

"I know it is," said Roach.

"It isn't over, you dumb bastard. This right here... this is just the beginning. You have no idea what's coming for you now. You think what you saw on that flash drive will help you? Heh. *Nothing* can help you now. Either of you."

"Honestly, Brandon, I barely looked at the damn thing. I wish I had never been sent it. I saw enough to know Becky was in danger. Everything else I looked at made little sense to me. Goddard told me most of what I know, and despite his penchant for talking crap, I believed him."

"That won't stop them from coming for you."

"I figured. Which is why I'll be hanging onto that drive for now. Call it an insurance policy. If anyone comes for me again, the entire contents of it get published online. I know a journalist who would love to go after the story."

He and Rebecca exchanged a brief smile.

"You know your problem, Roachford?" asked Crow.

Roach shrugged. "Enlighten me."

"You're too short-sighted. You only ever focus on the problem directly in front of you. You never look at the consequences. You don't look at the big picture, and like it or not... you're a part of it now. There's nowhere you can hide."

"I don't need to hide. No one else will be stupid enough to come looking for me. Not after this."

"Really? You think so? See, this is *exactly* what I mean! You're blind, Roach. You can't comprehend what's really going on here. Your ignorance will be the death of you and of your sister. Hell, I bet you haven't even thought about getting out of here, have you?"

Roach said nothing. He just let out a taut sigh.

"See?" continued Crow. "You beat me. You got me. Congratulations! Now what? Hmm? You're in my office, in my building. You killed, what? Ten of my men getting in here?"

"Eighteen, but who's counting?" said Roach.

"Oh, impressive. So, what do you intend to do about the remaining fifty? Huh? And there's plenty more where they came from. You can't hide behind the police. Not here. Not from me. The police don't bother us. If anything, they'll arrest *you*. We're just a security firm, trying to make an honest living. You're the psychopath that stormed the place with a goddamn shotgun! So, tell me, *Roach*... tell me your big plan for getting out of here. I'm *dying* to know!"

Roach smiled at him, then turned to his sister. He held out one of his guns, nodding to it.

"Here, take this," he said.

With shaking hands, she did. She held it awkwardly, confused and terrified.

Roach moved to her side and held his gun ready to fire.

"Hold it like this," he said to her. "A firm grip of the butt, then clasp your other hand around it. Steady and secure."

Rebecca mimicked his hand positions and body language.

He smiled, feeling oddly proud. "There you go. Keep your right arm straight, but don't lock your elbow."

"Don't these things have, like, a safety or something?" she asked tentatively. "I've never... I don't know what I'm doing, Will."

Her voice cracked as emotion betrayed her.

"It's okay. Just relax," he replied patiently. "Safety's always off when you're in a fight. Your trigger finger... that's your safety. Look."

Roach showed her how he rested his index finger flat against the outside of the trigger guard.

He continued. "Only hook your finger around the trigger if you intend to squeeze it. Any other time, it's outside, resting against it, okay?"

Rebecca nodded, following the instructions.

"If you need to shoot, don't pull. Just make a fist with your hand. Let your finger squeeze the trigger. Understand?"

She nodded again. "I... I think so. But why are you giving me the gun? Why tell me all this?"

"Because I need to make a call. I want you to point the business end of that at him." He pointed at Crow. "Shoot him if he moves."

Her eyes popped wide. "What?"

He smiled to comfort her, despite knowing it likely wouldn't work. "Relax. He isn't stupid enough to try anything. Besides, he's bleeding like a stuck pig. And if he *does* make a move, just remember how much of an asshole he is... it'll make it easier to shoot him."

Rebecca rolled her eyes and muttered to herself, "Jesus Christ..."

Roach holstered his gun and moved over to Crow. He frisked him, rifling through his pockets until he retrieved his cell phone. Then he reached into his own back pocket and took out a business card.

"Who are you calling?" asked Crow scathingly. "I don't think you can dial a miracle."

Roach smiled. "Depends on your definition of a miracle."

He punched in the number and paced over to the opposite end of the office, standing beside the dead bodies.

The call rang out. Once. Twice. Three times. He checked the screen to make sure he dialed correctly. As he did, he heard a voice. Female. Authoritative.

"Fisher."

"Julie Fisher? It's Roach."

The line went silent for a moment, save for the rustle of movement in the background.

"William? What the hell are you doing?" hissed Julie.

"You said to call you if I changed my mind. Well, I have. I'll help you. But I need something from you first."

"Yeah, I bet you do. Jesus, what were you thinking?"

He was confused. "What do you mean?"

"I mean you storming Tristar's headquarters like you're Rambo!"

"How do you—"

"Have you not seen the news?"

Roach sighed impatiently. "No. I've been a little busy."

"Yes, I know! The Gramercy Park Siege, they're calling it."

"Who is?"

"Everyone! Pick a news channel, William—you're on all of 'em."

"Oh. Well, what did you expect? You gave me that bag. You said you wanted to—"

"I said I wanted you to be discreet, asshole."

"And I said I would do whatever it takes to get my sister back. And I have."

Julie's tone softened a little. "You found her?"

"Yes, I did. I'm with her now. In Brandon Crow's office. He's been shot, but he's alive. I'm calling from his cell, so you have his number now too. I figured you might want to take him before the NYPD arrest him for kidnapping and murder."

"I mean, we do, obviously, but—"

"There you go, then. So, can you and Captain 'Roid Rage come down here and escort us out? There's a lot of real estate filled with a lot of angry Tristar guards between us and the exit. Get us out of here and Crow's yours. Along with the flash drive. Becky and I will disappear."

The line went silent again.

"Julie?"

The line crackled from the heavy sigh. "William... *Roach*, I... we can't help you."

His expression hardened. "What?"

"I told you GlobaTech couldn't get publicly involved. You've got a police cordon outside, a SWAT team sitting there waiting for orders to take the building, and two dozen news crews covering a three-block radius. We can't waltz into the middle of all that and start flexing authority that we don't have just to get you out of there, I'm sorry."

"You're being serious?"

"Yes. Of course, I am." Another sigh. "Look, as far as we can tell, the police don't know who they're looking for. Reports from scared employees just mentioned a lot of shooting and a lot of dead bodies. Tristar seem to have some pull with the local PD, so they're keeping a distance. You might be able to slip out unseen if you—"

"If I what, Julie? Fight my way back out through double the number of assholes I fought through to get in, with limited ammunition and my sister in tow?"

"Look, I know it's not ideal, but that's on you. You should've thought of that before you blasted your way inside."

"That's real helpful. Thank you."

"I'm sorry, but for now... you're on your own." She paused. "Roach, look. I—"

"You don't get to call me Roach. We're not friends."

He hung up and stared at the phone in his hand for a moment, stunned silent. He knew coming here was risky. He knew that he might not make it back out. But he had put together an exit strategy anyway, in case he made it far enough to need one.

It had hinged completely on GlobaTech helping him.

That was his mistake. He saw that now. After the conversation in the diner, he thought they had wanted the same thing he did. Perhaps for different reasons, but the outcome was the same. He thought they were prepared to do whatever needed to be done, just like he was.

He was wrong.

"Problem?" asked Crow, grinning with satisfaction.

Roach looked over, glaring at him with dark, empty eyes laced with venom.

"No," he said. "No problem at all."

He marched over to the desk and dragged Crow to his feet. He held him upright, then punched him hard in the top of the leg, squarely on the bullet wound.

Crow yelled out with pain. Roach took out his gun and moved behind him, placing the barrel to the back of his head.

"Will, what's wrong?" asked Rebecca.

"There's been a change of plans," he said. "Turns out our ticket out of here has expired."

She lowered her own gun, grateful to relax her arms. "So, what are we going to do?"

Roach held her gaze, trying to exude as much confidence as he could. "We're going to walk right out the front door."

30

"This is crazy!" Rebecca called after him.

Roach stormed out of the office and back along the corridor leading to the stairwell, pushing Crow forcefully out in front of him. He had a firm grip on both his neck and the gun held to his head.

"Will, can you..." She quick-stepped ahead of him and stopped, blocking his path. "Can you please just stop a minute?"

He did, without trying to hide his frustrations.

"Do you have any better ideas?" he asked tersely.

Rebecca held his gaze, her adrenaline causing her to breathe as if she were running. A tense moment passed.

"Well, no, but—"

"Okay, so we do this my way. You might want to stay behind me."

Her eyes misted with tears. "But I'm not you! I'm not a... a... whatever *you* are. A soldier, a killer, a... mercenary—I don't know!"

"Oh, he's a killer, all right," added Crow, laughing.

Roach pressed the barrel of his gun harder against Crow's skull. "You shut your mouth."

"And if I don't? You going to kill me, champ? You *need* me alive to get out of here."

Roach spun him around and pinned him to the wall, a hand wrapped tightly around his throat. "Listen to me, you sonofabitch. I managed to get in here just fine without you. You'll make it easier getting out, sure, but that doesn't give you a free pass to say whatever you want. You're a disposable asset at best. Understand?"

Crow struggled against the grip, wrestling to relieve any pressure he could. "And what about... your new... friends? Don't Globa... Tech want me?"

Roach chose his words carefully. "You're not their priority. You were a nice bonus but ultimately inconsequential to what they've got going on. Like I said, you're disposable."

Crow relaxed, distracted by the comment. His eyes grew wide and the color drained from his face. He believed Roach. He recognized the look of conviction in his eyes. He realized he had no bargaining power left. No real value.

He nodded hurriedly and clamped his mouth shut, a symbolic gesture of his obedience.

Roach pulled him back into place in front of him, then looked over at Rebecca. Her expression was a petri dish of emotion—fear, determination, sympathy, anger.

"Stay behind me," he said. "Move when I say. Find cover when I say. We'll get out of here, I promise."

She nodded once. "Okay."

"And remember what I said about your gun. Finger outside the guard unless you intend to pull the trigger. Don't hesitate. Make a fist to fire. Got it?"

She nodded again.

"All right, let's go."

They headed for the stairwell at the end of the corridor. Roach used Crow to push the door open. They filed through and descended the stairs. Crow stumbled and fell forward against the wall after the first flight.

"Hey, come on," said Roach. "You don't have time to bleed."

"I've been shot in the goddamn leg!" he protested. "Walking isn't easy."

"It also isn't my problem. Move."

He shoved him forward again, and they continued their journey down. Roach checked corners and doors as they passed them. He periodically looked up and down the stairwell for any signs of movement. So far, it was quiet.

"Where is everyone?" he asked.

"Oh, they're here," replied Crow cryptically.

They pivoted on the stairwell, taking the flight down that led to the sixth floor. Roach saw the pile of bodies, the river of blood, the charred floor and walls... all remnants of his journey up these stairs not one hour earlier.

"Oh, crap." He looked back to address Rebecca. "Hey, stay there a sec. Don't—"

It was too late.

Her scream echoed around the bare walls. She dropped her gun and covered her face with her shaking hands. She dropped into a crouch and rocked back into the corner. She took a deep breath, renewing her horrified howl.

Roach acted quickly. He slammed his gun into the back of Crow's head, sending him tumbling down the last few stairs. He landed heavily at the bottom, beside the severed legs of one of his former employees.

"Stay there," he said to him, then headed back up the steps two at a time to comfort his sister. He crouched in front of her. "Becky, it's okay. Don't look at it. Just close your eyes, and I'll guide you past it all, okay? You don't need to see it."

She moved her hands, revealing her tired, tear-stained face. "You knew this was here, didn't you? All that... death. You caused it?"

Her voice was firm and strong. Not accusatory. Not angry.

He nodded. "I came through this way. I was pursuing someone who came in here. I saw a squad of six Tristar operatives lined up. It happened fast. I went to throw a flash-bang, so I could—"

"Throw a what?"

"It's a non-lethal grenade that lets off a loud noise and a bright light on detonation. Designed to disorient and debilitate enemies."

She nodded past him, to the carnage at the bottom of the stairs. "Looks pretty goddamn lethal to me, Will!"

"Yeah, well, I was in a hurry and threw a frag grenade instead."

She looked at him, impatiently asking a silent question.

He rolled his eyes. "The normal kind of grenade that goes 'boom.'"

"Jesus..."

Her breathing began to slow as she calmed herself.

"I didn't intend to cause all this," he said. "But I still would've killed every single one of them to get to you. This ain't pretty. This ain't right, and I honestly hate it as much as you do. But this is war, and we're on our own, which means we do what we have to do. You can argue the morality of it all with me over a coffee, *after* we get out of here alive. Deal?"

Reluctantly, Rebecca nodded and got to her feet. She retrieved her gun and followed Roach down the stairs, doing her best to focus completely on the doors ahead of her.

Roach dragged Crow upright and guided him around to the next set of stairs. His movement was becoming more limited, with his injured leg trailing behind him like dead weight. They took one step, then automatic gunfire rang out from below. A hail of bullets pinged off the metal railing, punching into the walls above them.

Rebecca backed away in the corner, screaming once more. Roach fired a few blind rounds over the edge, then chanced a peek. A line of Tristar operatives snaked around the stairwell maybe two floors below them. He couldn't count how many.

"Shit," he hissed.

He yanked Crow back up the stairs and headed through the doors onto the sixth floor, propping it open with his back foot.

"Becky, let's go. Now!"

She followed without hesitation, taking a deep breath to subdue the wave of nausea as she stepped over the dead bodies.

Roach led them left, quickly moving out into the open-plan office space from earlier. He was surprised to see everyone was still there, hiding in their cubicles.

The woman he had spoken to earlier saw them approaching and got to her feet. She visibly hesitated when she realized it was Brandon Crow with them.

"Help me!" barked Crow. "All of you, stop this man immediately."

Roach hit the back of his head with the gun again. "Will you shut up?"

The woman smiled weakly and raised an apprehensive hand at Rebecca. A feeble wave.

"Are... are you this man's sister?" she asked.

Rebecca smiled warmly. "I am."

More people from around the floor started getting to their feet and wandering over. It wasn't long before a sizeable crowd had gathered around them.

Roach surveyed it skeptically, tightening his grip of both his gun and Crow.

Rebecca noticed the shift in her brother's body language. The tension and uneasiness.

The woman walked toward Roach, seemingly nominating herself as a spokesperson of sorts.

"W-what happens now?" she asked.

Roach relaxed a little. "There's a bunch of your operatives on their way up here, intent on killing us. You should find cover."

The woman hesitated, looking around the group of her colleagues.

"Seriously," urged Roach. "You need to get yourselves safe. Why are you all still here, anyway?"

She shrugged. "Protocol. Tristar run drills all the time. They sometimes use the office as a kind of training ground for their field operatives. No live fire, so we're told. But if we hear the alarm, we're to buddy up and take cover in the cubicles. Stay there until it's over."

Roach and Rebecca exchanged a look of disbelief.

"Are you serious?" he asked.

She nodded. "It's always been that way."

He had spent most of his time with Tristar overseas. He had trained in London and took contracts almost exclusively around Europe. Ironically, the first assignment he had outside of Europe was in Cambodia. But he had only been to the New York office a handful of times, and even then, it hadn't been for long.

He had no idea the company was so corrupt and unethical.

He shoved Crow, who landed hard on his knees. Roach moved in front of him.

"This is over," he said. "This company is done. You will pay each and every member of office staff a handsome severance package, then you'll rot in jail. Your operatives will find their own work, I'm sure. They're someone else's problem. But Tristar is done. You understand?"

Crow shook his head. "It doesn't work like that. Tristar is a privately-owned company. I don't run it. I'm just one of the directors. None of us can make that kind of decision. We answer to the owners."

"You mean Orion?"

"How did you—"

"The flash drive. Does Orion know everything that's going on here? All the illegal crap you do? All the killing and the off-the-books operations? Do they know about Cambodia? Do they know about me?"

Crow looked away, staring at the floor solemnly, like a scolded child. The reaction told Roach all he needed to know. Orion International were one of the biggest corporate entities in the world. If word got out they knew one of their subsidiaries was conducting illegal activities on their dime and did nothing, they would be destroyed. Their share prices would bottom out overnight. It could have a lasting effect on the global economy, such was their size and significance.

This just got a whole lot bigger than even Roach had realized, but he knew it wasn't the time to worry about it.

He looked at the woman. "Listen, this is what you would call a live fire exercise. This is real and dangerous, and your protocols could get you killed. I need you to leave. All of you. Take the stairs, ignore the dead bodies, and tell everyone on every floor you pass to do the same."

"Is that safe?" asked a man in the crowd. He was tall, disheveled.

"The operatives here won't fire on their own colleagues. Besides, for every one of them, there's, like, thirty of you. Safety in numbers. If you run at them, they can't stop you."

"What will you do?" asked the woman.

"Me, my sister, and this sack of crap you used to work for are going to take that fire exit in the corner, see if we can't bypass any more unwanted attention. Do you know where that leads?"

She glanced back at the door in the far corner, as if to refresh her memory. "They lead down to the lobby. Bring you out beneath the elevators on the right."

Roach nodded. "Perfect. Thank you. Now go—all of you."

Some of the crowd hesitated, exchanging worried looks. He took it as understandable sign of divided loyalty. He knew how difficult that must be. How awkward they must feel.

But he didn't have the time for moral debates.

He raised his gun and fired twice above everyone's head, careful not to aim directly at the ceiling.

"Go!" he shouted.

A mass panic broke out. The thunder of footsteps rose as everyone stampeded toward the doors.

Rebecca stepped closer to her brother for fear of being shoved to the floor.

Roach smiled apologetically to the woman in front of him. He placed a friendly, sympathetic hand on her shoulder. "Thank you."

She smiled with an ounce of uncertainty before pushing past him and getting lost in the crowd.

"Come on," he said to Rebecca. "We have to move."

He dragged Crow back to his feet, holding him steady to prevent him from stumbling too much. The three of them navigated the last of the panicked crowd and headed for the fire exit.

As they got to the door, Rebecca placed a hand on her brother's arm. When he looked at her, she smiled weakly.

"Tell me we're going to be okay," she said. "Tell me we'll get out of here, and I'll believe you."

Roach took a deep breath. It pained him having to put her in this position. To subject her to all this blood and violence. But he only did what he needed to in order to keep her safe. It was harsh, it was necessary, and if his plan worked, it was almost over.

He nodded. "We'll get out of here. Trust me."

She took a deep breath, steeling herself for whatever awaited them when they opened the door. "Okay. Thank you."

Roach pushed open the door and shoved Crow into the cold, narrow stairwell. The steps were bare concrete, stained with damp. The walls were exposed brick, unpainted. He looked up and down. He listened carefully.

There was no sign of life. No movement.

"Okay. Let's go," he said.

The three of them began their descent.

31

———

Roach pulled open the door enough to create a two-inch gap, then peeked through it. A wave of commotion greeted him. Roach held Crow tightly beside him, forcing the gun into his back as he looked out at the chaos. Hundreds of people, Tristar employees, flooded through the reception area and out onto the street. They were being met by police officers, EMTs, and a hungry media.

Just as he had hoped.

He turned to look at Rebecca and asked, "Do you trust me?"

The question confused her. She furrowed her brow. "Of course, I do."

"I need you to do what I ask, okay? No questions."

"Okay..."

He spun Crow around to face him. His complexion was noticeably pale, even in the poor lighting of the emergency stairwell.

"You're going to answer for your part in all this," said Roach. "One way or the other."

Slightly dazed, Crow shrugged. "I'd rather you just killed me now. It'd be easier."

"Oh, no. You don't get off that easy, asshole."

Roach smashed the side of his gun into Crow's skull, sending him crashing to the harsh, unforgiving floor, unconscious.

Rebecca shrieked, caught off-guard by the sudden attack.

"What are you doing?" she hissed.

Roach holstered his gun. He took hers from her hand and holstered that too. Then he placed both hands on her shoulders, holding her in front of him. He looked into her eyes. They were wide and innocent. Fearful but alive.

"You need to go," he said.

"What do you mean? I thought we—"

Roach shook his head. "For this to work, we need to split up for a little while, okay? If you run out there now, you'll be swept up in the crowd, and no one will know any different. You'll be safe out there, inside the police cordon."

"W-what about you?"

"Sooner or later, someone's going to look at the security footage. I'm not innocent, but what I did was justified, and I think if I talk to the right person, I can get them to see that. That's the only way I'm going to walk away from this."

"But... but how?"

He gestured to his outfit. "I'm wearing a GlobaTech uniform. I can pass myself off as one of them, say I was here to secure a terrorist." He pointed to Crow. "If I'm dragging that asshole behind me, I can make sure he's arrested and maybe talk my way past the police before anyone thinks to ask too many questions."

Rebecca sighed. "Will, that's a risky plan. How do you know it will work?"

"I don't, but it's the best chance we've got. Now, I want you to head east, away from the cordon, maybe three blocks. Find somewhere safe and wait for me. If I'm not there in thirty minutes, I want you to leave. Get out of the city and lie low in a hotel somewhere. I'll find you."

She stared vacantly at the wall behind him. "This is insane. I mean, how? How will you find me?"

"Because I'm good at that sort of thing, I promise."

He smiled to offer comfort. She returned it, then wrapped her arms around his neck and hugged him tightly. For a long moment, they embraced, enjoying the feeling of relief that they had made it out.

They parted and Roach kissed her forehead. "Now go. I'll see you soon."

He opened the door to let her out. She smiled at him one last time before turning and running toward the entrance. As he had anticipated, she was quickly lost in the crowd.

Roach hoisted Crow upright, threw an arm around his neck, and dragged his unconscious body out of the stairwell. He headed along the short corridor and out in the reception area, on the opposite side of the steps that led up to the elevators. He could see the bodies he had left when he arrived. People were still pouring out from corridors and down the stairs.

He took a breath, then dragged Crow over toward two NYPD officers standing just inside the entrance, directing people outside.

Here goes nothing.

Heading directly for them, he stared until he caught the attention of one of them. The officer immediately rushed toward him, a hand hovering over his weapon. He was calm and in control. He carried himself with an air of experience.

"Hold it right there," he said, his tone confident and authoritative.

"I'm with GlobaTech," said Roach. "I'm here on behalf of the U.N. This guy's a known associate of a terror cell believed to be planning an attack. I was sent here to apprehend him."

The officer hesitated. "Is this for real?"

Roach nodded. "His name is Brandon Crow, and I need to secure him for interrogation."

The cop looked around. "Do you know what happened here? This... siege?"

"There wasn't much of a siege. This asshole resisted and called in a bunch of Tristar operatives to protect him. I was forced to defend myself. There are a few dead bodies lying around here that are on me. I'll file a report and make sure GlobaTech sends you a copy, if it would help?"

The cop frowned, clearly unsure what to do. Roach had no idea if anything he was saying made sense. But it sounded good, and he knew bullshit was more appealing if said with confidence.

"What's your name, Officer?" he asked.

"Franklin."

"Okay, Officer Franklin, this guy I'm holding up is really heavy and needs medical attention before he's detained. Can you figure out what you're meant to do *after* you've helped me get him out of here? It's been a long day."

Franklin seemed to snap back into the moment, regaining the focus and confidence that had momentarily wavered. He took a step forward.

"Sure, let's get him—"

A loud gunshot rang out. A heartbeat later, a cloud of blood engulfed Roach's face. Startled, he dropped Crow and stepped back, quickly wiping his eyes clean. The screaming and commotion around him intensified. He blinked hard and squinted ahead, his vision still temporarily impaired by the blood. He looked down to see Officer Franklin lying awkwardly at his feet, a wide, vacant gaze on his face. There was a sizeable exit wound in the center of his forehead.

"What the hell?" he muttered.

He looked over at the entrance in time to see the other officer collapse to the sound of a second gunshot. Standing there, silhouetted by the influx of daylight flooding in from behind, was Jay.

Roach felt a rush of adrenaline and a wave of anger as he laid eyes on her.

She shuffled forward, holding her gun low by her leg. As the shade of the interior hit her, Roach saw her face properly. It was shredded from their first encounter. A shower of dried blood droplets covered the right side of her head. It looked as if she had been in a car accident.

She brought her gun up, aiming it at him. "Payback's a bitch... and so am I."

"You can't win here," he said. "Your boss is done. There are hundreds of witnesses, not to mention police and news crews outside. You're done. Just... go."

Jay hesitated. Her aim dropped a little. "You think I *want* to walk away? Would you honestly let me, even if I did?"

Roach shrugged. "You and I have some unfinished business, sure. You can bet your ass we'll get square one day. But today isn't the day." He edged closer to her, keeping his hands high, away from his guns. "You said to me you never truly know someone until you fight them. That doing so reveals their true nature. Well, I reckon we got to know each other pretty well earlier. I don't think you want to go down protecting a piece of shit like Brandon Crow. I don't think you have as much loyalty to Tristar as you make out. I think if you could get out of this world altogether, you probably would. This is your chance. We don't need to go another round. Neither of us has anything left to prove. I did what I came here to do. After this, I'm a ghost. Maybe you should be too."

He stopped a couple of feet away from her. Over her shoulder, he saw police and SWAT officers moving into position. There was still enough of a crowd piling out through the entrance that they couldn't effectively move in just yet. He still had a little time.

"Do you... do you mean that?" she asked.

"I'll never forgive your part in my sister being taken," he replied. "But I'm willing to forget it. Revenge isn't as high on my list of priorities as disappearing is."

Jay's expression softened. She held his gaze. For a moment, he thought he saw a flash of gratitude in her eyes. Of respect. Then her mouth formed a smile laced with the sickness and evil he had seen before.

"Sorry, big boy. But revenge is my only priority!"

In the split-second that followed, he anticipated her firing. He ducked away as she did. The shot left his ears ringing. He grabbed her wrist and pushed her arm upward, aiming the gun away from the crowd.

"Don't... do... this," he said, struggling for position against her seemingly endless reservoirs of strength.

Jay said nothing. She brought a knee up and connected with his waist, just below the ribs. That weakened his grip enough for her to break free. She swung a left hook that connected with his head, sending him staggering back.

Roach saw her take aim. He recovered quickly and lunged forward, dropping his shoulder and spearing her to the floor. Her gun flew from her grip, skidding away across the reception area. She lay on her back, her legs wrapped around Roach's waist as he postured up and began raining fists and elbows down on her face and body. She twisted and writhed, deflecting as many of them as she could.

Roach grabbed her throat in one hand, shuffling his own knees forward for balance, which brought their bodies closer together. He felt her legs tighten around him. Her hips pressed against his. He fumbled for his own gun with his free hand, continuing to squeeze with his other, trying to restrict her breathing.

Jay felt her eyes begin to roll back in her head as she struggled to defend herself. Both hands were wrapped around his wrist, but she could do little to relieve the pressure. She felt a rush of blood in her head. She looked down, still wriggling her hips against him, trying to gain some momentum so that she could turn away from him, get the advantage. She saw him reaching for one of his guns.

Then she saw his tactical vest.

She used the heel of her foot to jab down on his hip, trying to deaden his leg. After three or four blows, his grip weakened. She scratched at the flesh on his forearms, easily drawing blood with her dark nails.

Roach felt a rush of pain up his arms. He let go, rocking back on his haunches to recover.

Jay seized the opportunity. She jerked up as if doing a stomach crunch and snatched a smoke grenade off his vest. She pulled the pin, then rolled back, bringing both legs to her chest. Then she pushed forward, kicking him with both feet in his chest.

He fell backward. She dropped the grenade beside him and scrambled away as it popped and hissed, engulfing him in thick, gray smoke. He disappeared almost immediately. The only evidence he was still there was his persistent coughing.

The entire entrance was lost in the cloud in a matter of seconds.

Jay found her way over to Crow. She slapped him hard across the face, trying to bring him around. She heard a faint, disoriented murmur, confirming it had worked.

"Come on," she said. "We need to go right now."

She helped him to his feet, and the two of them shuffled awkwardly into the last group of employees trying to flee. They were quickly consumed by the smoke and confusion.

Roach fumbled around on all fours. His chest felt tight, and his stomach muscles ached from intense dry heaving and coughing. He had inhaled a significant amount of the smoke grenade.

He got to his feet and held his arms out, feeling blindly for the walls and doors. A moment later, he fell out through the entrance, stumbling into the arms of two SWAT team members.

"On the ground now!" one yelled.

"Hands! Show us your hands!" shouted another.

Roach complied, quickly realizing he had no other choice. He lay flat and immediately felt a knee on his back, which made breathing even more difficult. He continued to cough and splutter.

"Hey, wait," said a voice nearby. "He's with GlobaTech. Look."

A second later, he was lifted upright by two pairs of strong arms and led down the steps to the street.

"Sorry about that," said one of the SWAT officers.

Roach rubbed his eyes and took a few deep breaths of refreshingly clean air. When he looked up, he saw a face obscured by a tactical mask and goggles.

"You okay?" asked the officer. "What happened in there?"

Roach leaned against a nearby car and shook his head. "I was attacked, and one of my smoke grenades went off in the skirmish."

"Yeah, looks like you took a lungful of it. I'll get an EMT to check you over. You see who hit you? We'll see if we can find them."

"It was a... a woman. I think she made off with my prisoner."

"A woman? Seriously?"

Roach looked directly into the man's mask. "Don't underestimate her. She's as violent as they come. She killed two NYPD officers and carried a near-unconscious man with a gunshot wound out of here on her own. She's dangerous, so you boys watch yourselves."

The SWAT officer nodded. "Yes, sir. I'll get someone to come look you over."

"Honestly, I'm fine. I just need to get back to work." He pointed to the Challenger. "That's my car. You mind clearing me a path out of here?"

"Of course. Give me a minute."

He wandered off, immediately directing people out of the way. Roach looked around. The noise and the chaos outside dwarfed what he had just gone through inside Tristar's building. There were people everywhere, covering the street and sidewalks. Police and emergency services, then news reporters, then the public. Overhead, he heard the distant whirring of choppers. He didn't look, figuring it was either the police, the news, or both.

There was no obvious sign of the woman or Brandon Crow.

He reached into his pocket and felt for the flash drive. It was still there.

"Hey," called the SWAT officer. "You're good."

Roach waved a *thank you* and headed over to his car. He gunned the engine and pulled away from the curb, carefully navigating the narrow path through the sea of people and away from the carnage he had created.

Once clear, he headed east. The traffic was light. Word must have gotten out that the streets around there were closed. After a couple of minutes, he spotted Rebecca up ahead, standing in the doorway of a building.

He pulled over in front of her and got out, resting on the open door.

He caught her eye and smiled. "Need a ride?"

"You made it," she said before losing control of her emotions and bursting into tears.

Roach opened his arms, and she ran into them. They embraced, enjoying the moment of freedom. "Told you I would."

She moved away and looked at him. "Are you okay? You look like crap."

"I feel it," he said with a weak smile. "Come on, let's get out of here. You're driving."

He made his way around the vehicle and slid into the passenger seat. Rebecca climbed in beside him and started the engine. "Where to?"

"Anywhere. Just... go."

She pulled out and was quickly just another car on the road, lost in the daily traffic.

Roach allowed himself to relax. He let every inch of his body melt into the seat. It amplified every ache and pain, but he didn't care. He had been permanently tensed and engaged and on the move for over a week. He was tired.

He looked in the side mirror, watching the bedlam he had left in his wake disappear into the distance.

He let out a heavy sigh and closed his eyes.

When he opened them again, the scenery had changed. The skyline wasn't as cluttered. Buildings were low enough to be obscured by the trees proudly lining the interstate. He looked at the clock on the dashboard to see an hour had elapsed. He turned to Rebecca, who was focused on the road ahead.

"Where are we?" asked Roach.

Rebecca smiled. "Hey, Sleepyhead. We just passed through Stamford."

"Connecticut?"

"Uh-huh. Figured getting out of New York was a priority. How are you feeling?"

"Like I need a vacation."

She laughed. "That sounds good to me."

"Yeah, sadly, I don't think it's an option."

Roach shuffled in his seat, sitting straight. He took the flash drive from his pocket and held it between his finger and thumb, regarding it quietly.

"Is that it?" she asked. "What all this has been about?"

"It is."

"So, what's our next move?"

He looked over at her. "Our?"

She shrugged. "I'm involved in this just as much as you are. Like you said, this is a story that needs to be told. A story the people have a right to know. If I'm going to take this to my editor, I need to all the facts. I'm not backing down now."

Roach watched her for a moment, impressed with her

resolve and immensely proud in a way only an older sibling can be.

"Fair enough," he said. "The way I figure it, we won't be left alone until Tristar is gone for good. Maybe this drive can help. Maybe not. I don't know. All I know is, we aren't out of the woods yet. People will be looking for us. Our only option is to take the fight to them. We need to go after the people responsible for this. I don't care how big they are or what resources they have. We need to bring them down and make them pay for everything they've done. That's the only way we get out of this."

Rebecca glanced over at him. She could see the determination on his face. His mind was made up, but she knew he wasn't thinking straight. Not just yet. Not after everything he had been through.

She sighed. "Look, Will, I know you don't want to be involved. I know that choice has been made for you, and you hate it. But we need to be smart here. We need to thoroughly investigate everything on that drive and build a case out of it. You saw how frightened Crow was back there. Hell, the whole world has heard of Orion International. If they are somehow involved in what Tristar has been doing, they're not the kind of people you can just threaten until they stop. And what you did to rescue me won't help, either. We don't even know if all that back there will actually stop Tristar. We're in over our heads and need to regroup, figure this out."

Roach stared intently at the dashboard until his vision blurred. His jaw muscles pulsed and clenched. His head ached from his deep frown. His mouth was a thin line of conviction. He felt a pressure cooker of anger rising in his chest. He heard what his sister had said, but it didn't matter.

"No," he said without looking over at her. "You got it all wrong. I'm not talking about Orion."

"You're not? Then who?"

He looked across at her. "I'm talking about the people who involved us in all this. The people who betrayed us. Rebecca, we're going after GlobaTech... and I'm going to bring their entire world crashing down around them."

THE END

EPILOGUE

The intercom buzzed on the desk. A weary finger reached out to press the flashing button. The voice of the secretary sitting just outside the Oval Office spoke.

"Sir, your ten o'clock is here. Should I send him in?" she said.

President Schultz sighed. "Yeah, sure. Thank you, Nancy."

He stood and walked around the Resolute desk, straightening his tie. A moment later, the door opened. His secretary entered and moved aside, holding the door open. Behind her, Moses Buchanan walked in, wearing a dark suit. He approached the president and held out his hand, which Schultz shook warmly.

"Good to see you, son," he said.

Buchanan nodded. "You too, Mr. President."

"Please, take a seat." Schultz looked over at Nancy. "That'll be all. Thank you."

She nodded. "Thank you, Mr. President."

She left, closing the door behind her.

"Drink?" asked Schultz.

"I'm good, thank you," replied Buchanan.

Schultz took his seat again. He leaned back against the soft leather, resting his elbows on the arms and bridging his fingers in front of him.

"Did you see what happened in New York last week?" he asked.

Buchanan nodded. "I did."

"And?"

"I'm afraid it's worse than we feared, sir." He sighed. "Tristar was just the beginning."

"You got any evidence?"

"Nothing we can use. Not yet, anyway."

Schultz let out a heavy, impatient breath. "Goddamn it, we need something, Moses. How in the blue hell can we know so much and still be five steps behind the bastards?"

Buchanan smiled sympathetically. "Red tape, sir. Feel free to remove some of it."

Schultz huffed. "If only it were that easy. This is an election year. I'm fighting more wars than just this one."

"I hear that. I've got my best people on this, sir. We're doing everything we can."

"D.E.A.D.?"

Buchanan nodded.

"Well, it goes without saying that discretion isn't optional here, Moses. I know your team gets the job done, but I also know they ain't too fond of diplomacy."

"I can't disagree, sir, but in my defense, you picked them."

"Yeah, I guess I did."

Silence fell between them. Buchanan looked around the Oval Office absently. He had only ever been in there once before, and the awe of the iconic room never lost its impact. Eventually, he looked back at the president, who sat stroking his chin thoughtfully, contemplating a whole host of problems that would drive most men insane.

He cleared his throat. "Sir, can I ask... how is the new project coming along?"

Schultz looked up at him and rolled his eyes. "How do you think? You know who's running it."

Buchanan grinned. "Yeah. I figured you might find it a challenge. Do you think they will be ready?"

He nodded. "Of course. I don't like the son'bitch, but you can't deny he's effective. The only question is, will they be ready in time?"

"Let's hope so," said Buchanan. "For all our sakes."

A MESSAGE

Dear Reader,

Thank you for purchasing my book. If you enjoyed reading it, it would mean a lot to me if you could spare thirty seconds to leave an honest review. For independent authors like me, one review makes a world of difference!

If you want to get in touch, please visit my website, where you can contact me directly, either via e-mail or social media.

Until next time...

James P. Sumner

CLAIM YOUR FREE GIFT!

By subscribing to James P. Sumner's mailing list, you can get your hands on a free and exclusive reading companion, not available anywhere else.

It contains an extended preview of Book 1 in each thriller series from the author, as well as character bios, and official reading orders that will enhance your overall experience.

If you wish to claim your free gift, just visit the website below:

linktr.ee/jamespsumner

AFTERWORD

What follows is a bonus chapter I wanted to share with you. Originally serving as a prologue to this book, it tells the events of the incident in the Cambodian warehouse.

This is a critical part of the Thrillerverse. You briefly saw what happened here from GlobaTech's perspective in *Crossfire*. It's also referenced multiple times throughout this book, as it serves as the launchpad for Roach's own story.

It's also a thank you for purchasing the print edition of the book!

Enjoy.

BONUS CHAPTER

September 26, 2019

They weren't really there. They never entered the country. They never entered the building. For a period of twelve hours or so, the four men didn't exist. That's how the unknown benefactor of this particular mission wanted it.

They each traveled separately, arriving at pre-arranged times over the last seventy-two hours. They were under strict instructions to wear their masks at all times during the mission—full balaclavas with only thin slits for their eyes.

The four men moved through the large warehouse, conducting a final sweep before moving out. It was a simple structure—large and spacious, bordered by makeshift metal paneling and a roof comprised of wooden slats. The entrance opened into a wide-open loading area. Four aisles began a third of the way inside, formed by racks of empty shelving.

They moved with practiced synchronicity, an unwavering line that headed along each of the four aisles with measured footfalls, light but firm on the dusty floor. Their jet-black uniforms merged with the shadows and poor lighting, camouflaging them into their surroundings. Each man had a thin rucksack over both shoulders. Their rifles hung around their necks, held close to their bodies with an expert grip. Holsters were strapped to both thighs—a silenced pistol in one and a combat knife in the other.

Outside, the sound of the truck starting its engine and driving away filled the small, secluded compound. The crates had been loaded into the back of it twenty minutes ago.

"How are things looking?" asked One into his comms unit. His voice little more than a rough whisper.

"Looks clear," replied Three. "You?"

"Same. What about you, Two?"

"Yeah, same here," said Two. "The recovery team did a good job. I've got nothing but empty boxes."

"Good. Four?"

"Nada," came the response for the aisle farthest away from him.

"All right. Let's wrap this up," said One. "Head back to the entrance. Let's get out of here."

The men turned and retraced their steps back to the loading area, regrouping by a stack of empty crates in the middle.

"Goddamn, it's hot as hell," sighed Three.

Two shook his head. "You're in the middle of the Cambodian jungle. What do you expect?"

Three shrugged. "A little AC wouldn't go amiss. Just sayin'."

"Come on," said One. "We're done here. Let's head for the RV. Exfil will be here in a couple of hours."

The group turned toward the entrance. As they did, a

flash of red caught One's eye. He snapped his head left, resting his gaze on Four's shoulder.

"What the hell is that?" he hissed.

The men stopped and looked at each other, confused.

"What?" asked Three.

One pushed past them to confront Four, pointing an accusatory finger at the logo of their employer still emblazoned on his uniform. "That!"

Four twisted his arm to see. "Shit. Sorry."

"Never mind *sorry*, asshole. We're supposed to be incognito here. No names. No faces. No markings. You've jeopardized this entire operation!"

Four took a step back, subconsciously adjusting the grip on his rifle. "Hey, take it easy. I forgot, okay? It's no big deal."

"No big... Are you kidding me? If anyone finds out we're here or who we work for, we're dead. Do you understand that? Dead!"

"Will you relax? Jeez. There's no one here. We got what we came for. There's no security. It's fine."

"Yeah, ease up, man," added Three. "We're good here."

One turned, pointing a finger in the man's masked face. "Don't tell me to ease up. I'm running this op, and I'll tell you when we're good." He looked back at Four. "We're not good. Do you understand?"

Four shrugged. "What do you want me to do, man? I've apologized already."

Without another word, One lunged forward and grabbed Four by the collar, allowing his own rifle to swing loose around his neck.

Four instinctively took a step back, raising his arms. "Hey! Are you out of your damn mind? What are you doing?"

One said nothing. He clutched at Four's shoulder and

tore a piece of the material away, removing half the logo of their mutual employer. He discarded it without looking, then shoved his teammate away.

Four stood his ground. "Are you kidding me? What the hell?"

One took another step toward him, prompting the others to move between them. He gestured to him over the shoulders of their colleagues.

"You're done. Do you hear me? I'll make sure you're finished after this, you incompetent prick."

Four held his gaze, his eyes nothing more than slits in the narrow holes of his mask. "You touch me again, *I'll* finish *you.*"

"You're dead!" One yelled. Two and Three held him back, keeping the two men separated. "When this is over, you're dead. Do you hear me?"

Four flipped him a middle finger, further antagonizing their assumed leader.

The commotion of four voices shouting echoed around the deserted warehouse. Reason gave way to testosterone. The scene descended into a four-way shoving match, which lasted until a distinctive sound drowned out the scuffle.

The group stopped. They repositioned themselves into a line, staring out through the open entrance. The distant plume of dust approached them, bringing with it the growl of a loud engine.

"What the hell?" asked Two. "We got more support?"

One shook his head slowly. He stepped back, his mind switching from directionless anger to professional clarity.

"Whoever that is, they're not with us," he said. "Let's move. Now!"

With their confrontation instantly forgotten, the men moved quickly out of the warehouse. The blistering afternoon sun assaulted them as they scattered to seek cover in the surrounding forest. One and Four went left; Two and Three went right. They all crouched in the shallow undergrowth as they silently awaited the new arrivals.

"Hold your positions," One muttered into his comms. "Nobody does anything until we know who this is."

A couple of minutes past filled with silent tension. The road was little more than a wide path formed by years of tire tracks and footsteps, forcefully embedded in the landscape and adopted by all who lived and worked in the area. The vehicle kicked up grit as it slowed, sliding to a halt in front of the entrance a moment later. It was an unmarked white Range Rover. The windows were tinted. All doors opened in unison and four men climbed out. They were all dressed the same, but one wore a tactical helmet with a forward-facing camera attached to the side. An unmistakable logo adorned their arms, chests, and legs.

GlobaTech.

"Shit," hissed Two.

"Quiet," urged One.

The men looked on as the GlobaTech unit entered the warehouse. They exchanged looks to their sides and across the dusty path.

"We know what we have to do," said One.

Without a sound, they stood and moved over to the building, taking up position on either side of the entrance. One and Three were at the front of their respective duos. They each peered around the corner and exchanged a nod.

"They're talking," confirmed One. "Sounds like one of them is reporting in."

"What shall we do?" asked Two. The nervous energy was evident in his voice.

"We let them finish. Then we take them out."

"Is that wise?" asked Four. "I mean, not for nothing, but that's GlobaTech, man."

One glanced to his side, addressing his teammate. "I swear to God, if you question me one more time..."

"I'm just saying."

"Well, just don't."

One glanced inside the entrance one more time. The huddle of GlobaTech personnel moved along the second aisle from the right. It was quiet.

Into his comms, he said, "Okay. Move in, on me. Quick and clean."

One by one, they filed inside, silently drawing their suppressed sidearms. Using rehearsed hand gestures, One directed his companions. He sent Two and Three down the aisle to the left of the GlobaTech men and Four down the right. He took cover at the end of central aisle, looking on at the men he was about to kill.

The team drew level on either side, using the handful of crates that still lined the shelves for cover. They took aim and awaited the order to fire.

The GlobaTech team stopped. On either side, the men stopped a few steps behind.

One took a single breath to calm the adrenaline.

"Now," he whispered.

The muted splutter of bullets punched relentlessly into the group, caught by surprise in the narrow shooting gallery. The man at the back dropped to his knees, watching in horror as the rest of his unit collapsed in front of him, lifeless and bloody. He turned, desperately scrambling for distance and safety, but he was met by a bullet between his eyes. One stood over him, aiming his pistol unwaveringly as a wisp of smoke escaped from the barrel.

The rest of the squad appeared behind him.

"We clear?" asked Three.

"Almost," replied One as he walked over to the pile of fresh corpses. He stood over the one wearing the helmet and stamped his boot down on the camera, smashing it against the man's skull. "Now we are. Let's move out."

"What about these guys?" asked Four. "We can't leave them here for someone to find. It's GlobaTech. You really want to bring that kind of heat down on us?"

"I know." One looked across at Two. "Drive their Range Rover inside and then rupture the fuel tank. We'll blow this place as we leave."

"Can we do that?" he asked.

"Our orders were to secure the tech and leave no trace we were here. Can you think of a better way of doing that?"

Two shrugged and headed outside. A moment later, the Range Rover pulled to a stop inside the warehouse. As the engine died, Three set to work on the fuel tank, quickly creating a puddle beneath the vehicle that began to expand across the dusty floor.

Four turned to One. "Listen, about before. I'm sorry for leaving the logo on my gear, okay? I should've been more careful."

One held his gaze for a moment and nodded.

"Forget about it. We're good here. Now do me a favor, would you?" He gestured to the dead GlobaTech employees with his pistol. "Check the bodies. See if there's anything useful. Take any IDs, et cetera."

Four nodded. "You got it."

He crouched beside the first body and began rifling through their pockets.

"Oh, one more thing," One called over.

Four looked up. "Yeah?"

One took aim and fired, hitting Four's thigh. He sprawled onto the floor, clutching the wound.

"What are you doing?" he screamed.

One said nothing. He just took aim again and put a second round in his chest. Four fell backward, motionless and silent.

One turned to see Two and Three staring at him. "What?"

They both shook their heads, keeping their peace.

He pointed at Three. "Turn around."

One reached inside his colleague's rucksack and retrieved a block of C4 and a detonator. He then walked along the aisle occupied by the dead GlobaTech operatives, stopping next to a crate sitting alone on a shelf level with the bodies. He attached the C4 to it, connected the detonator, and set the timer for three minutes. He pressed a button, activating the countdown.

He walked back, completely ignoring the body of his former teammate.

"Let's go," he said.

The three men walked outside and turned right, quickly dissolving into the thick surrounding forest as they headed for the extraction point.

Four's eyes snapped open and he gasped in shock. He instinctively moved a hand to chest, seeking the comfort of his Kevlar vest. The bullet had missed it, striking him where his shoulder meets his pectoral muscle. The wound was superficial, but that didn't stop it sending a wave of pain across his body.

But it was the leg wound that concerned him more. He

shuffled himself upright, resting back against the shelving. He removed his mask and threw it to the floor beside him. He looked over at the bodies of the four GlobaTech men.

"Damn it," he sighed.

Then his eyes moved to the low beeping noise coming from the crate on the shelf opposite. He saw the C4. He saw the timer.

His eyes widened. "Oh, crap!"

He scrambled to his feet but crumpled back to the floor the moment he put pressure on his injured leg. He let out a grunt of discomfort and frustration. He glanced over his shoulder. There was less than a minute left on the timer.

He discarded his rifle and crawled across the floor as fast as he could. He reached the Range Rover and used it to hoist himself vertical. Resting all his weight on his right leg, he looked down at his left. He needed to stem the bleeding, but he knew he didn't have the time. He just needed to move.

He limped toward the entrance but never made it over the threshold.

The explosion tore through the warehouse, consuming everything inside and destroying the fragile walls in its powerful blast.

Four felt a wave of intense heat smash into him, lifting him off his feet.

Then his world turned black.

ACKNOWLEDGMENTS

To say 2020 has been a challenging year for everyone would be an understatement of epic proportions.

I've been fortunate in that I've found a renewed focus on writing, which has given me something to aim for and feel positive about.

This book is a product of that. While it has been planned and in development for over a year, the actual writing phase took me a little over seven weeks—a personal record!

Having spent much of this year indoors, I want to take a moment to thank the people who have made sure that being alone didn't feel lonely.

The last three months have definitely been transitional for me, and I suspect 2021 will be much the same. My friends and family are incredibly supportive of both my writing and my other businesses. But I want to take this moment to thank my big brother, who has been there for me with advice and a friendly ear, to give me some perspective and clarity when it was needed the most. We've always had each other's backs, and I couldn't do this without him.

Finally, as always, I want to thank my readers. Their support and dedication (and patience!) make all this both possible and worthwhile.

Thank you all.

Printed in Great Britain
by Amazon